The Sea Inside His Head

The Sea Inside His Head

Theresa Le Flem

ROBERT HALE · LONDON

© Theresa Le Flem 2012
First published in Great Britain 2012

ISBN 978-0-7090-9567-5

Robert Hale Limited
Clerkenwell House
Clerkenwell Green
London EC1R 0HT

www.halebooks.com

2 4 6 8 10 9 7 5 3 1

Typeset in 10½/14¼pt Sabon
by Derek Doyle & Associates, Shaw Heath
Printed in Great Britain by the MPG Books Group,
Bodmin and King's Lynn

Chapter 1

1974

Bradley stood with the back door open, watching the winter sun sink over Silt Edge Colliery. He looked out on a fertile land; the Kentish fields have produced cider-making apples, beer-making hops and cereal crops for generations. Its hard-working people were once united in their defence of Britain. As Spitfires ripped across the skies over Dover, miners underground threw their backs into hauling coal from under its chalk-laden fields to fuel the machinery of war. Although the coal mines were deep and prone to flooding, for as long as there was coal to harvest, Bradley knew that men like himself – men like his sick father, Ralph Shepstone – would go underground and work because that's what they were born to do.

Coal: that precious black gold that power stations devoured by the ton to drive the manufacturing industry. Coal: that dirty black stuff that families simply needed to heat their homes. And yet, as he turned his head in concern at the distressing sound of coughing coming from within the house, he longed for so much more out of life than those dark underground tunnels could offer him. He wondered to himself – would he ever escape the pit?

The coughing grew louder and Bradley tore up the stairs to find his father out of bed, swaying near the window and struggling for breath. He was just in time to see the man plunge his massive fist through the glass in desperation.

'Give me some air! God help me!' cried Ralph, gasping at the freezing night air. Bradley struggled to hold him upright.

As footsteps sounded on the stairs, he shouted, 'Is that you, Doctor? Come quickly!'

'Take it easy now,' came the gentleman's soft voice as he entered the room. The doctor released an oxygen mask from the cylinder by the bed and placed it over Ralph's face. Rumblings deep in his chest quietened and his eyes turned opaque and dreamy, like an infant at the breast.

Seeing him relax, Bradley sighed with relief. A cold draught was blowing in through the broken window and after helping to move him back into bed, he thrust some clothing into the gap. There was a cut on Ralph's hand and the doctor began tending it, pouring antiseptic and filling the room with its pungent smell. Once the dressing was applied, Bradley tucked the covers more closely around his father as the room had taken on a chill. He sat down by his bedside as he had done many nights before, watching the doctor take his pulse and write-up the notes on his pad.

'Where's your sister?' he asked Bradley.

'Downstairs.'

'Perhaps you'd better call her,' he said quietly.

Bradley looked up, read his expression with some alarm and went to find her.

Kim was hiding in the cupboard under the stairs as she often did at times of trouble; she had done this ever since she was a child.

'Comin' up to see Dad?' he asked, peering in. 'He's bad – doctor says for you to come.'

She shook her head, her fists clutching the ends of her sleeves, her thin arms wrapped around her knees. 'I ain't goin' up,' she whined.

'But he'll wanna see yer, Kim! What if—'

'No!' She put her hands over her ears.

Something inside him wanted to protect her from what was about to happen and he left her and climbed the stairs again. His father appeared to be sleeping.

'She won't come,' Bradley whispered. 'He's bad, is he?'

The doctor nodded. They both remained in the room, perfectly still. The only sound was Ralph's torturous breathing and occasionally the creak of a chair.

Presently the doctor put a hand firmly on Bradley's shoulder and held his gaze. With a quick shake of the head he said, 'Be good and run for the priest, lad.'

Taking one last look at his father's face, he descended the stairs and went to ask his sister once more.

'You'd best go up an' see 'im. The doctor's sent me to get Tom. Go on, Kim, you know what that means. . . . You've got to see Dad – he ain't good at all.'

'I don't wanna see 'im, do I!' she cried, tears streaming down her face as she hugged her knees in the semi-darkness of the cupboard. 'Let me alone, will yer!'

'But Kim!' he pleaded, peering in at her white face.

'Leave me alone!' she wailed.

It was useless. Not wanting to waste any more time, he left the house hastily. It was after midnight now and having forgotten his jacket, the cold January air stung his skin. Sprinting through several streets, the towering headgear of Silt Edge Colliery bore down on him in the moonlight and he winced under its mocking presence. He couldn't help but stare up at it with hatred, feeling an overwhelming sense of remorse that it was about to consume yet another innocent life.

Arriving at the presbytery and seeing it in darkness, he hammered at the door and shouted, 'Tom? Tom!' Hearing him, the Catholic priest got up, saw Bradley standing on the doorstep, put his overcoat on over his pyjamas and went straight out and started the car. They were both back at the bedside within twenty minutes.

Bradley tried yet again to get Kim to come out of the stair cupboard but she refused and went to bed, pulling the covers up over her head. Tom blessed and lit one of the old pit candles, and the three of them – Bradley, the doctor and Tom – sat huddled together around the bed like a coven of witches, murmuring prayers. All night they sat there.

At first light the doctor stood up, snapped his bag shut and heralded the dawn with finality:

'I'll need to open the surgery soon I'm afraid. Call me if there's any change.'

When you lift a paving slab, you see the effect on grass deprived of light. Ralph's dying face was yellow now, faded by years of working in the dark. He was all they had left – their mother had deserted them years before. Since then, Bradley had tried to shelter his sister as best he could, but some sense of the girl's own self-worth seemed to have gone missing.

Soon after the doctor left, Tom began to administer the Last Rites. But as though from the dead, Ralph suddenly came to life. He threw off the oxygen mask and struggled to sit up, dropping a hand as heavy as a shovel on his son's shoulder.

'Don't you let 'em get you like they got me, Brad!' he gasped. 'You get yerself out of that damned pit. Go to sea, work on the land, anythin' to get a bit of fresh air in yer lungs! Promise me, boy!' With that he fell back and coughed up the last remnants of Kentish air until his pillows were scattered with rose petals.

'I promise, Dad,' Bradley murmured, but it was too late. The great chest gave up the contented sigh of a dead-tired labouring man as he breathed out for the final time. The priest's thumbs closed the last chapter on his life and gave his blessing to the soul which at last was free.

Long before Bradley was old enough to go down the pit, their mother was still at home and Kim had not long started primary school, his father had often taken him out sea-fishing at night off the coast of Dover. Bradley could remember him saying, *This is the life, boy, not buried alive down that godforsaken pit.* He remembered the fearful excitement they had shared, pushing off from the shore in the pitch black. Ignoring the seeping cold, he'd learnt how to tie and bait the hooks with numb fingers, plunging his hand into a clammy nest of live worms and hearing his father's reassuring voice. *'Like this, lad,'* he'd say, slipping each razor-sharp hook through the wriggling flesh and casting off. Bradley remembered seeing pin-holes of lantern light from fishing boats miles out in the English Channel, thrilled by the sense of freedom he felt and yet wondering at their vulnerability – their own boat was only a small craft.

*

After the funeral, which Kim refused to attend, their father's bedroom was kept locked and the curtains drawn. People had told Bradley that's what you did out of respect and he had no other way of knowing how you dealt with a death in the house. He had been unable to contact his mother to inform her – in fact he had no way of knowing if she herself was still alive. There was no word in his vocabulary for how he missed his mother. When she had gone away, that had been like a death. Grieving for her had become a part of his growing up. Now the memory of his father would join hers.

Starting back at work down the pit, a few days after the burial, Kim followed Bradley downstairs one morning and challenged him.

'You're not goin' to work an' leavin' me with our dad's body still layin' dead in there, are you?' she shrieked. Quiet as a squirrel or as loud as a stricken rabbit – that was Kim.

'Don't be daft, girl! He's not still in there, is he! He's buried up in the churchyard!' He felt he could have laughed but he didn't because she looked so afraid, half like a ghost herself.

'You should've come wi' me, an' seen 'im laid to rest. Would've settled it in your mind. Oh, come 'ere, you poor kid!' he said and, crushing her in his arms, he had to stifle his own unspent tears. He tousled her hair. 'Silly mare, worrying yourself like that,' he whispered, hugging her. His throat ached because he so desperately wanted to cry too.

Leading Kim upstairs, he threw open their father's bedroom door and flung back the curtains, letting the light flood into the room. It showed the sickbed stripped and bare, the bedside cabinet no longer crammed with medicines, no oxygen cylinder, and no more tubes or alien medical apparatus; it had all been cleared away. Where the window pane was broken, a thoughtful neighbour had stuck a piece of cardboard across to block the draught. Wrenching up the sash window, he let the freezing wind gust into the room. Holding her close, he was at last able to let go of those tears backed up like rocks in his throat for so long. Brother and sister clung to each other. Mourning the past – harsh though it was – had thrust them unprepared into an unknown future together. While the wild cruel world spun around them, they both wept.

*

For a few weeks the Irish priest, Tom, often stopped by with a bag of groceries or some meat or chocolate he'd saved for them. Rolling up his sleeves, he would start the evening meal in preparation for when Bradley returned from work. In an absent-minded flurry of masculine domesticity, he went about the chores cheerfully, whistling to himself. He would wash up, fetch the coal in and light the fire. His presence made the house seem homely again.

'I'm no cookery expert, mind,' he mumbled to Kim one day. She had just returned from school and was sprawled lethargically on the sofa, eating bread and jam.

'They didn't teach me anything useful at that Catholic Seminary,' he complained. 'Just as well my old parents taught me a thing or two about looking after a house when I was a boy, eh! They've never had much money but they always make the best of it, so they do.' He was busy clearing the ashes from the grate and looked up at her for a response. 'Eh, Kim?' he prompted.

She gave a twitch of a smile and shrugged her shoulders.

'Suppose so,' she said.

By the time two months had passed by, Bradley, being the head of the household, was working long hours down the pit to pay the bills. Tom's helpful assistance in the house had been replaced by the presence of Kim's schoolfriends, so when Bradley finished work he would often arrive home to find the girls chatting and cluttering up the place with clothes, nail varnish and hairspray.

One of Kim's friends was the practical, pretty and motherly Helen. Helen was older than Kim and in her last year at school. She easily fell into the domestic role the priest had carved out, and she began to bustle about in the kitchen after the other girls had gone, while Kim remained curled up on the sofa staring at the television. She began to organize their food and turn out kitchen cupboards. At first she commiserated with Kim, chivvied and nagged her, but it didn't do any good – the practical side of Kim's nature seemed to be non-existent.

'There seems to be no motivation in your sister,' she confided in

10

Bradley one night, as he sat at the kitchen table eating the beef casserole she had cooked for them. 'You'll have to talk to her; get her to help out a bit in the kitchen, do some washing and stuff. I won't be around for ever, you know.'

Bradley paused in his chewing and looked up at her. 'No?'

He thought for a moment; somehow he hadn't envisaged Helen leaving them. Shrugging his shoulders, he said, 'What can I do? I'm earnin' money to pay the bills, ain't that enough? I don't think Kim knows how to cook an' clean anyway – never seen 'er doin' it.'

'Then she'll have to learn, Brad!'

His dark eyes glowered under a moody brow. Raking a hand through his black hair, he pushed his empty plate forward and folded his arms in front of him on the table. Helen's sympathetic tone, he realized, was changing.

'You'll stick around a bit longer, though, won't yer?' he asked.

'I might be going to college soon, university even one day if I can. If I do well in my exams I might go and study in London or something. I can't be stuck around here all my life, can I? What future is there for me here in Silt Edge? It's a dump!'

Bradley had never spoken to anyone about his own desire to get away. He had shared his dreams with Kim as a child, but they had only been dreams. To hear Helen talk with such assurance about leaving the place made him feel uneasy. He agreed with her, of course he did. And yet, the world she craved was not his kind of world – the world of studying, of college or university. Escaping Silt Edge for him meant making for the open sea, or for the countryside, and to be able to cultivate the soil and breathe fresh air. He longed to be far away from having to endure hours underground in the stifling heat of the pit. It was a freedom he hardly dared hope for, a dream to keep him going through the long winter nights.

While Helen's concern for their domestic arrangements had no effect on Kim's behaviour, Bradley began taking extra care with his appearance. After changing into his gear down the pit at the start of a shift, he found himself folding his clothes neatly before putting them in his locker so they wouldn't be creased when he came to put them back on. Showering and changing at the end of the day in the wash-house, he started putting on aftershave and styling his unruly hair with Brylcreem. The lads began to tease him.

'Blimey, Brad's comin' up smellin' o' roses!' they all laughed, lifting their arms and patting under their armpits in exaggerated mimicry.

'Get lost, you lot!' Bradley chuckled. He was impatient to get home. Without realizing it, Helen had become his focus. One night, he found himself picking a handful of spring flowers to give her. The evenings were getting lighter. Snowdrops had sprung up along the side of the footpath to the colliery, worn bare by years of miners' boots. Hanging back so as not to be seen, he picked a few and felt he was holding a living thing with a beating heart. Afraid he might damage their white waxy heads, he took a dock leaf and curled it around them, totally absorbed in preserving their perfection.

Going in the back door and stamping his feet on the mat, he found Helen at the sink wearing his mother's apron. It was the same faded cotton apron that had been hanging on the kitchen door for years, ever since the day their mother had left.

'Kim's in there, is she?' he asked.

'No, I've sent her up the shop for some lard. It's about time she did something to help.'

'I picked these for you,' he said, holding the small posy out towards her, his pulse accelerating.

'Oh, right!' she laughed. 'My mum's got loads of those in the garden – they grow like weeds, you know!'

He stood holding them, waiting for her to come and take them from him. All day he'd thought of this moment, imagining her soft breath against his face, her fingers touching his as she took the delicate flowers out of his hands.

'Mind yourself out the way, Brad, I've got to get to the oven,' she said. 'And you've still got your boots on! Take them off – I've just washed this floor!'

'But the flowers,' he said, offering them to her again.

'Oh, stick them down there – can't you see I'm busy?'

So he put them on the draining board, knocked sideways by her dismissal, and went out into the back yard. But by then, it was already too late. He longed for her approval. As each day passed, he had found himself falling more and more in love with her.

As he left the kitchen Helen paused, watching him pass the window. She saw his downcast face and his moody eyes flaring with indignation, and a smile played around her lips. Taking up the small posy of snowdrops, she marvelled at the thought of his big clumsy hands gathering them and she put them in a jam jar of water next to his knife and fork.

Chapter 2

1984 – Ten Years Later

Bradley had the sea inside his head. The waves were roaring, crashing to the shore in his mind and dragging with them tons of gravel. Propelled by the strength of this tide, he hurried past the allotments in the half-dark, out towards the copse up by Madden's Farm. How he thirsted for the sea air now! How he longed to fill his lungs with the salt tang and feel the buffeting wind drive him. But he was a prisoner to this hot humid night with its dumb cloud obscuring the moon. 'I'll get away, Dad!' he whispered under his breath. 'Somehow I'll get out of this mess!'

He had had a few beers with the lads, and having arranged to meet them later to go poaching, he feared it would cause another row with his wife, Helen. But he felt he would go mad if he didn't do something soon. He was so hungry, but he wasn't just hungry for food – he was ravenous for life and freedom. He felt trapped and helpless in the deadlock of the strike.

Since the National Coal Strike had begun three months before, memories of the dark consuming tunnels gnawed away at his soul, threatening to draw him down, to smother his nose and mouth with thick black dust. He was quickly developing an aversion to going underground ever again. In his head, his late father's voice echoed back to him down the years: *'Anythin' to get a bit of fresh air in yer lungs! Promise me, boy!'*

Frustration triggered his anger; it wasn't Helen's fault, he thought. But since her enthusiasm for the Miners' Wives Campaign had taken over the house, any feelings she might have had for him seemed as bare now as their kitchen cupboard. He walked faster, filling his lungs with the scent of blackthorn and wild garlic, mentally rolling in it like a sheepdog anxious to be rid of domestic smells on his coat.

This was what he loved. His body responded to the wild spinning of the wind; the scent-laden night air fired up his muscles. This was where he was born to be.

'A man can't live and breathe down the pit,' he murmured. 'I'll get work on the land somehow.' As an owl hooted, his dead father's approval seemed to come from somewhere across the sky. 'I'll not be buried underground any more, Dad. I'll get another job, nothin' special, but I'll get out of that pit like I promised you!'

Far away across the rooftops, the whinnying of a pit pony gave a poignant response to his pledge. The ponies had been retired from the colliery years before; he would never forget the day they were brought up above ground for the last time. When he first saw them turned loose, he'd felt akin to their joy and he could have galloped across the grassy field with them. Casting his mind back to the closeness he and Helen used to share, his body ached for her. 'Where did it all go wrong?' he asked himself. Looking up into the charcoal emptiness of the sky, embers of the hot day scorched into his soul. Where was the love they used to share? Now all her love and caring concern seemed to have been stolen away from him by the campaign. She was always so busy, she had no time for him any more.

Walking quickly through the dark trees, Bradley's shirt soon became soaked with sweat. Carrying an empty canvas fishing bag slung across his shoulders, his clothes hung off him. He checked his fishing knife was still tucked under his belt, and a thrill of excitement ran like a shock of electricity up through his body. It felt good to be out at night with a task ahead of him.

Breaking from the thicket came the sound of a low whistle. It was that unmistakable sound miners use to communicate when they are down the pit. When he gave the answering note, his friend Gavin emerged to meet him out of the darkness, put a finger to his lips and gestured for Bradley to follow him. For once, Gavin had left his dog at home. This was a task requiring stealth and skill, one wrong move could give them away. Already the night was swallowing them up, the lights from the windows of the village receding. The only sound was the brush, brush of their pitboots moving through the long grass. After half a mile or so, two more miners joined them. They didn't utter a word. They moved as one man, silently, deliberately, with sharpened senses – every small sound was amplified by the night air.

The men were heading for Fell's Cross. It was a small copse about two miles distant. The traps had been set the previous night. Gavin was wearing his old raincoat with numerous pockets perfect for carrying twine, wire and small pliers; it had deep pockets in the lining for concealing rabbits. He had travelled with gypsies before settling in Silt Edge and from them he had gained the knowledge of survival, but he didn't boast about it. The way he followed animal tracks and handled poacher's tools, he earned the men's respect.

Following in Gavin's footsteps, Bradley trailed him like a shadow. Dampness seeped through his clothing. Occasionally, an owl shrieked or a disturbed bird broke cover. They were striding automatically now as Gavin set the rhythm. A sense of unreality began to come over Bradley. The adrenalin was rising, he could hear his heart pounding in his ears, and with this energy came long-lost memories of warmth and comfort. It reminded him of when he was a small boy, longing for his mother to come home at night. *If only she would come when he called her: 'Mother! Mother!' At last he could hear her soft footsteps on the stairs! She would put her cool hand on his forehead and sing to him as he savoured her fragrance. Her singing voice was as musical as a blackbird's song.*

Another sensation suddenly took him by surprise – he began to desire his wife. Recalling the natural perfume of her skin, the cool weight of her naked body pressing against him – such feelings overwhelmed him so urgently he lost his concentration. It had been so long since they had lain close, since he had felt that tingling excitement: those slow movements of her fingertips, the flutter of her tongue as delicate as a butterfly's wing. Loving words, quick breaths and sighs as she traced the shadows of his quickening desire. Oh, how he longed to run home to her now! 'Forget the past!' he would say. 'Forget the campaign! Damn the strike! It can't come between us, Helen, it can't! It mustn't!'

A sudden tug on his arm brought him to his senses. There was a torchlight ahead. Someone was standing there in the darkness. They all stopped still, not daring to breathe. One false move, a scuff of leaves, and they would be betrayed. If challenged, they knew they would be lost: no one would be walking through private property legitimately, near on midnight. The gamekeeper flashed his torch about and a metallic reflection revealed the shotgun under his arm. Not breathing, the poachers became as tall and still as trees. If the man had a gun dog with him, they knew they would be lost.

With relief, they heard the rustle of his footsteps receding. Still they remained like standing stones until Gavin finally gave a low whistle: the signal for the 'all clear'. They were climbing now, up a steep bank laced with sinews of tree roots and ropes of tangled ivy, which they grabbed to haul themselves up. As he reached the top, Bradley found Gavin already crouching over a trap. He saw him lift a limp animal form and bundle it into his coat. They all spread out, checking the traps, releasing the taut wire loops which held the last few seconds of a rabbit's life. Bradley soon had two in his bag and was just about to release a third when he felt warmth. At his touch the soft thing shuddered, kicked violently and gave out a piercing scream. It was caught cruelly by its hind leg, the tight wire cutting into its flesh.

He jumped back as the animal flipped around horribly. Looking up, Gavin's stare met his own. Masterful was Gavin, he knew the business; there was no trace of compassion in his lean face. The muscular spasms of the rabbit were as nothing in Gavin's hands. He took hold of its body firmly and with one swift backwards jerk broke its neck. With a nod of satisfaction, he gave it back to Bradley and moved on.

Within thirty minutes all four men had filled their bags and re-set the traps. On Gavin's command they moved out, back down the steep bank. Tree roots threatened to trip them as their weight carried them half-running down through the trees. Ahead, they came upon a small flock of sheep, separated from them by only a few strands of barbed wire. Sheltered on one side by the steep rise of the hill, the sheep began to bleat softly as the scuffing of their boots descended on them. The men stopped and eyed each other. Gavin took out his knife purposefully, facing Bradley with a question in his eyes.

So unexpectedly, hunger pangs leapt out and snatched blood from those tender living throats. It would be so easy. Bradley hadn't eaten roast lamb for months; his stomach churned. Menace flooded the night air but he grew afraid. Sheep rustling was serious; it wasn't like taking a few rabbits. Suddenly appalled at the idea, he shook his head and, turning, appealed to the other two. One of them glanced back over his shoulder, judging the distance between them and the gamekeeper. Gavin looked up at the moon and, seeming to change his mind, relaxed his grip on the knife. He jerked his head and they left the sheep and moved on.

Just as they neared the border of the village, they found the curfew had sparked some activity. Police were everywhere, manning the roadblocks and stopping cars. The men skirted the village and made for the pit-head – a beacon shining across the fields like a lighthouse. Just before they parted company, Gavin gave Bradley an affectionate thump on the back. 'Enjoy your supper, old mate!' he whispered. 'Thanks,' he replied. They were the only words they had spoken to each other all night.

It was well after midnight when Bradley got home but there was still a light on in the kitchen. She must still be up. His earlier physical desire was now forgotten; the prospect of a confrontation with Helen made him shudder. He was able to enter his back garden by leaping the back fence and in a moment he was at the back door. Finding it locked, he tapped on it, calling, 'Helen, it's me!'

The door flung open and bathed him in light. She stood staring at his filthy blood-streaked clothes in horror. 'Brad! What have you been doing? Look at the state of you!'

Lowering his bag of loot to the floor, he sank into the nearest chair.

'Where d'you think I've been, murderin' someone?' He felt exhausted. 'I've been out with Gavin. Now don't start, look – I've brought us some fresh rabbit for our dinner tomorrow.' He opened the bag and revealed a mass of brown fur, white down and rabbits' ears. 'We've easily got enough for two or three days here once I've skinned an' cleaned 'em. A nice rabbit stew wi' some carrots an' that from the allotment – it'll be grand.' He looked up at her eagerly but was shocked by her expression.

'How disgusting! I'll tell you what you can do with those, Bradley Shepstone – go and bury the poor things up your precious allotment.' Turning away, she stormed up the stairs, adding, 'I'm going to bed.' He stared after her, feeling a million miles away from anyone who would ever understand him.

Upstairs, Helen was close to breaking point. Their raised voices had disturbed the baby and almost thankfully she had picked him up and cuddled him, soaking up the comfort from his babyish smell.

'And so, it's war,' she murmured, gazing out of the bedroom window, with the baby on her shoulder. Headlights from cars in the street outside were striking into silhouette the figures of policemen exercising the curfew – stopping drivers and asking questions. In several police vans parked by the roadside, she imagined boyish faces peering out, waiting for something to happen, sleep-deprived young men, bored and hungry for action.

Holding Sam on her shoulder, she let her eyes wander around the room, seeing it as though for the first time. She saw homely but shabby, mismatched furniture. It was still in essence Bradley's parents' place, she thought; there was hardly anything new, nothing she would have chosen herself. 'Oh, Sam, what's going to happen to us?' she whispered into the baby's damp hair.

Thinking back, as a lonely and quite morose youth, Bradley had appealed to her like no other. He was uncommonly detached, not like the lads in Ebbingsfield where she had grown up. Grieving the loss of his father, he had retained a certain vulnerability, but also he had a wildness about him, which meant that when he came home from the pit, angry and scowling at life, instead of recoiling from him she had felt inexplicably drawn to him. Coupled with the fact that he and his sister Kim were in effect orphaned, she had also felt needed. But now, carrying Sam to the mirror, she asked her reflection: Why do I always step in and try to mother the unfortunates? But a sudden rush of guilt made her turn away from the mirror. It's not Brad's fault, she thought. He's a good man at heart, he hasn't changed. It's me who's changed. But I do want more out of life than being a miner's wife! No excitement, nothing to look forward to! Please, dear God, help me!

Downstairs, in the silence of the house, Bradley sat and waited for Helen to come back. A procession of words, fragments of conversations drifted in and out of his mind. Finally, realizing she wasn't coming back down, he took the rabbits and went outside. He topped and tailed them with his penknife and skinned them as Gavin had taught him. Then, slitting open their bellies, he cleaned them under the running tap in the yard. Going back indoors, he took a heavy saucepan from the pantry, jointed the meat, ran cold water enough to cover it and added a good measure of salt. In the morning, whatever Helen said, he would pull some onions from his allotment, dig up some carrots and cook them a good hot stew.

Working down on his allotment in fine rain a few days later, Bradley paused and looked up. The trees were beginning to sway and in a shudder of excitement he sensed the winds of change. Something was in the air. It was as though he had soared upwards and was looking down on himself. Such a small insignificant human being, digging away on a pathetic portion of the earth! He caught his breath. It occurred to him that if God was up there, perhaps he had just lifted the lid to take a closer look at him. A sense of providence fired up his blood and he cast about, seeing clumps of natural chalk shining white against the iron-rich soil. A sweep of seagulls screamed overhead as storm clouds gathered, wrapped in pinkish-grey vapour, pierced by shards of sunlight. As a fisherman loves the freedom of the sea, Bradley exalted in feeling fresh air in his lungs as the cold rain showered his face, trickling down his neck and sleeves. It mingled with his sweat and, tasting its saltiness on his lips, it took him back to his boyhood days out fishing with his father.

Resuming his digging, he saw a figure approaching: it was Gavin with the collie at his heel. One thing he missed about working was the companionship of his workmates. Shouting a greeting, he stood watching him leave the perimeter of the allotments and take the path towards him. While he waited, he started to clean the clagging clay from his boots with the edge of his spade.

'How y'doin', ole mate?' Gavin called when he was still some distance off. 'You're still at it then?'

'Yeah, you all right? Them rabbits were real tasty, y'know, the other night. My missus did her nut but still – nothin' beats a good stew when a man's hungry.'

'Too right. What's that you're plantin' out then?'

'Some cabbage an' Brussels sprouts an' that,' Bradley replied, digging again with renewed energy. 'You still growin' some?'

'I do a bit,' replied Gavin, 'but I ain't got mouths to feed like you have. Only Skip here. He doesn't take too kindly to Brussel sprouts, do you old boy?' At his voice the dog looked up curiously and pricked his ears. 'Mind you, some nights all he's had is a bowl of potato peelin's cooked in broth – all I've had for him, poor fella. But he doesn't mind, he's a good lad.' He cuffed the dog affectionately. 'Better than a woman any day, eh, old chap!'

'You can say that again!' Bradley replied. 'I've been thinkin', Gavin, I might go for getting out of here altogether and gettin' a bit of land.'

'What, the allotment's not big enough for you, eh?' Gavin teased.

Bradley looked up from his digging and grinned. 'I'm serious! What would you say to me goin' for a smallholding to make a livin' out of it, proper like?'

'Like in *The Good Life*, y'mean? Can't see your Helen falling for that one!'

'No,' Bradley said, 'nor can I.' There was a silence between them for several minutes, interspersed with the sound of Bradley's spade slicing into the wet soil. Gavin stood with his collar turned up against the wind, watching his friend's progress through half-closed eyes. The aggression with which Bradley attacked the soil didn't go unnoticed.

'You're serious, aren't you?' he said.

'I'm deadly serious, Gavin, I need to get out of the pit. I'll fight my way out if I have to!' He stood up and, taking a deep breath, filled his lungs with the rain-soaked air. 'I can't stand this deadlock, and what's worse, when the strike's finished, I can't bear the thought of goin' back down underground for the rest of my life. I'd rather die, here and now, while I can still see a bit o' green.'

'You told Helen you wanna get out?'

'No,' Bradley chuckled, shaking his head. 'No point, not till I've got half a chance of doin' anythin' about it. She'll cut me down, mate, before I even open my mouth.'

'She might not,' Gavin muttered, gazing down at his friend's thinning hair. Bradley worked on in silence, throwing each heavy spadeful with relish.

'What I need,' he gasped as he let another load fly, 'is some real money behind me so I can say to her: "Look, we've got some cash now, why don't we do this or do that." ' He paused. 'Hey! I'll show you!' He thrust the spade into the ground, felt in his jacket pocket and brought out a small newspaper cutting. 'It's a smallholding to let, on a lease, in a remote part of the Welsh hills. It ain't too expensive and look at its barns, Gavin, and the stone cottage – it's got several acres! That's what set me thinkin'!' His eyes shone with delight.

Gavin studied it for several moments. 'Looks great, but get real, mate – where are you gonna get that kind o' money?'

'I'll put in for redundancy, of course! Voluntary redundancy! They're asking for names, I know they are.' He took up his spade again and rammed it back into the soil with all his strength. 'That's my answer, Gavin.'

The dog was bored now, nosing around and following a trail back along the path. Gavin watched him silently, thoughtfully, not whistling him back. After a few minutes he said carefully, 'Brad, old mate, there's only one problem with that, y'know. You can't put in for redundancy – the Coal Board won't accept it, not unless you go back to work first, that is.' He waited for the information to register. 'You'd have to break the strike.'

Bradley paused, stopped digging and straightened up. His heart missed a couple of beats. He looked his friend straight in the eye. 'You sure about that?'

Gavin nodded. 'I heard our gaffer telling a chap up the Welfare; they won't even give you the time of day. Back to work first, talk after, that's what he said.'

Bradley fell silent and Gavin, sensing the conversation was over, whistled his dog and made to leave. 'Take it easy, old mate, eh,' he said. 'I'll be seein' yer.'

Bradley watched him striding away towards Fell's Cross and his heart turned to stone within him. Could he ever bring himself to betray Gavin? To go against Helen and all his mates, break the strike and return to work? He crumpled the newspaper cutting up in the palm of his hand and was about to fling it into the freshly dug soil but suddenly changed his mind and thrust it back into his pocket. Something in him just couldn't give up the dream, not just yet.

Chapter 3

'I thought being a priest was hard enough, but my God, having to sit on the fence and say nothing!' complained Tom, sitting at his old typewriter. Bradley was sprawled opposite him in an armchair.

'So they don't want you preachin' politics from the pulpit then, Tom?' Bradley remarked, taking a gulp of beer. He grimaced and looked twice at his glass. 'Bloody hell, Tom, what did you put in this?'

The priest regarded him soberly. 'Maybe it could have done with being left to ferment a bit longer,' he commented. Turning again to his sermon, he declared resolutely, 'No, I'm to "sit on the fence and remain impartial", that's how the bishop put it.' He compressed his lips glumly. 'What he doesn't realize is, there's nothing else but the strike on anyone's mind around here. How can I ask my congregation to give money for digging wells in Africa, for goodness' sake? People just aren't interested in that sort of thing at the moment. They've no spare cash anyway, God help them.' He typed laboriously for several moments, mumbling to himself.

'Tell me about it!' replied Bradley, who was well aware his debts were mounting by the day.

Several weeks had elapsed since his poaching escapade had driven yet another wedge between himself and Helen. Stretching out his legs, he put the beer glass down and wiped his mouth on his sleeve.

Tom peered at his work again, wrenched it from the typewriter, screwed it up and hurled it towards the bin. Bradley kicked out at the paper with his steel studded pit boot and tossed it like a ping-pong ball. It missed the bin and rolled under a cabinet.

'So why don't you stand up and say what you really want to?' asked Bradley mischievously. 'Folks round here would respect you for it at least!'

'What do I really want to say though, Brad? That we've all got a duty to stick together in this strike and put on a united front? Give me a break! Some of my parishioners, who I won't name, God bless them, are dead against the strike. They won't admit it, of course, or their lives wouldn't be worth living.' He scratched his grizzled head, looking genuinely perplexed.

The sight of his tragic face caused Bradley to smile involuntarily. 'So why don't you just tell the bishop to stuff it!' he chuckled and downed a hearty gulp of the homemade brew.

Tom straightened up and removed his glasses. 'You know, Bradley, sometimes I'm very tempted, God forgive me. It's at times like these I wonder where my vocation came from, or rather, where it's gone. My dear mother would be horrified to hear me say that, but it's true.'

'Don't beat yourself up about it, Tom. We're only human – we can't all be perfect, can we!' He finished his beer, dragged himself up from the armchair and, leaving Tom to struggle over his sermon, made his way to his allotment. There he knew he would find peace of mind. Digging and turning the soil gave him a sense of otherness. While many of his fellow miners spent most of their waking hours picketing, sounding off about the strike or sitting around drinking up the working men's club, he felt at least he was doing something positive by growing food. Also it got him out of the house. People were constantly coming and going, the phone was always ringing and Helen usually had her head buried in a pile of papers. He feared she was turning their home into a mini-headquarters for the Miners' Wives Campaign and he found the atmosphere difficult.

Leaving the allotments two hours later, Bradley shouldered his spade like a rifle and set off for home. A fence of policemen had gathered along the street – a peculiar sight – with arms interlocked, forming a barrier to protect the rebel miners making their way to work. Lined up like lead soldiers, the only moving target happened to be Bradley and he felt their eyes on his back. Suddenly the ghostly memory of his young workmate, Neil, came into his mind. His eyes looked dusty and unseeing, like the bird they'd once found behind the fridge that the cat had brought in. Tragedy had struck at the coal face. *'Just pass us that drill, would you, Neil?'* he heard himself say. A deep rumble made them both glance up, as though a thunderstorm threatened. *'Oops! Somethin's going on up there!'* chuckled Neil, his playful laugh preceding an enormous roaring sound. Desperately they lunged towards safety, but the underworld that had allowed them to creep under its eaves came crashing down on them.

When the earth moves underground, something always rushes in to take its place. Gas, carbon monoxide, water, toxic dust – never anything life giving. Neil had only been working down the pit three months. He was small boned for his age, no muscle on him, not much more than a kid really. Where he had stood minutes before, smiling impishly, was a shifting pile of rock and timber eight feet high.

After the explosion of noise – silence. Bradley was on his stomach, winded. *'Neil! Neil, are you there, lad?'* Silence. *'Neil! For God's sake, answer me!'* He listened again. Dear God, let him be all right. Silence. Nothing, only a tremor as the dust shifted and settled. Gradually Bradley had become aware of the pain in his legs; he tried to move but found they were pinned under a beam. Not daring to try more force in case the whole lot came down on him, he waited. Any voice, any movement might mean a sign of life. Twisting his neck around and gasping with the exertion, the beam from the lamp on his hard hat at last found a glimpse of Neil's face. He was still; he looked like a plaster cast, his head and shoulders completely covered in grey dust.

Miners give their lives to the pit. They don their working clothes and descend underground not just as a team, but as a family. Each man has to look out for all the others, they are all like limbs of the one body. They have to care enough for their fellow man to shoulder and support a falling beam if it means it will save his life – beams that might hold ten tons of rock under a collapsing roof. Each man's life is in the next man's hands. It's a shared life. Each breath of oxygen is shared, it has to be, because every hint of danger affects everyone and therefore it has to be made known. If gas is suspected, everyone has to be ready to sound a warning: one tiny spark can cause an explosion and a rolling ball of fire that will consume the whole tunnel in seconds. So it's a shared life, it's not your own life.

It had been twenty hours before the rescue team reached them. All Bradley remembered of it was a timeless, womb-like darkness of pain, which was savagely interrupted by the blinding lights of the rescuers. As soon as he had heard sounds of their approach he had roared with renewed strength: *'We're here! For God's sake we're here!'* And then their bright eyes, their faces full of life and excitement. *'Leave me!'* he had cried. *'Get the lad out! Neil, they've found us!'*

'We're on to it mate, don't worry,' they had told him. *'We'll have him out in no time! Easy now, here: drink this, just a sip, no more.'* They had moistened his parched lips and he had yielded to a sinking faint as the medics injected something into his arm before manipulating the beam to release his legs.

Relief! To be lifted out of the grave and carried up into the light. Pain came, deep in the marrow of his bones, and a rush of life-giving air that had made him cough and heave. Born again.

'One of the saved,' murmured the crowd. *'Thanks be to God.'* Bradley's eyes stung, they seemed full of pepper and stinging sand. He tasted blood; his chest was as heavy as lead. Such relief to be surrounded by Helen's soft arms, to sense her smell, to feel her warm tears on his face. *'I thought you were gone, Bradley, love!'* she had sobbed, shouting as though he was still down the end of a dark tunnel.

'Was Neil with you?' begged Helen. *'His poor mother's going frantic here.'*

'Yeah, he's coming,' Bradley had replied. *'Just behind me.'*

Neil was brought out three hours later, like a shadow detached from the living boy. Neil's mother was there and she kept calling him her 'baby'. He was all dried up; he looked like nothing more than a roll of old carpet. But suddenly he had moved and coughed.

'He's still alive!' The crowd started cheering. Press cameras flashed. But as the fresh air went tumbling into his lungs something happened – it seemed to explode his young heart. Perhaps the shock of being born again was too much. His mother clung to him hysterically. He was supposed to take a breath and cry, but he took a breath and died,

without even opening his eyes. He was still born. And the midwife crowd wept.

Bradley walked on purposefully, ignoring the line of policemen as best he could. It reminded him of what his dad had taught him: '*When you encounter a vicious dog, lad, look straight ahead and keep your hands in your pockets – meet their eyes and you're done for.*'

A rumble of rowdy voices and laughter broke from the open windows of the working men's club, distracting the policemen's attention. They turned their heads as though to a single command.

'That lot sound happy don't they!' he heard one say.

'Striking must agree with 'em,' scoffed another.

On hearing this, a surge of anger made him shout, 'Just look at you lot! What are you all waitin' for? You make it look like goin' to work's a bloody crime!'

'S'pose it is, sir,' replied a copper near him. 'To that lot in there it is, anyway! Mates of yours, are they?' he sneered, eyeing him up and down. 'They'd soon have you, you know, if you turned up for work on the shift tonight, wouldn't they? Ha! You couldn't call them friends of yours then, could you!' Ugly laughter rippled down their ranks.

'Get lost!' shouted Bradley. 'Wish I could go to work, at least I'd be damned well earnin' something.' He kicked a stone because the thought of going back underground filled him with dread.

'Don't think your missus would like to hear you talking like that!' laughed a policeman. 'She's a bit of a local hero, so we've heard,' he added, winking at his colleague. Snakes' eyes watched for his reaction. So they'd seen his Helen on the television news. Getting right carried away, she was, he thought, with her banners and everything. God knows he could do without that.

'Oh, she's got her head full of politics all right,' he found himself saying out loud. 'I've told her we can't go on living on handouts and charity for much longer but what's the use? She won't give in. Bloody stupid strike, I'm sick of it! They said it would be over in a month and now look – four months and still no sign of an end to it.' He knew he shouldn't be complaining to a load of coppers but he couldn't help it.

He didn't care. No one understood anyway. No one would listen. Nobody.

The policemen exchanged amused glances but remained silent. Perhaps they were thinking of their own wives sitting at home. Perhaps they had already joked about being paid to stand around doing nothing in a quiet village street. As he walked on, Bradley felt their eyes on his back, weighing up his spade with bored suspicion. One copper he seemed to recognize and he realized it was the local builder's son. 'Expecting trouble tonight then are you, Colin?' he called amiably.

The young policeman eyed him strangely. Suddenly he broke free from the line – and with a lunge towards him – kicked the spade out of his hands. He stormed him, crushing his face against the wall, yanking his arms behind his back.

'What do you know about any trouble then?' he hissed in his ear. 'Heard something have we, mate?'

'Get off me! Bloody hell, don't yer recognize me, Colin?' he hissed as more policemen surrounded them, heaving their bodyweight against him like the massive flank of a horse.

'Look,' gasped Bradley, trying again. 'If the others recognize you, your life won't be worth living round here. Get off of me and I'll say nothin'. Count yourself lucky it's only me has seen yer.'

The copper's pale blue eyes dilated. He shrugged his shoulders, muttered something to his colleagues and they shoved him aside like a worthless sack of clothes. Bradley hit the ground, winded. In case their boots came in, he scrambled to his feet hastily, grabbed his spade and made off to the sound of their sniggering. Once at a safe distance, he walked on slowly, too tired to be angry any longer. Would the coppers being here make any difference? He didn't think so. What a waste of time and money! Would the strike save the pit? He didn't know or care – it would close down eventually, he knew that. 'And good riddance to it,' he muttered under his breath. He loathed the noise and dirt. The suffocating dust seemed to swell up in his lungs at the thought of it. Don't they know that just because I'm a miner, it doesn't mean I'm on the miners' side? He didn't feel he was on anyone's side any more – only on his own side. Completely alone.

Bradley left the police behind and made his way home. He was a lean wolf of a man, as sharp as a hunted fox. His eyes were scarred raw, watchful for the slightest movement in hedgerow or thicket. Carrying his undernourished frame loosely, he tried desperately to relax. At ease in his own body, it was his anger which made him as alert as an animal; if anyone stood in his path he would spear them with one flash of his dark eyes.

Beneath the landscape he loved lay the black coiled serpent of the pit. He dreaded its dark places and its poisonous jaws. The time would come, he knew, when its ugly coal face would gape open to reveal the vacuum that had swallowed man and boy alive. That ugly womb, snatching back the babies that had once been born and suckled. It choked him to think of it. Looking out across Silt Edge from the footpath, he could see a panorama of terracotta-coloured roofs, Mediterranean-looking in the orange glow of the evening sun. In the midst of those houses was his own home, built and owned by the Coal Board and let to employees of the colliery. Miners and their families had once travelled on foot all the way from Wales to work in the Kent coalfields; they had come tempted by promises of better wages and working conditions. Leaving behind outdoor toilets and gas lighting, they moved into houses with all the 'mod cons'. Their children ran from room to room, switching the lights on and off and squealing in delight. They had never known houses like them, with bathrooms and hot running water.

In the distance Bradley glimpsed the landscaped grounds of the big manor house of Chalkfield Hall, nestling in the neighbouring village of Ebbingsfield. With its neat bungalows and detached houses, this was where Helen's mother lived and where its only pub had a sign up in the window: 'No miners admitted'.

Not visible from where he stood, but less than twenty miles away was the English Channel and the white cliffs of Dover. When the sea fog rolled in, the low booming sound of the cross-channel ferries could often be heard at Silt Edge. His father's voice came back to him again: '*Listen, son, hear that boom? Put your jacket on – the weather's turning.*' Overhead, seagulls flocked inland, screaming their raucous cries across the miners' rooftops as though to herald a storm, their greedy eyes seeking out dustbins to ransack. But not much was surplus to requirements in the mining village; prosperity had turned to famine. The gulls circled redundantly on the warm air currents, with pink-lidded, hungry eyes.

Now Bradley caught sight of washing left to dry in the humid heat. He could hear parents' voices calling their children indoors. Their shouts ricocheted between brick, slate and slag heap. No one was allowed on the streets after nightfall. Not all obeyed the police, of course: they moved between houses like thieves in the night, meeting relatives, pickets planning attack and scabs making their secretive way to work.

Sometimes, late at night, the sound of pit boots tramping towards the pit gates could be heard. If recognized, the faces of men who had broken the strike would never be forgotten. They were considered traitors, all of them. They would never be forgiven. All these thoughts went through Bradley's head as he came to his own front gate. Hatred for a scab was an inherent part of belonging to a small mining community. This was their common denominator: to be united against the enemy.

He had already made up his mind to go to the NUM* meeting that night, to see if anything new was up. But he dreaded going home to get a shave and change in case Helen was in one of her enthusiastic moods. It was impossible for him to enthuse with her about the strike campaign or to care about the pit's future, he hated it so much – the pit that had killed his father and his friend. If he couldn't get away, he felt it would rob him of any hope for a future too. So wrapping his feelings up as he went, he braced himself for what Helen might say, stood his spade up against the wall, opened the back door and went inside.

Helen was counting out piles of leaflets. She stood up as he entered and Bradley went to give her a hug but she turned away, wrinkling her nose.

'Get off, Brad!' she said. 'You're disgustingly sweaty!'

* National Union of Mineworkers.

'I've been working,' he said. 'The cops are a bit edgy out there tonight, aren't they?' Receiving no reply, he took the stairs two at a time and went to the bathroom. Emerging a few minutes later with a towel around his waist, he was surprised to find her waiting for him.

'Let's see if we can't get something sorted out tonight, Helen, eh?' he said, aware of having to avoid her eyes. He began dressing as he tossed more words into the vacuum between them. 'The strike's been goin' on for months now after all.' Putting on a clean white shirt, he noticed the collar was looser than usual. Deciding against a tie, he tucked the shirt into his trousers and picked up a comb. 'It can't go on much longer though, can it, love?'

'It'll go on for as long as it takes,' she replied, rather too quickly, he thought. 'We're not going to back down now, are we, Brad, not till it's all sorted.'

He glanced at her but said nothing. Turning towards the mirror, more to see if his face was successful in concealing his temper than anything, he checked his appearance and looked himself in the eye.

'We're managing brilliantly, aren't we?' she continued. 'Everyone's being so generous – the supermarkets, and the schools – it's incredible!'

He tried a gentle response. 'I need to get on and earn some wages though, love, or the bills won't be paid again, y'know that. And the rent's overdue. We don't wanna get evicted, do we?' Already sweat was breaking out again on his back. 'Wish the union wouldn't make such a meal of it! All their talking never gets us anywhere, and all we'll do is end up losin' more pay at the end of the day.' Now he could see in the mirror the reddening flare of frustration creeping up his neck. He turned away from his reflection in time to see her stand up, folding her arms defiantly.

'Don't talk like that!' she retorted. 'We've got half the country on our side. If we keep up the fight like we're doing and stick together, well, they won't dare close the pit down, will they!'

Bradley attempted to defuse the situation. He sat down on the edge of the bed and appealed to her common sense. 'So why do I feel the strike's so wrong then, love? The industry's so out of date – it's like the old days, like sendin' little kids up the flamin' chimney! We can't

32

go on scrabblin' around in the muck and dirt like flipping animals for much longer, not in this day and age. It's filthy dangerous work, Helen, you know it is! It's had its day, you have to admit it!' A nervous amusement almost stole his nerve but he persevered. 'I don't think we've got a bat in hell's chance of keepin' it going really, so what's the point in fightin' it? The pits will close eventually. You know it, I know it, the men know it, and y'know what, even the union bosses, I bet even they can feel it in their bones! That coal is best left where it lies, dead and buried – dead and bloody buried – and the sooner we get out of that pit the better.'

Helen was unmoved. 'What about all those who have gone before you then? You think they've worked their backsides off for nothing? You think they have given their lives for something that's not even worth saving?'

'I do, yes,' he said, 'and ain't it about time someone had the guts to turn round and say, "Hey look, it's not a great industry any more – it's an old cog in an old clapped-out machine that should have been shut down years ago". Trouble is, no one's got the guts to stand up and say it. If they still want the coal got up, then open-cast mining's the only way forward. Let the machines take the sweat, that's what I say.'

'You do come up with some rubbish sometimes, Bradley Shepstone! The country will grind to a halt without fuel to keep the power going. We'll have the government on its knees begging us to return to work before the year's out, you wait! They'll be no electric, nothing to power industry—'

'Helen, there are other ways. They know it, they know there's the nuclear power stations, there's ways of gettin' power out the wind an' the sea. They want coal all right but just want it easy, they want it cheap – and they don't care! If some men are fool enough to crawl about in the dark on their hands and knees then they'll go along with it, so long as it's bringin' enough money in. If they can't have our coal then they'll get it from abroad, cheap stuff from Russia, or anywhere where they can get the poor sods to fetch it up. That's how loyal they are to us mine workers! It all comes down to money in the end!'

He hadn't meant to, but Bradley realized he'd opened his heart to her and now she knew just what little faith he had in the strike. 'Anyway, I'd best get up there or I'll miss the show,' he added bitterly.

'So, they still need our coal so why are they trying to close the pits then?' she persisted. 'All the men want is security. They wouldn't be talking about shutting us down if they still needed the coal!'

'They're only closin' the uneconomic pits, Helen, and ours is one of 'em. Stands to reason – when it takes more money an' manpower to get the coal out than they can sell it for, well, it's pointless. The Kent coalfields are always floodin', the seams are thin and hard to access, it gets too expensive. Not like Nottingham: there the seams are rich, easy pickings. Give you three guesses why that lot in Nottingham haven't joined the strike! They know their jobs are safe, that's why.' He sighed, tired now. 'We can't win, Helen, so what's the point in trying? I just wish we could have got out years ago. I could have got a job on a farm or somethin' instead of being stuck here like a pig in mud.'

Impatiently she began tidying the bed which was already made, flicking the covers and tucking in the sides. 'There you go again, dreaming, as usual! What kind of wage would you get on a farm round here anyway? It's all casual work, fruit picking – that's OK for students but it's not like having a proper wage, Brad. We can't raise a family on that, can we!'

'I know, I know,' he sighed, 'but there must be another way.'

She came and rested her hand briefly on his shoulder. Relief flooded through him at her touch and he grasped her hand and gave it a squeeze. Like an exhausted offshore swimmer, weakness swept through him. He would have given anything to have taken her in his arms, to feel she was with him and not against him. 'We'll sort somethin' out, love,' he said gently. 'Don't worry.' He could have kissed her, but when he brought his face towards hers, she didn't respond – she was miles away.

'Right, I'd better go,' he said.

'Perhaps I ought to go too, you know,' she called as she descended the stairs after him. 'We've got to show that lot we're not going to give in easily. If anyone gets an inkling we're not a hundred per cent behind this strike, it could all fly back in our faces.'

He turned back in surprise. 'What do you want to go for? It'll only be that man from the union going on and on, and the Coal Board arguing their case – it'll be dead boring! It's not exactly a night out, is it!'

'You've got to tell them we're not open to compromise,' she said importantly. 'Tell them we're managing. We've got plenty of money in the kitty and support from all over the country. We'll get by, so long as we stick together, for as long as it takes. Let that Maggie Thatcher know she's got a real fight on her hands! I'd like to stand up and say we're behind them a hundred per cent – the strike's not just about money, it's the principle of it! We want prospects! Job security! Oh, Brad!' she cried, reaching out and grasping his upper arms with firm hands, her eyes shining. 'We want jobs for life, don't we! It'll be worth it in the end!'

'You just don't see it, do you? Haven't I toiled away long enough already? Do you think I enjoy haulin' tons of rock in that heat with every bone in my body screamin'? I've had years of risking life and limb, seein' men go down for a day's work and never comin' up again. A job for life, you say? Didn't help my poor old dad, did it! Didn't help young Neil.' The words were out before he had time to stop them.

She thrust him away. 'Trust you to say something so callous,' she whispered.

He hated her then, for the way she turned words into weapons against him, making him look thoughtless and cruel. There was nothing he wanted more than to bring Neil back from the dead or to have his dad back and hear him curse the pit. Suddenly he couldn't wait to get away from her. Taking his jacket, he walked towards the door. Turning, he said quietly, 'Please yourself, Helen. Go along if you like, it's up to you. But I'm going to hear what they've got to say to us, not the other way around. Prospects? Scrapin' a living out of that black dead-end coal hole the rest of my life – you think that stands to mean I've got prospects? You seem to be forgettin' one thing, love,' he added. 'I'm the one out on strike, not you! When the strike's over, I'm the one who's got to go back down underground, not you. If it were a hundred years ago, you might be down there too, draggin' carts on your hands and knees for a pittance. Would you be callin' that prospects? I doubt it. Oh, look, love,' he sighed, 'you don't know half of it, really you don't.'

But she turned her back on him and folded her arms. So he went out, closing the door behind him, desolate.

Chapter 4

Hearing a faint knock, Tom opened his front door to see a girl on the doorstep.

'Excuse me, Father, I shouldn't be here really,' she whispered, staring with frightened eyes, 'but could I ask you somethin' though?' She glanced over her shoulder as if afraid to be seen there.

'Of course, come along inside,' he said, swallowing a mouthful and casting a forlorn look in the direction of his half-eaten dinner.

'No, I hadn't better.' She took a step back. An older face than her teenage appearance, he thought. There was something familiar about her.

'Come across to the church then?' he suggested.

He took the church keys and watched her walk down the path hugging herself. Here's another waif and stray, he sighed, with hungry eyes and a sad tale to tell. I wonder where she's sprung from?

She was standing inside the church-porch when he got there, like a stray dog waiting to be let in. He unlocked the door and led her into the dimly lit building. It was cool and shady after the heat of the day; pigeons cooed in the hollow recesses of the roof. The girl sat in one of the pews: Tom sat in front and turned to her.

'Now tell me, you're in some sort of trouble, eh?' he asked. 'What's your name, child?'

'It's Kim,' she replied, looking surprised. She broke off from chewing the cuffs of her cardigan which were pulled down over her small hands. 'Kimberley, y'know, Bradley's sister?' she said, staring at him expectantly.

'Kim!' the priest exclaimed. 'My word, it's years since I've seen you. And your brother never said you were back! I must confess I'd never have recognized you!'

The girl shrugged. 'I ain't been around long. Didn't he tell you I was workin' in London? I got a job with this girl I knew, in a hotel, only cleanin' an' that, but I've chucked it in now. After me friend went off wi' this bloke, I moved back here. I ain't goin' to Mass though, not now I'm with—' She trailed off and fixed him with an anxious stare. 'You helped us right, me and me brother, when Dad died? I don't know who else to ask.'

Tom ran his fingers through his greying hair, waiting patiently for her story to unfold. 'So, are you in some sort of trouble, Kim?'

'Father,' she began, 'if you get pregnant, right, and you've got nowhere to go, is there somewhere where they'll have you, you know, to have the baby, like, without no one knowin'?' Her eyes flashed a glint of hostility.

'Do you mean a Christian house or a convent, Kim? Yes, I dare say there is such a place, especially for a young girl such as yourself.' He smiled to reassure her.

'Oh no, it ain't me! It's me friend – I was just askin'!' she exclaimed, her cheeks flushing a vivid red.

'I can't help you unless you're completely honest with me, Kim. So who is this girl in trouble? Do I know her?'

'No, you don't, her name's um . . .' Kim's imagination failed her. A silence ensued. While Tom looked on curiously, her eyes flitted about nervously for inspiration. Finally, she relented. 'Oh, all right then, it's me, right – but don't go and tell no one, will yer?'

'Of course not. I'll keep it under my hat.' He touched his forelock with an index finger. But any attempt to help her relax failed. She crumpled into tears and he watched the top of her once-blonde head sadly as her body shook with sobs.

'Kim! Come now, no need to upset yourself. We'll sort something out. Now, the father of the baby, does he—'

'Danny?' she cried. 'Danny won't want no baby! He told me before, if I forget to take that rotten pill again he'd land me one – an' he will as well.' Recovering herself, the girl snorted and Tom fetched a box of tissues from a table by the church door, which he offered to her.

'Danny?' ventured Tom.

'My boyfriend. I met 'im in a pub when I was in Dover last summer an' he was startin' work down the pit. I've moved in wi' him now,' she explained, blowing her nose savagely. 'He's got a council place here, up the road.'

'Oh, Danny Stuart!'

'You know him?' The girl looked up in alarm.

'I know *of* him, that's all.'

'He'll kill me if he finds out I'm pregnant. The doctor said, if I want to, he can get rid of it for me though. I've thought about it. He wants me to come back an' tell him, and he said he'd sort it for me with the clinic an' that but—' She faltered. 'But I sort o' like babies – they have all them pretty clothes an' toys an' that.' She sniffed, her eyes flooding. 'You won't go an' tell Danny though, will yer? He won't let me 'ave it, he'll kill me first. He hates kids.'

Tom's features softened. If only babies were born complete with all their pretty clothes and ribbons, he thought, and perhaps a crock of Irish gold thrown in for luck. Poor girl. It was as though someone had promised her a present – like a new doll for Christmas – and that was all she had to look forward to.

'A baby is God's gift to us, child, and whatever our circumstances, it's a gift to be cherished. I give you my word, Kim, I promise I won't tell a single soul.' She caught the compassion in his eyes and gave a shuddering sigh of relief.

'Do you love Danny, Kim?' he asked gently.

She stood up abruptly. 'I've got to go,' she said, nervously tugging her short denim skirt down over her bony knees.

'Your brother, Bradley, you know he's a fine fellow. I'm sure he would help.'

'You won't go an' tell me brother, will yer, Father? Oh, you mustn't tell 'im! You promised!' she cried, her cheeks flushed with sudden fury.

'No, it's all right, I won't breathe a word, Kim. Now listen, I'll sort something out for you, and your baby. I'll make a few phone calls, so don't you worry. And you can tell Bradley yourself when things are a bit more settled, eh? Now, where shall I find you?'

'In Danny's stinkin' place, up the road there.' She tossed her head. 'But don't look for me there.'

'Well, will you come back here to see me, say in a day or two? I should have some news by then.'

She agreed, turning to leave. 'I do love Danny,' she said, 'but he's horrible to me though. He's all right 'til he gets drunk an' then he knocks me about.' She sniffed, wiped her nose on her sleeve, and without warning threw her cardigan off of one shoulder, revealing a startling purple and yellow bruise. 'Look,' she said.

'Dear God in heaven, child!' exclaimed Tom. 'Did Danny do that to you?'

But in an instant she was gone.

He watched her go, carrying all the hurts wrapped up in her thin torn clothes. Buffeted by loneliness and cruelty, she seemed to be drifting helplessly like a small boat on the open sea. He vowed he would throw her a lifeline if he could.

Kneeling down to pray, he had begun to make plans for her when those terrible doubts rose up in his head again as though to crush him. How could he lecture a child like this on Catholic teaching? That 'rotten pill' that the poor child had forgotten to take would be enough to bar her from receiving communion. How could he bring himself to enforce such rigid rules? When a child's so vulnerable, and life hasn't blessed her with any comfort, surely a tiny pill couldn't condemn the girl to hell! Where is Christian compassion in all this? He held his head in his hands, praying in anguish. Just lately the doubts in his vocation had really begun to bite. So often, when he started praying, he began trawling over a whole junk room full of doubts and now his mind doubled up in confusion. How can I help the girl when I'm in such a turmoil myself?

Cursing himself, he was distracted by loud voices in the street. He stood up, opened the church door and, seeing a crowd, stepped outside. There was a group of swaggering, well-built miners, including Bradley himself, walking up the street in the middle of the road. 'Coming up the club for the meeting, Father?' one of them shouted. 'It's starting soon!'

'Right you are, lads, I'll be there shortly,' Tom called back, noticing that young Kim was still in the distance, dawdling up the road obliviously.

Helen watched Bradley go from the the window. Just as well I didn't tell him about Danny then, she thought, he'd really have hit the roof. Relief washed over her like a warm wave as she saw him take all the tensions with him, bundled up under his arm like a plumber's tools. It was so like him not to realize she'd want to go too, and yet she couldn't help loving his funny, obstinate character. A smile played around her mouth as she recalled his intensity. Such a proud man, so single-minded and protective of his world!

'Mum?' she said, holding the receiver. 'I know it's short notice but could you pop up and babysit Sam for me? There's a meeting I want to go to.'

If only I could hear what was being said instead of having to wait for when he came home, she thought. Why should I wait on his every word and only hear what he chooses to tell me? If I didn't have the campaign work to do, and the girls' company up the Welfare, what would I do? I just wish the strike would go on for ever, even though the rent's now so in arrears we could be evicted if the Coal Board change their minds. If only Brad and I could talk without it turning into another row!

She went to check on little Sam, who was sound asleep in his cot. Having brushed her hair and changed her T-shirt, she washed up a few cups left on the draining board. Within minutes there was the sound of her mother's car.

'Hello, darling, there's hundreds of miners out there – I thought I was going to be mobbed,' exclaimed her mother, collapsing dramatically into a chair.

'They're all going up the Welfare, Mum,' said Helen. 'It's a meeting with the NUM.'

'Ugh! Is that where you're going, dear? I don't know what you see in that lot!'

Helen didn't even try to explain. 'Mum, have you stopped

41

colouring your hair?'

'Oh, I stopped dyeing it at least six months ago. I thought it was about time I grew old gracefully. No woman over sixty has blonde hair unless it's out of a bottle.'

Helen sat down near her. 'Mum, I've got to go in a minute, but can we talk?'

Beatrice looked at her, concerned. 'It's Bradley, isn't it?' she said.

Helen nodded. 'I just can't seem to get through to him, Mum. Whatever I do is wrong. You'd think he'd be pleased with me keeping the soup kitchen going, all the money we collect and all the work us girls do. You'd think he'd be proud but no, not him! I don't know what to say to him half the time now. He flies off the handle at the slightest thing.'

'It's the strike, dear. It can't be easy for him when he's got a family to support.'

'Yes, but I daren't tell him the latest thing. You know Kim's boyfriend – Danny Stuart – well, he's only gone back in and become a scab. Brad will murder him if he hears, he's so touchy these days. He won't even come up the Welfare for his hot dinner now. Too flippin' proud, he is – he'd rather starve.'

'Well, what's his name, Danny, if he's started back to work I think he must have some sense. Your Bradley ought to take a leaf out of his book and go back too, earn a decent living again. All this business about striking, it's all a waste of time and money if you ask me.'

Helen was looking at her incredulously. 'Mum, no one will think Danny's done the right thing in going back to work! He's a cheat and a coward and he's let us all down.'

'Well, I think he's been very brave and sensible,' Beatrice announced. 'I wish your husband had as much guts. I'm sorry dear, I know I shouldn't say that but I do! I've a good mind to tell him so myself.'

'Mum, please!' Helen remonstrated with her in horror. 'Please don't say that. Brad's mad enough already and—'

'And what, dear? It really is high time he was told.'

'Mum, listen!'

'Helen, darling!' her mother began, putting a firm hand on her daughter's arm. 'You know, your poor father and I, we had such hopes for you. You were so clever at school! We both expected you to go on to university. With the results you had, why, you could have become a teacher like me, or even a lawyer. And then, just as you reached the crossroads in your life, you go off and marry a coal miner! A coal miner, of all people!'

'I fell in love, Mum, and he needed me. I know I should've listened to you and Dad, but I wanted to do what Bradley wanted, settle down and start a family. I didn't want to keep slogging away studying for a career, it didn't seem right, being ambitious. Well, it wasn't part of his world, if you know what I mean.'

'Unfortunately, I know exactly what you mean,' her mother replied. 'Helen, love!' A tear came to her eye and she swallowed hard. 'When your father was alive, he always said that you can't be pleasing other people all the time. If you're not sure what to do at any given time, just do what you feel is best in your own heart. And that's exactly what you did. He was very angry with you, yes, and in principle he wasn't entirely wrong, bless him. He was just a bit selfish sometimes I suppose. He wanted you to do what he thought was best.' She looked back at Helen and smiled, and an expression of such sadness crossed her face that Helen rose and went to hug her as words suddenly seemed inadequate.

After a few moments, releasing her mother and recovering herself slightly, Helen said, 'Just lately, with all the fundraising I've been doing, I've surprised myself how much I get out of it, Mum. The other girls, well, it's amazing, they don't even know how to write proper letters or anything! Now you've given me your typewriter, I've been able to – Oh!' she broke off excitedly. 'I've had an answer back from Downing Street!'

'No!' Beatrice cried in amazement. 'From the prime minister?'

'Yes! I asked Maggie Thatcher if we could go and talk to her, just us girls – the miners' wives – tell her how we're coping, tell her to save our men's jobs and not to close the pits down. She wrote back personally. Wait, let me show you her letter!' Helen dashed upstairs and retrieved the precious document which she had hidden from Bradley in her undies drawer.

Beatrice felt the texture of the paper and gazed in admiration at the printed letter heading. 'Helen,' she whispered, 'look at the quality of that paper and look – her signature!'

'Mum! Mum, read it, read what she says!' cried Helen impatiently, watching every nuance in her mother's face, waiting for her reaction as she read those few words which had engraved themselves in her memory – those words that ran through her head day and night, words she had longed to share.

Beatrice read aloud: '*Arrangements will be made by my secretary for a mutually agreeable appointment . . . looking forward to meeting you. . . .*' She stared at it in disbelief. 'She's invited you to go to Downing Street to meet her!'

'Yes, Mum! Isn't it fantastic?' At last Helen could indulge herself in the pure joy she felt. 'We've had a meeting, us girls, we've arranged the day with Mrs Thatcher's secretary, and we're going up at the end of this month on the train.' She could hardly contain her excitement.

'Oh, well done, my girl!' Beatrice gave her a hug. 'I'm proud of you, my darling. Anything I can do to help, just let me know. I'll have Sam for you, of course. What does Bradley say?'

Helen's face fell and a shadow crossed her brow. 'I haven't exactly told him I'm going yet. He still thinks it's only a rumour, about Downing Street. I know he won't want me to go. He's funny, Mum, he doesn't seem to understand.'

'It's different for him, love.' Beatrice patted her hand. 'He's not the sort for politics and discussions. He's a "yes" or "no" kind of man.'

'Well, it's "No" most of the time these days!' said Helen. 'I don't know how I can persuade him to let me go without causing another row.'

'Helen, you're going and that's definite. Let me deal with Bradley – if he makes a fuss I'll speak up for you, my girl. I'm used to dealing with boys, remember? Now, isn't it time you were off? I'll go up and check on the littl'un. You take as long as you like.'

'Thanks, Mum,' cried Helen, slipping out of the door, her heart pounding with excitement.

Tom locked the church, returned to the presbytery and put his dinner, now cold, in the fridge. Heat still radiated from the pavement as he hurried to catch up with the lads. A noisy crowd, they were all laughing and preening themselves, like boys out on the town.

'How y'doing, Brad?' someone shouted. 'Didn't recognize you with a clean shirt on – what's up wi' yer?' He heard Bradley's rebuff, blinking as though he had just come up from under ground.

'Hey,' called Tom, breathlessly, 'thought I might come along and see what's happening. Sorry, lads, mind if I join you?' he asked, falling in beside them. It was a characteristic of his to apologize at every opportunity.

'You're all right, Tom,' replied Bradley. 'Come along if you like but I bet it don't do us no good!'

Tom was wearing his dog collar, and trousers hitched over, rather than under, his ample belly. A tweed jacket concealed a pair of braces in Irish tartan green. As they neared the entrance, cars and motorbikes were arriving from all directions, parking both sides of the street.

Bound together by untapped energy and testosterone, the miners all began converging on the Welfare Hall. An odour of sweat, aftershave, beer and cigarette smoke carved out a space for them as they swaggered and shouted, laughed and shoved each other. But as a smart black chauffeur-driven limousine cruised past them and drew up at the entrance, the mood changed. There were low whistles and curses as the men exchanged glances.

'There goes one big union fat-arse who's done all right for himself,' cursed Bradley under his breath. 'Would he pity us poor sods wi' no strike pay and nothin' to eat? Would he hell!'

They converged at the door. Bradley stepped back respectfully to let the portly Irish priest go in before him. The volume of noise inside greeted them with a roar and the waft of beer and sweat was almost overpowering. It was packed with men standing shoulder to shoulder.

'Funny they haven't put any chairs out,' said Tom, and stood with his chest heaving.

'There's a few at the back,' observed Bradley, nodding to some men already standing on them to get a better view. 'Gone to town on the decorations haven't they?'

Tom puffed out his cheeks as he gazed at the stage where a long banner declaring solidarity to the National Union of Mineworkers sagged like damp washing. Looking around the hall, Bradley saw that there were a few women dotted about and he felt glad his Helen hadn't come. Tom nudged him, interrupting his thoughts by lifting his eyebrows towards the stage where some activity was commencing. Perspiring, Tom hadn't removed his jacket but was blotting his forehead with a linen handkerchief.

All heads turned towards one small platform with a pedestal placed at the front of the stage. Two men were fiddling with some wires, adjusting the height of a microphone which was fixed to a stand. As they tested the microphone it kept emitting amplified snatches: 'Testing . . . Two . . . Three. . . .' Bradley caught Tom's eye, raised his eyes to the ceiling and muttered, 'What a palaver!'

More and more men were piling into the hall, which was already full. The priest was struggling in the heat.

'Take your jacket off, you'll be cookin' in this!'

'In a minute. Shh, think they're starting,' Tom replied, but then a second parade of sound technicians seemed to descend.

'Our Kim's back, by the way,' said Bradley. 'She's moved in with her boyfriend, just up the road.'

'Has she now?' replied Tom, puffing, biding his time. 'Will she be coming along to Mass with you on Sunday? T'would be nice to see how she is – how long is it now?'

'Since she was here? About ten years, I s'pose. Still like a kid though.'

'Settling down, is she? Here in the village, I mean?' asked Tom. He never felt very good at play-acting. But the confidence of the confessional, or in this case, the church pew, was sacrosanct.

'Don't ask me, Tom, she seems. . . . Oh, I don't know. Helen says she's old enough to look after 'erself but—'

'Losing your father like that didn't help, Brad.'

'Yeah, too late to worry about that now,' he replied and whistled through his teeth. 'Oh, I wish they'd get on with it. It's so bloody hot in here!'

Tom agreed. 'Ah, this wretched thing,' he mumbled, loosening his dog collar. 'I don't know why I put it on tonight. Heh, 'tis warm in here, enough to turn the milk.'

'No ventilation either,' replied Bradley, looking up at the dirty windows, which were covered in thick steel mesh. Flies and wasps buzzed lazily, trying to escape. Everyone was getting impatient. Shouts rang out from the crowd and someone shouted, 'Come on, let's be havin' yer then!' followed by rhythmic stamping of feet and laughter.

Suddenly a deafening roar went up as a figure appeared on the rostrum at the front of the stage: formal in appearance, tall in stature, and balding.

'That must be the speaker,' hissed Bradley. 'That suit must 'ave cost 'im a bit.'

All eyes were on the man in the black dinner-jacket, white shirt and cream tie, in complete contrast to the miners' attire. As he stepped up prettily onto the platform and raised a manicured hand to the crowd, a gold bracelet flashed in the spotlight.

'Bet he's not short of a few home comforts,' Bradley whispered in Tom's ear. The irony of the situation brought a flush of anger coursing through his veins. The man standing on the rostrum, he thought, probably hadn't seen the back of a hard day's work for years. The speech was punctuated by deafening whistles from the microphone's feedback but eventually the two roadies seemed to get their act together and the voice became clearer.

'We won't agree to a single pit being closed!' roared the speaker. 'Why should we, when there's good men like you and me willing to do an honest day's work!'

Thunderous roars of agreement rang out as he continued, 'The seams are running rich with coal beneath these Kent coalfields, and we won't let them get away with it!'

Applause exploded all around them. The miners were not only clapping but stamping their feet until the vibrations travelled through the floor. Bradley didn't join in the applause. He stood solidly, legs apart, with his sun-bronzed arms folded against his chest and his eyes burning into a miner's broad neck in front of him. Beside him, Tom was now inflating his cheeks absentmindedly in childlike concentration, causing the grey whiskers on his chin to quiver like an otter's.

The speech intensified, punctuated by pauses in which he held his audience in rapt attention, looking around to catch the eye of every person present. Bradley looked at the floor.

'We want,' the speaker continued in a murderous whisper, 'good honest pay for an honest day's work for all our miners in the coalfields of Britain!' The applause took off into such deafening volume that the man was unable to make himself heard for several minutes. He waited, looking around the hall with satisfaction before sipping a glass of water delicately.

Still Bradley stood with his arms folded, refusing to applaud. His mind wandered back towards the fields, where ragwort grew in clumps on the barren slag. He thought of the footpath he liked to take, round the back of the slag heaps which took him in sight of the allotments. Rabbits in their hundreds burrowed into these dusty hills and the ground was strewn with their droppings. He'd go out and take a few more soon. Rabbit stew, hot and nourishing, was one of his favourites. Taking a deep breath, he imagined he was breathing in the soft dewy air, treading the damp meadow grass where the breeze was laden with the scent of wild garlic. He couldn't wait to get back out there. The atmosphere in the hall was stifling.

The speaker began asking for questions. Many hands went up. Turning to the priest abruptly, Bradley hissed into his ear, 'I'm goin', Tom, I've heard enough of this shit. Are you coming?' Without waiting for a reply, he started pushing his way towards the door.

Seeing a path opening up, Tom took advantage and hurried after him. Outside the evening sunlight dazzled them as they found several men already out there smoking. A stocky man offered them his packet of Woodbines as they emerged from the hall.

'No thanks. I knew it would be a waste of time,' growled Bradley, waving the cigarettes aside.

He was looking pale now, as they came into the light. 'It's only money the big bosses are interested in, not really coal at all, or our jobs – they don't fool me.' He gazed around in the dry heat; even outside the hall there seemed to be no air to breathe. Depressed at the boarded-up shops and the broken tarmac, the steel police barriers and the graffiti, he turned to Tom.

'Well, what a waste of time that was!'

Tom nodded good-naturedly. 'I'm glad I went, so I am. Showed the lads a bit of support, heh!' He smacked his lips with satisfaction. 'To be sure that man has the gift of the gab!'

'I'd shut 'is mouth for him all right. Excuse me, Tom, but I would.'

'It's OK, Brad, I know you wouldn't really.'

Bradley looked at him quickly and looked away.

The word 'Pigs' was scrawled on walls, pavements and litter bins alike. 'Kill the Scabs' or 'Scabs Out!' also adorned almost every exterior surface of the Welfare Hall.

'That union bloke, he looked as if he was doin' all right for himself!' spat one of the men, dragging on his cigarette. 'Someone ought to stand up an' tell 'im where to get off, the bloody fat bastard!'

'We can all keep fightin' and shoutin' and wastin' our breath,' said Bradley, 'but it won't do no good, I'm sure of that.'

'But there's plenty of support now, Brad, don't forget, all over the country, so they say,' said Tom, putting his hands into one pocket after another, as though he was searching for something.

'They don't need our coal, Tom, that's the truth of it. You heard 'im, didn't you? The government's secretly stockpiled enough to last till Christmas and if that runs out they'll get it from abroad – you heard the man!' Bradley kicked the dust angrily.

'Take it easy, ole mate!' The stocky one slapped him on the back. 'Don't let 'em get to yer!'

'Hey, did you see Danny in there?' asked Bradley suddenly. 'Thought he'd be here; he's not one to miss a good fight.'

'No, haven't you heard the news, Bradley lad?' replied one of the group. 'He's gone back in. Went back to work this morning he did, the bloody creep. Said he's fed up of havin' no beer money.'

'What?' exclaimed Bradley. 'Danny Stuart? You're kiddin' me!' He couldn't believe it. The news shocked him rigid. 'Surely he wouldn't dare! He's one of us lads, ain't he?'

'He's always been a bit of an oddball, mate,' said another. 'Wouldn't like to get on the wrong side of 'im.'

Something about the news made Bradley stop in his tracks. While the others rattled on, he tried to make sense of the implications. It was so unexpected, it sent his mind reeling. He took a deep breath and whistled in amazement.

'Phew! Wait till I tell my Helen that bit o' news!' Leaving Tom and the others, he went striding off. There was only one blinding thought in his head and though they would never have guessed it, that thought alone isolated him from the crowd. He wasn't actually thinking about Danny at all.

Breaking the strike and going back in? Was it a real option after all? If other miners in Silt Edge could dare, could he? Should he? Doing something positive about the stalemate position he was in suddenly seemed within his grasp. He needed time alone to think.

Chapter 5

Danny Stuart lay on the bed, half naked and wearing oil-streaked jeans. One muscular arm lay across his hairy chest, his other held a can of beer from which he took long draughts now and then. Occasionally he burped loudly.

'Come 'ere girl,' he said, patting the bed. 'You're always starin' out that bloody window!'

'I was just looking,' replied Kim, laying down beside him. She rested her face on his bare shoulder and began absentmindedly fingering the black hairs on his torso.

'Ain't nothin' to bloody see out there, girl,' he said, moving an arm to draw her slight body closer.

'I used to watch out the window all the time when I was a kid,' said Kim, planting a kiss on the smooth skin of his throat. She started moving her lips like a butterfly across his body, in a teasing submissive bid for his mouth.

'All the time?' Danny laughed. 'Christ, you 'ad a good childhood then!'

'I used to be lookin' out for me mum comin' home. Wish you'd seen me mum,' she continued, flickering her tongue against his neck. 'She looked nice all dressed up to go out, an' she 'ad pretty clothes an' that. She used to go out workin' in a pub at nights and sometimes I think she went dancin' – when she came home she 'ad all glittery bits in her hair. Was your mum pretty, Danny?'

'She was OK.' He took a long drink from his can. 'She was a bit like you, I s'pose, small. She 'ad flamin' red hair, done up in a – y'know.' He made a circling gesture above his head. 'An' she kept the 'ouse spotless, always cleanin', dustin' an' polishing.' His dark eyes narrowed as he peered into the past. 'House proud she was, bit like you!' he teased, suddenly gripping her and planting a full kiss roughly on her mouth.

'Oh, yeah, right!' giggled Kim when she was released. 'Good she ain't 'ere to see this mess then!'

'Yeah,' drawled Danny. 'She's a cow though.'

'Perhaps she'll come an' visit one day, Danny, an' yer dad, come back down from Glasgow to see yer?'

'Come 'ere?' Danny laughed uproariously. 'You're jokin', aren't yer? Wouldn't let 'em in 'ere!'

'Don't say that, Danny!' Kim cried, rolling herself over to lie on top of his massive body and teasing him with her kisses.

'Ger off me, woman!' he roared, shoving her aside. 'I could be dead for all they care!' He took a slurp of beer. 'I messed it up wi' them big time, got myself in a right bloody hole.'

'Why? When did that 'appen then?'

'Oh, way back. I 'ad a lot goin' for me once, girl – got my exams, went to university. Could 'ave been a lawyer.' He turned and looked her in the eye. 'Can you believe that – me a bloody lawyer?'

'You'd 'ave made a good lawyer!' Kim giggled, dragging her fingers through his thick head of hair. 'You'd look nice in a posh suit an' tie.'

But Danny was looking morose. 'The grant ran out, didn't it, an' I had no money for nothin'. Couldn't afford my food an' lodgin' – couldn't get the books. I was doin' the work, pretendin' I'd read the books an' writin' rubbish. Ha!' He laughed thunderously, an ugly, bitter laugh. Crushing the empty can, he flung it across the bedroom, hitting the far wall. 'So, I got a job in a bar to get some cash, nights an' weekends, but I 'ad too much to drink one night an' lost the bleedin' job.'

Kim was half sitting up, watching him nervously now, with a mixture of amusement and dismay. 'Didn't your parents help you out though? They 'ad some money, didn't they?'

'I went an' asked my dad, just to borrow a bit, to tide me over till I found another job. He wouldn't give me a soddin' penny.'

'What did you do then?'

'You don't wanna know all that crap! Shut up and go an' get me another beer, will yer?'

Danny stared at her. She slid off the bed and went down the stairs, returning minutes later with another can in her hand.

'So then you went on the oil rigs, is that it?' she asked, settling herself down again beside him to listen, like a child. She was safe while he was talking.

'If you must know, girl, I went out an' got blind drunk.'

'You didn't have no money to get drunk!' she laughed.

'I got the money, right. I got it, that's all you need to know.' Kim looked at him. His face had closed up and he stared straight ahead of him.

'Danny!' she protested. 'Come on, how'd you get the money then?'

'If you must know, I went back that night an' took my dad's wallet. Crammed it were, with twenties, and he wouldn't give me a bloody fiver when I'd asked him. So served him right. I took some of Mother's precious jewellery as well. Flogged it!'

'Danny!'

'Shut up. Then I put the whole wad of it on the horses and lost the bloody lot.' He pushed Kim aside and, rising from the bed irritably, began to pace the floor. 'Don't know why I'm tellin' you all this crap!'

Kim uncurled herself from the bed and sat on the edge, her eyes shifting about. 'I was only asking.' She shrugged, afraid now that he had stopped. He towered over her as though to strike her, before he went and stared out of the window.

'Anyway, I tried to pay 'im back. I dropped out of university, got a job on the rigs; you can earn a load on the oil rigs. So, about a year later I goes back to my parents all apologetic like. I owned up to it. Apologized. I offered 'em the money back and some more besides – I had a bit by then. Felt rotten about what I'd done. Said I was sorry, said I'd been desperate. They wouldn't listen though, the bastards!' He spat on the floor. 'They called the police, didn't they, had me locked up in prison for three years.'

Kim stared wide eyed. 'They turned you in to the cops?'

'Mother came to the prison to visit me once. You know what she says to me? "*Curse you!*" she says. "*You're no son of mine. If you ever have kids, God help 'em. I hope they hurt you just like you've hurt me and your father.*" That's what she said.'

'Danny, that's terrible,' said Kim. She moved as though to get up and hug him in sympathy but then checked herself. Instead she stayed sitting on the edge of the bed, chewing her cuffs and staring at him, afraid.

'So, I says to her, "*Don't you worry, I won't give you the bloody satisfaction, woman! I won't never 'ave no kids so you won't have that pleasure.*" ' He turned to look at Kim and the expression in his eyes killed any hope she might have retained. 'I bloody hate kids anyway, all of 'em. So don't you ever go sayin' to me you're pregnant or I'll ring your bleedin' neck.' His eyes were loaded with evil. He took a step towards her, bending down and putting his face up close to hers. 'You hear me, girl? Don't you ever dare come tellin' me you're havin' a bloody kid!' he roared. Crashing away from her, she heard his footsteps demolish the stairs. As the front door slammed behind him, she fled to the bathroom and vomited violently.

Having intended to go straight home after the NUM meeting, Bradley had soon lost his resolve. He stood staring at the pit head's towering presence. 'I'll get away from you one day,' he said quietly. 'You won't get me, I'll see to that. You an' me – we're finished.'

Instinctively, he came again to the balmy hedgerows that bordered the allotments. Everywhere was ablaze with quickthorn, honeysuckle and ivy. Sheep's parsley sent up clusters of mist as he brushed past. Mosquitoes thronged in the dampness as he came to his own plot, with its rows of vegetables and framework of sticks for the runner beans which were already climbing and showing a few scarlet flowers. An idea was germinating in his mind which sent his blood racing.

Still he didn't head for home. A vivid red sunset slashed across the sky. Crimson crossroads opened up above him with jet trails skimming across in all directions. Yes, he would get away. It didn't matter where. He started to run, spurred on by his excitement he ran down the footpath like the miners run when they come up after their shift. Faster he ran, as before him lay the open countryside and the fields of freedom. There were times, he remembered, when he had run down this path as a boy, heady with the freedom of school holidays, carrying tadpoles in a jam jar and shouting to his sister to hurry and catch up.

Before he realized it, he was heading back towards the police curfew, but he wasn't far from home and his reaction to Danny's betrayal was almost forgotten. He had Helen's questions to face about the meeting and he was too tired for it all. Too tired to cope with her politics, too tired to fight her.

The houses ahead were close to Danny's place; it would become a target once word got out that he had become a scab. Maybe he should see if his sister was there and warn her; it would waste a bit more time before he had to go home. If Danny answered, he could always pretend he hadn't heard and play it cool.

Their council house looked a sad little place. It had its front gate broken and was standing at an angle half buried in the long grass, which was overgrown with nettles. Blue paint on the front door was peeling off and the front-window curtains were drawn against grimy silted-up windows. Rubbish littered the path. He went round and tapped on the back door. Inside he could hear a loud television. Presently a bolt was drawn back and Kim's face appeared round the door.

'Hi,' she said, wearily, looking at him in a bewildered fashion.

'You all right?' he asked.

Nodding faintly, she replied, 'Danny's not here.' She opened the door wider and Bradley stepped into the kitchen. It smelt of rancid rubbish.

'Too busy workin' I hear,' said Bradley quickly.

'How d'you know that?' Kim swore. 'Don't take long for news to travel, does it!'

'The lads told me, when I was up the meeting.'

'Didn't know there was no meetin',' Kim said. They were in the sitting room now. It was stuffy and dark in there, the curtains blocking any remaining light. *Z Cars* was blaring out on the television. Kim turned the volume down but didn't switch it off. They sat down, he on the grease-stained sofa, she in the armchair. She had pulled the sleeves of her thin cardigan down over her wrists and sat clutching them over tight fists pressed against her mouth. Her legs were curled up under her and her eyes never left the television screen as she spoke.

'He went off to work this mornin', didn't tell me, like – that he was goin' back – just got up, really early it was, still dark. He woke me getting his clothes on, so I asked him where he was goin', an' he says summat like: "To work so shut yer gob." I hate 'im sometimes I do. Don't know why he's so nasty all the time.'

'Eh, he's a dark horse all right,' Bradley said. 'You OK though?'

'Yeah, but he might come back soon. He stormed out not long ago – in a right mood he was. You'd better go.' For the first time she turned and looked at him, her pale eyes shifting.

'Yeah, I'd better be off, I s'pose, Helen will be wonderin' where I am.' But still he didn't move. Life didn't offer his sister much, he thought. She had such a pitiful unappetizing portion of life on her plate – no excitement, no new clothes or days out. He began recalling how they used to dream about their future together as kids. Their dad would be at work such long hours down the pit, often doing a double shift just to get the money – and their mother, they didn't know where she was half the time and she often arrived home late, singing quietly to herself. He could remember her perfume as it enveloped them and hung around in the room afterwards like a ghost. Sometimes they would lay in bed and hear their father's voice shatter the peace. He would be shouting a string of complicated words: angry words, frustrated words, and they would hear crashing sounds and breaking glass and then their mother, weeping.

One night she didn't come home at all. In the morning their father didn't mention her, just went off to the pit as though everything was normal, but he had expected to see her there when he got home from school. He could remember telling little Kim not to worry, she was sure to be back soon and he had asked his father that night where she was. '*Gone away,*' he had said, '*and don't mention your mother to me any more – I don't want to hear it.*' She never did come back and Kim was only seven years old. . . . With a jolt he returned to the present.

'Remember the dreams we used to have as kids, Kim? About building a tree house on a beach somewhere? We'd pretend we were livin' there, wouldn't we, by the seaside. We'd make a bit of a fire in our back yard, when Dad was at work, and we'd cook some bread an' bacon drippin' in an old tin.'

'Shut up, will ya! Makin' me feel hungry! Look, Danny might be back in a minute.' She stood up and, drawing back the curtain a little, looked up the road. A shaft of evening light streamed in. 'I wanna get away from this dump of a place, Brad,' she said, peering out of the window as if through the bars of a prison.

'Does Danny know that?'

She shrugged her shoulders. 'Don't know that he's bothered. I do love 'im though. At least, I think I do,' she added, giving a self-conscious giggle.

'If he loves you he's got a funny way of showin' it.'

She didn't respond. 'The lads,' he added, 'they won't let it rest, you know, him going back to work, I mean.'

'It's up to him, ain't it, whether he works or not?' she replied. 'What's it got to do with them?'

'Don't be bloody stupid, girl! You know what they do to scabs! They say we've all got to stick together in this strike or the bosses'll do what they like, sack us all, an' close the pit down. Then we'll all be out of work for good. That's what they say.'

'Good riddance! It's a stinkin' dump anyway,' she murmured. 'You hate it too, Brad, don't yer! Why don't you just get another job anyhow?'

'Wish I could. I've been thinking about that, but it's not that easy. Wish it was.' He stood up and walked towards the door. 'Oh, if I had the chance I'd get a job miles away from here, you try an' stop me,' he said. 'I'd find a job on a farm, or get myself a bit o' land or a smallholdin' – somethin' of my own. We could have chickens an' all sorts then – could keep us all goin' in food, no problem, me an' Helen and Sam and you too if you like.'

'Yeah, keep dreamin', Brad.'

'Just bolt the door when I'm gone, there's a girl. You never know,' he said, walking into the stale kitchen where a pile of dishes stood in the sink and the bin was buzzing with horseflies.

What made her stay with Danny Stuart of all people? When their mum and dad were arguing, he remembered Kim curling up in the cupboard under the stairs. He used to try and coax her out, tempting her with a few sweets he'd save up specially. She'd always dreamed of living in a better place too. Poor kid. He'd tell her stories about what they'd do when they were grown up and rich; give her some dreams to fill her head with, before the reality of another dark hungry night came down on them.

When he had left school and started work down the pit, his father had warned him he would never get the coal dust out of the pores in his skin. '*It's like a tattoo,*' he had told him, '*that's still there in your lungs for years, even if you do get away.*' Bradley remembered seeing the colour of the bloody phlegm, poisoned with coal dust, that his dad had coughed up, how it had stained the bedclothes.

It was getting late. He was nearing home but Helen still seemed way out of his reach. He wished she'd relax like she used to, wandering the cornfields with him for hours, their arms entwined, her long hair falling across her face. One day, he told her, he'd buy her a house on the mountainside, and she used to listen with her brown eyes glowing. She believed everything he said in those days, laughing and covering her ears when he mimicked the sea birds, calling across the empty fields to the sea. The sea! The sea was inside his head again.

Wasting more time, he decided to take the footpath that ran along the back of the slag heaps. These were a range of grey barren mountains of coal spoils that towered on every side of the village. It was infertile slag, valueless. It wouldn't burn. Nothing but ragwort and a few straggling silver birch trees would gain a foothold. Alongside these were the pit ponies' fields, dry, close-cropped earth littered with rabbit droppings, sparsely covered with nettles and fenced with makeshift posts, support beams retrieved from the mine.

This path was worn by hundreds of miners' feet walking to work over the years, with their steel-tipped boots, dragging themselves home again after a ten-hour stint. The siren sounding the change of shift could be heard for miles around. Men would come swarming out of the mouth of the mine, carrying their snap-tins and flasks, owlish white eyes peering from blackened faces, dazzled by the daylight. They would crowd into the wash-house to shower and change. Once through the pit gates, some would break into a run, or clamber onto motorbikes; they didn't speak, once out in the open. They were temporarily inward, as if disorientated and anxious to be home for a hot bath and a good meal or a pint down at the club. All of them were desperate for sleep.

It was almost dark; hunger pains gnawed at his stomach. Suddenly a familiar figure came striding across the field.

'Hey, Gavin,' he shouted, 'you all right?' The man raised his stick in greeting and made his way over, whistling his dog. When he came closer Bradley saw how gaunt he looked, his wax jacket hanging off him, his shoulder muscles wasted.

'I've just been over the woods,' Gavin said, 'just to clear my head. You OK, mate?'

Bradley shrugged his shoulders and stooped to scratch the dog's ears. 'Don't know what to put my mind on, Gavin, if y'know what I mean. It all boils down to the same thing. You heard any more?'

'No, nothin' doin'. I saw you up the meetin'. They're all sayin' the same: we're stuck between a rock an' a hard place.' Gavin looked away thoughtfully. Stepping closer, he lowered his voice. 'The traps are sprung,' he growled under his breath. 'Come out with us again tonight, ole mate, be a full moon if the skies stay clear. They'll be rabbits just sittin' there waitin' to be taken. Get some more meat for your supper, eh?'

Bradley shook his head. 'Love to, but not tonight, Gavin. It's already late an' I'd best get back.' He placed a hand on his friend's shoulder. 'Helen won't have it, you know. She'd be on at me again. I just can't hack it at the moment. You know what these women are like.' He tried to laugh but the humour wasn't there. 'Thanks, anyway, old chum. Next time, eh? And good luck,' he added.

*

Finally he arrived home. He could hear Helen moving about upstairs. He hung up his jacket and sank down into his chair. One of Helen's folders was open on the settee. There was a vase of sweetpeas on the table; her mother must have been. He sighed.

She came downstairs with a smile he couldn't match. 'He woke up screaming. He's teething, poor little mite, but he's gone out like a light now, bless him! What's the news about the meeting then? You've been such a long time, Brad, I thought you'd have been home ages ago.' She filled the kettle in the kitchen and came through, expecting a reply.

'Nothin's movin',' he said, 'and the lads all say the same. Nothin' new an' it's the same old jargon. While they're happy battling it out, the government an' the Coal Board an' the unions, it's us who has to bloody suffer. I'm fed up of it.'

'It'll be worth seeing it through to the end, though, won't it? They won't shut us down, not when they've spent so much modernizing it with new shower blocks. We can hold out – hey, the girls were on TV again tonight!'

Her words stung like salt in his wounds. 'I don't care! I need to work now, Helen!' he exploded. 'We need the money now, you know we do! I just feel my hands are tied, like I'm useless. I must do something soon!'

'You'll just have to be patient and wait it out like all the rest. It's our long-term future we're fighting for. Remember that, Brad.'

This was too much. 'Future?' He stood up. 'Look where it got my old dad – in his grave without a breath of life in him before he was forty-five! Is that your so-called future? Is that what you want for me, and for our Sam?' He stared at her. 'Well is it?' Striding across the kitchen, he opened the back door, unable to cope. Without stepping outside, he stood leaning on the door frame looking out, as the chill evening mist crept up the garden and into the house.

She came softly, standing behind him, and put her arms around his waist. 'I'm sorry, I didn't mean it to sound like that. But what choice have we got, love? Mining is your job, after all.' She reached up and

60

kissed the nape of his neck, where the salt and pepper hairs curled at random. He couldn't answer, although he longed to turn and hold her in his arms, to throw himself into that warm place where thoughts stop and time dissolves. His body ached for her, yet he stood staring out across the garden, choked and unable to respond.

Chapter 6

Tom pulled up on the gravel under the shade of the yew trees; it was a cool hollow in the churchyard, bordered by the walled gardens of the Chalkfield Hall estate. Parking the car, he was tempted to just sit there, lulled into a peaceful reverie by cooing pigeons. But climbing out, he stood and gazed up at the ancient wall where it bulged noticeably, bearing the swell of so many tree roots. In the hot sun, the moss was so dry it had lifted off the wall a little, making a tiny cave from which ants scurried to and fro. Further along by the church path, tombstones were pitched at eccentric angles into the grass. He pulled at his dog-collar where the sweat was chafing his neck, sighed and looked up into the shady canopy of horse chestnut and yew. It was late afternoon in the village of Ebbingsfield, a drive of ten minutes or so from Silt Edge. Tom had come to check all was well at the small subsidiary church of St Joseph the Worker, for which he was also responsible. Casting a quick eye over the building, he went to test the door, leaning his weight against it.

A blackbird's warning note pierced the air as footsteps approached and a stooped woman appeared, her puffy face framed by a headscarf. Her progress was impeded by thickened bandaged ankles and a bowed spine. As she walked, she strained to peer upwards at the church roof, squinting against the sun, the skin under her chin stretched taut like a turtle. At her heel panted an elderly Labrador.

On hearing her approach, Tom ducked out of the shadowed porch to greet her. 'Good afternoon, Winnie!'

'Oh, my goodness, Father, it's you!' the housekeeper exclaimed. 'I didn't hear your car.' She peered at the priest in good humour. 'I was just coming to check the church but as you're here, I can see that all is well!'

'Very kind of you to say so, Winnie!' he replied. 'How are you today? It's a fine afternoon, is it not!'

'I'm well enough, thank you, Father,' she said, smiling.

'Is Edith at home by any chance?'

'She most certainly is! And I'm sure she'll be delighted to see you!' Turning to the dog, she called, 'Come on, Ben,' gazing back at him patiently. 'He's such an old boy now, but none of us are getting any younger, eh?'

'You're not wrong there, Winnie,' he replied, as though she had just revealed a solemn truth. As the dog had flung himself down on the path to cool, they both waited while he struggled to his feet and made a supreme effort to follow them. The path led to a cast-iron side gate, giving access to the kitchen garden, which Winnie unlatched.

Everywhere lay remnants of a bygone age. They made their way around a wrought-iron table and chairs, rusty and covered in lichen. Several terracotta pots stood by the path, mildewed and trailing geranium plants; an air of decay and neglect hung over the whole garden. Some french doors stood open, offering glimpses of the elegant drawing room and chintz curtains but they proceeded further, to the back door.

'Soon be teatime,' Winnie disclosed. As soon as they were inside, she announced loudly, 'So kind of you to drop by, Father!' for the benefit, presumably, of Lady Edith Ashby, who ruled the house like a duchess. Chalkfield Hall and the grounds surrounding the manor house had been in the Ashby family for generations. Winnie had been its trusted housekeeper for countless years.

Aged in her mid-eighties, Edith's skeletal frame was always exquisitely dressed and a diamond flashed from every finger. In Edith's presence people behaved with extravagant politeness – her manner demanded it. Among the faded décor and the abundance of antique furniture, visitors were fixed with an honest stare from portraits of ancestors which were hung at intervals up the stairwell.

Paying guests frequently occupied all nine bedrooms and the

housekeeping was done on an elaborate scale. However, currently there were only three guests. Winnie coped with the work alone, working from dawn until dusk without complaint, always abiding by the house rules, which Edith was keen to point out to any newcomer. She was sometimes known to remind guests with a scolding reprimand: 'There's no excuse for sloppiness, I can't abide it!' Visitors were required to dress formally for dinner, which was served promptly at six. The rigid routine was changed only in exceptional circumstances, such as for general elections or state funerals. Time was always allocated for polishing the silver and brasses, airing the bed-linen and other domestic tasks that Edith considered essential.

In spite of Winnie's declaration, there was no response from within. Tom took advantage of the nearest chair in the kitchen and eased himself into it, breathing heavily. Preparing to make tea, Winnie pulled the heavy kettle across the top of the range to the hottest part. This ancient appliance was kept alight constantly, providing heating, hot water and cooking facilities, summer and winter alike.

As the kettle began to sing on the hob, Winnie shuffled off in search of Edith. Standing up, brushing himself down and preparing himself for his introduction, Tom wandered into the hall. There he caught sight of Edith herself, sitting at her bureau by the window in the drawing room. It occurred to him that she must have observed his arrival earlier and not stirred from her seat. He waited respectfully until his presence was announced, fidgeting with his tweed jacket buttons until Winnie's footsteps on the cool tiles preceded her summons.

'You may go through, Father,' she announced. 'Lady Ashby will see you now.' Tom entered the drawing room making a self-conscious gesture, something between tipping his forelock and bowing.

'Do take a seat, Tom, for goodness' sake!' commanded Edith, regarding him with some amusement over the top of her glasses.

'Thank you, ma'am, thank you,' he muttered, sinking his bottom cautiously into a voluptuous armchair. Perspiring profusely, he remarked on the hot weather. Edith drew his attention to the fact that he was wearing his woollen tweed jacket. Until that moment Tom hadn't realized why he felt so uncomfortable. He agreed with her observation, made as though to remove it and then changed his mind for fear of knocking something over.

In the kitchen, Winnie set out a tray with bone-china teacups, and gingernut biscuits and began to stoke the Aga. The dog was again flat out, panting, on the cool linoleum floor. It was indeed very warm. Presently Winnie came through and set the tray before them. Tom, relaxing, gave out an audible sigh, causing his host to glance up at him curiously. While Edith poured the tea with elaborate elegance, Tom apologized for coming into the house with his muddy shoes on, although they were in fact immaculate. Holding his cup and saucer carefully, he began relating a story characteristic of his apparent lifelong battle with mud and carpets. Edith interrupted him impatiently, waving his apology away as one would a fly. Making sure Winnie was quite out of earshot, she began to address him in a lowered, conspiratorial tone:

'Now, tell me, Tom, are you standing up to those miners? The fools, if they think they can bring the country to its knees – well, they're wrong I tell you, wrong!' Her powdered cheeks wobbled, setting her diamond earrings sparkling.

Tom took a sip of his tea, smacked his lips and gave another deep sigh while he considered his response.

'Do they think we've fought two world wars only to be brought down by a few colliers!' she continued, flushed with indignation. Taking her own cup and saucer, her hand shook. Looking grave, Tom helped himself to sugar, stirred his tea and took a deep breath.

'They're putting a brave face on it, ma'am, but it's a struggle for them, I can tell you. They need to work, that's for sure.'

'Work! I've heard about how they're behaving with their – what do they call them – picket lines! Trying to stop decent men doing an honest day's work!' she said crossly, putting her cup down and fanning herself with an envelope.

Tom decided to alter course. He shifted his position in the armchair by way of an introduction to his new subject. 'I had a girl on my doorstep recently,' he began, clearing his throat. 'A local girl. I know her brother – he's a miner, of course. She was in a state, I can tell you, heh!' He shook his head at the recollection.

Edith swallowed, gazing at him over heavily marbled lids. 'After money, I presume, like all the rest of them.'

'She has a lot on her shoulders, ma'am. The women up there, they do have a hard time of it, that's for sure.'

Edith snorted. 'I really don't have time for sentimentality, Tom – as well you know!'

'This girl,' he continued bravely, 'she's a sweet girl, a poor girl.'

'Mmm . . .' Edith regarded him dubiously.

This was a delicate situation. A lot depended on him choosing his words carefully – in fact he had been rehearsing this conversation all the way over in the car. 'She's a good girl,' he paused, eyeing Edith cautiously, 'but she's in a bit of trouble.'

'Pregnant!' Edith announced triumphantly, smiling broadly at him. Nothing he could say would ever surprise her.

'Yes, she is, as it happens,' he replied forlornly. 'But—'

'And you want me to help her, is that it? I've told you before, Tom, I refuse to give those ridiculous striking miners a single penny of my hard-earned money. Why should I when—'

'Lady Ashby,' Tom interrupted impatiently. 'Will you please listen to me for one minute and I will explain!'

'Oh, very well, Father, go on,' she said meekly. A feminine and quite pretty blush softened the features of her once-beautiful face. Occasionally she seemed to enjoy being corrected by the priest.

'The girl's . . . um . . . chap, he's a miner who's broken the strike and gone back to work.'

'Quite right too!' she interjected. 'I should think so!'

'Yes, and because they live together I'm a bit worried she might—'

'They're not married?' Edith blurted out. 'Oh, typical!'

'Lady Ashby! Edith, please, with respect,' he added, 'please let me finish.' Tom was beginning to get annoyed.

Edith folded her small hands in her lap like a scolded child. 'Very well,' she said.

'This girl, because her boyfriend's broken the strike, well, she's likely to be victimized and made an outcast in the village.' He persevered while he had her attention. 'To cut a long story short, I wondered if I could ask you to take her in for a while?'

'Take her in?' exploded Edith. 'Take her in, here? In my house?' she demanded, staring at Tom in disbelief. Her eyes travelled from his face to the sofa, to the window, and around the room as if the girl had already taken possession of the place.

'Edith, I wouldn't ask you if I didn't think it was absolutely necessary,' he explained. 'Things being the way they are.'

She looked past him in silence, her lips moving involuntarily. She seemed to drift off into a reverie. 'Has the girl nowhere else to go?' she asked quietly after a while. Tom gazed at her and slowly shook his head. She swallowed, her opaque eyes taking on the colour of the sky.

'Forgive me, but what I was thinking, ma'am, was that perhaps you could find a position for her here? She can cook and clean. It would be a help to Winnie; it wouldn't necessarily be charity.' He watched her face moving through a series of emotions while he sipped his tea.

'What's the girl's name?' asked Edith, calm now, thoughtful.

'Her name's Kimberley Shepstone. We call her Kim for short.'

'Kim,' she repeated. 'Mmmm.' They sat in silence for several minutes while Tom puffed out his cheeks and stared at the gingernuts, holding his breath.

'My health isn't what it was,' she ventured, 'and nor is my purse, unfortunately, especially with the building work starting soon.'

'Ah, indeed!' Tom shifted awkwardly; he hadn't really contemplated a second solution to Kim's predicament. He wasn't on the best of terms with the bishop, he reflected, especially after arguing with him about his stance on the strike; he was hardly in a position to ask him for any favours.

Much as she tried, Edith couldn't quell the sudden surge of memories raging within her. It was 1917, and the First World War had already claimed thousands of lives when Edith had waved to George, her first love, as his ship set sail from Southampton. An officer in the navy, he had wooed her with elegant charm, promising to ask for her hand on his return. She remembered getting up early every morning to intercept the postman down along the lane to ask for his letters. The foreign postmark was bound to arouse suspicion. Even the cook was primed to hide them in her apron pocket if Edith happened to miss him. Then, mysteriously, she began to feel unwell in the mornings.

Tom ran a finger round the inside rim of his dog collar and pursed his lips, waiting. Wondering whether to risk taking a gingernut, he took another sip of his tea and found himself looking at what appeared to be a stocking half-hidden under the sofa. It was unusual to see anything out of place in that house, least of all an item from the bedroom. He glanced up guiltily, but Edith was staring into the distance, trapped in the past.

Young Edith's mother was balanced on the edge of the sofa, weeping into a handkerchief. Beside the fireplace stood the rigid figure of her father, Colonel Ashby, the muscles on his jaw twitching, his whole body vibrating with rage. The family doctor was standing five feet away, holding his surgical bag. He had felt it was his professional responsibility, it appeared, to inform Edith's parents that their daughter was carrying an illegitimate child. A mournful scream accompanied her mother's flight from the room.

Edith suddenly grasped the arm of her chair, shocked by the vividness of her recollection. She took a deep breath in a fluster, trying to steady herself. Clearing her throat, she declared:

'I will give the matter some thought, Tom, but I won't promise anything; one can't be too careful these days.'

'Thank you, Edith.'

The deed done, he felt a huge sense of relief. Experience had taught him that she would reflect on the matter and possibly, in a day or two, concede to his request. Probably she would put the suggestion to Winnie as if it were entirely her own idea – to offer a poor homeless girl a foothold on the precarious cliff of life as a gesture of goodwill. He felt satisfied that he had done his duty and fulfilled his commitment to Kim – the rest would transpire in time. Deciding it would be better to change the subject while he was ahead, he embarked on another topic:

'There was a big meeting in the village, with the NUM,' he said, smacking his lips. 'They had a good speaker – he had a lot of support.'

'Huh!' puffed Edith. 'A Communist probably.'

Tom looked at her quickly and continued, 'There's a lot of division, that's for sure. Yes, 'tis a nasty business.'

'Well, I'm pleased you attended, Tom. Someone needs to speak up for the decent working people of this country. Well, I ask you, why should we taxpayers pay to keep the darned pits going anyway? Especially when those fool miners can't even get off their backsides to lift a shovel. It's a scandal! How Maggie puts up with them I don't know. I'd fire the lot of them and that would be the end of it!' Edith, overcome with exasperation, took a handkerchief from inside her sleeve and held it to her forehead like cooling balm.

Tom, feeling out of his depth once more, sighed in a resigned fashion. 'Ah, 'tis a grand cup o' tea Winnie makes,' he remarked. 'Just like home.'

Edith smiled an ambiguous smile and reaching forward, offered him a biscuit. 'You should drop in to see us more often, Tom,' she advised. 'There's only so much good-shepherding a man can do.' She looked at him knowingly for a moment and Tom, not often quick on the draw, accepted a gingernut gratefully. Fearing it might appear rude to dunk it in his tea, he bit hard into it, nearly breaking a tooth.

Minutes later he made an excuse to leave, thanked Edith profoundly with the exaggerated politeness she was so fond of, and let himself out of the front door. Leaving dough to rise and seeds to grow was his favourite occupation, after all.

Winnie, with her own cup of tea, had sat down in her old armchair beside the range. A look of discomfort flickered across her face and she winced. Sitting there with her whiskered chin resting on her chest and her tea on her lap, she allowed her eyes to close for a few minutes. Her heavy legs were bandaged under thick brown stockings and her slippers were flattened at the heels to accommodate her swollen feet. She must have dozed off because suddenly she jerked awake and spilt her tea. Struggling to get up and 'tut-tutting' at herself, she reached for a cloth.

'Your mum's getting clumsy in her old age, eh, Ben!' she complained. The dog's tail thumped on the linoleum.

Preparing vegetables from the kitchen garden was her next job. There wasn't so much harvested from the garden of late. Winnie had mentioned it to Edith, fearing their arthritic gardener, who had tended the estate single-handedly for forty years, was finding the work too much. But Edith had replied, 'He's been busy with the roses; the kitchen garden is still awaiting his full attention.' Winnie knew her too well to contradict her. Alfred worked hard, but often she had watched him from her kitchen window, struggling to push the heavy wheelbarrow and she knew time wasn't on his side.

Winnie had just begun to scrape the potatoes when she heard the priest's parting voice in the hall. 'Oh, gone already,' she declared, 'and I was going to give Father a jar of my strawberry jam!' Edith, she noticed, was back at her bureau with her pen poised, so she returned to the vegetables.

But Edith didn't write. Instead she sat as still as a waxwork while her memories continued to torment her. So many letters she had exchanged with her officer in those early days of the First World War. She had kept them all, tied up with a length of lace, in her dressing table. While Edith's baby grew in her womb, their love swelled in the distance between them. Of her pregnancy, not one more word was spoken; she was allowed to rest, wander the grounds of Chalkfield Hall at will, or sit and read. The cook would bring her any delicacies she could filter from the stark war rations, although their house menu was already plentiful by comparison to what their neighbours survived on. Supplemented profusely by what was available by being shot, bartered for or received as gifts, the household enjoyed a secluded and somewhat favourable existence. Edith had noticed, though, that her parents had grown peculiarly quiet: they didn't reprimand her, they didn't demand anything of her. Actually they barely spoke to her. But her days were peaceful and tranquil enough while she longed for her lover's return from duty, and for her child to be born.

One day her parents sent the cook to fetch her. She was sitting in the sun out in the orchard, reading through her lover's letters. Both her parents stood facing her when she entered the drawing room. The ambience was as electric as a threatening storm; her womb lurched in apprehension.

'Father?' she asked. 'What is it?'

He took a telegram from inside his jacket and handed it to her. 'Prepare yourself, Edith,' he said sternly, 'War makes its own judgement.'

There had never been a silence like the silence in that house. Taking hold of the telegram, she saw her lover's name. Such a trembling took hold of her as she read it:

'Regret to Inform. Stop. Commanding Officer George Henry Marton. Stop. Killed in Action. Stop. Fourteenth Day of May 1918.'

'Sixty-five years is long enough, goodness knows,' Edith muttered to herself. 'Surely now it's time to forget my darling George and yet I can't!' And memories continued to torture her, soundless words moved her lips as her eyes searched the peaceful scene outside for some measure of comfort. But time surged forward cruelly to when her baby daughter was just three weeks old. . . .

'Torn from my arms!' she whispered as mercury tears swelled in her eyes. She could see the nuns before her, like the beast in the Apocalypse waiting to devour her child.

They had brought the Catholic priest to baptise the baby. Standing all around her, the nuns whispered to each other, their faces held rigidly in starched veils. A candle was lit, and one of the nuns took the baby from her and held her out towards the priest, who poured holy water over her forehead and began to speak: 'I baptise thee. . . .' He paused, turning towards Edith.

'What are you naming the child?'

'I've decided to call her Georgina!' she whispered eagerly. To speak the baby's name for the first time thrilled her.

'Margaret,' said one of the sisters flatly. 'It has been decided, the child will be called Margaret.'

'No, no!' protested Edith. 'I want to call her Georgina! Father, please?'

The priest gazed at her. He looked from the young mother's face to the older, harder woman and sniffed. Putting down his Bible he took the tiny baby into his own arms. Raising his right hand once more he said in a loud voice, 'I baptise thee Georgina, in the name of the Father, and of the Son, and of the Holy Ghost and the grace of our Lord Jesus Christ be with you always.' And having said this, he made a sign of the cross with a firm thumb on her little forehead. As he did this, Georgina let out a piercing cry that seemed to herald a terrible danger. Handing the baby back, he rested his hand on Edith's head for a moment, and gave her his blessing.

Moments later, one of the nuns snatched Georgina from her arms. 'We will take care of the child. We've found the perfect home for her.'

Suddenly Edith fell out of her memories and found herself alone in the drawing room. 'And my breasts ached to feed her, for days afterwards!' she whispered.

Chapter 7

Fundraising with her friend Jean in the hot sun, Helen took some lemonade from the back of Sam's pushchair and passed it to Jean. 'Here,' she said, 'after you. I went up the meeting, y'know. Didn't see you up there.'

'I saw you,' Jean said, drinking thirstily. 'Does your Bradley know you were there?' Helen's haunted expression gave Jean her answer. 'Right, playin' it safe then!'

'Oh, Jean, wasn't it fantastic!' Helen exclaimed, her eyes shining.

Jean looked at her soberly. 'It were only a meetin', Helen, everyone having their say and saying nowt, most of them. They won't decide to go back to work just like that, you know, it'll take weeks, months probably. Oh, I think I'm getting too old for this lark. I wish they'd just get on and sort it out so the lads can go back in.'

Helen regarded her with mild alarm. 'Why? I know I shouldn't say this but I don't want it to end – the strike, I mean. I love all this, going out collecting, all the cooking and sharing out of stuff, and everyone so friendly. It's just great!'

'You daft bat!' Jean laughed. 'Wait till Christmas! What'll you do then wi' no money to buy toys an' presents? You won't be laughin' then. Nor will poor little Sam I bet!'

'We'll manage somehow,' Helen replied. But when she glanced at her friend again, Jean wasn't smiling at all. 'Oh, yeah, great fun I'm sure,' she said coldly.

It was then Helen began to fear the strike ending. She couldn't justify the excitement she felt, carrying the banner in the frontline of the march, being rushed off her feet with all the work. It was so exhilarating!

She pictured their noticeboard: letters of encouragement, donations, pictures from children who had even sent their pocket money. Some donations had been breathtaking in their generosity, and it made her heart swell with pride. Newspaper cuttings of their marches. She didn't want the battle to end, ever.

'I can't wait for my Roger to start back,' Jean's voice broke in. 'Either he's hangin' round my feet like a flamin' puppy or he's sat in the bath moanin' about his rheumatism. The day he actually gets back to work he'll probably phone in sick! Honestly, Helen, he's getting as fat as a penguin in a fish shop!'

Helen tried to smile; the reality of slipping back into the role of miner's wife, cook and cleaner filled her with so much dread she felt the tears in her throat. But she couldn't cry – not in front of Jean. Casting an eye over that future, when the time came, she didn't know how she was going to cope.

It was after eleven at night yet Tom was still in his study replying to the bishop's letter. Tom recalled their last conversation, when he had told the bishop he couldn't avoid mentioning his parishioners' problems in his sermons any longer. The bishop had slammed the Bible down on his desk, shouting:

'This is your reference book, Father, not the ten o'clock news! Read the parable of the workers in the vineyard and then tell me your parishioners have been treated unfairly!'

Tom had held his tongue. But now he muttered to himself: 'Heh! Tis hopeless! Tis a mess we're all in with this strike, a real mess. God bless us and save us!' Suddenly there came a frantic knocking on his front door. 'Who the hell can that be at this time of night?' he asked himself.

'Father! Are you there? Please help, Father!' came a shrill female voice.

'I'm coming, I'm coming!' he shouted, flinging open the door.

'They're after us! They've beat him up, Father, look!' The girl was bent under the weight of a man with an ugly gash on his face, bloodied and dirty.

'Bring him in, steady now,' he said. 'That's it, lean on me. Close the door quickly, Kim, that's my girl.' The trio made their way into the sitting room. 'Who was it, Kim?'

'Dunno! They come after Danny when he got off the coach!' she wailed. 'I didn't know what to do!'

As they lowered him into the armchair, Tom said, 'I'm glad you came to me. Let's have a look at this now. Tis nasty,' he said, inspecting the wound, 'but not too deep. Wait while I fetch something and I'll see to it.' He dived into the kitchen, rattling drawers, and soon emerged with a bowl of water and antiseptic. 'You've been and had a lucky escape – Danny, isn't it?' he asked, swabbing the wound with cotton wool and peering into it for traces of dirt. 'I don't think it's bad enough to need stitches. Tis a nasty gash though.'

Danny made a gesture as if to wave the hand away. 'I'm OK, Father, thanks.'

'Can I fetch you a cup of sweet tea?' asked Tom. 'Tis good for the shock so they say.'

'Scotch,' Danny said, 'if you've got any.' He turned his bloodshot eyes up to Kim. Tom poured him a drink.

'Thanks.' Taking the glass, he downed it in one gulp, held it out again and wiped his mouth on his sleeve. 'The bastards!' he swore savagely.

Kim jumped. She was hugging herself, trembling, and she started to cry, the tears leaving her in great sobs that shuddered through her body. Danny ignored her. Seeing this, Tom said gently, 'Come on, lass, a hot sweet cuppa will sort you out, eh?' and taking a blanket from out of the stair-cupboard, he put it around her shoulders before going to put the kettle on. Some minutes later, while Kim sat clasping a hot mug of tea, Tom refilled Danny's glass for the third time and began by asking what had happened. The young man replied in a strong Glaswegian accent, while holding his ribs with a massive forearm.

'We'd just finished our shift. Ten or so of us got on the bus. Bleedin' pickets were there at the gates as usual throwin' muck an' stuff, creatin' hell. When the bus stopped to drop me off, I thought I was OK. Then a bunch o' thugs came out o' nowhere. Kim here, she came out an' started hollerin' at them but we couldn't get back indoors – they were everywhere – so we made a run for it.' Danny broke off coughing, holding his rib-cage. 'Well, I'll be ready for 'em tomorrow, I'll bloody show 'em.'

'You can't go in tomorrow, Danny!' wailed Kim. 'They'll kill you,' she cried, grabbing hold of him and letting the blanket fall to the floor.

'Shut up, will ya! Let go of me, woman,' he snapped, throwing his arm up between them to break her grip. She collapsed back in tears.

'There, there, don't upset yourself, Kim,' Tom said. 'I'll just give your brother a ring, see if he'll come round and see to you. He could at least walk back with you, eh?' He made a move towards the phone.

'No!' cried Kim, leaping to stop him. 'Don't get Brad, please! I'm all right, really!'

Danny made a move to stand up, but when Kim went to help, he pushed her away again. 'Get out of it!' he swore. 'All I want is do my fuckin' job.'

'Danny! Don't speak like that in front of Father!'

'Oh, give me a break,' spat Danny. 'I ain't no churchgoer. Aye, an' I bet you'd swear yerself sometimes if yer could, Father.'

'Believe me, lad, I'm often tempted,' replied Tom, 'but that's just between ourselves, eh? Now, Kim, finish your tea and we'll see if the coast is clear.'

'I shudder to think what's in some of those!' said Bradley. He was driving Tom's Ford Escort, sharing the long drive back from the Midlands.

'Heh! I'm sure the women will make good use of it, whatever it is. I never expected them to give us a cash donation as well, did you? They must be struggling too.'

Bradley shrugged. 'Who knows?' He wasn't able to offer any explanation. 'We're not far off home now, Tom – just passed Ashford back there.'

'That's grand,' Tom replied. 'I can't wait to get to my bed tonight – it's been a long day.'

'We'll leave takin' the food up the Welfare till the mornin' then, shall we?' He was thoughtful as he drove, trying to understand how those striking miners could *afford* to part with some of their own funds – and why.

Tom had other things on his mind. Taking a deep breath, he began, 'I've been meaning to tell you, Brad – I'm going away for a bit. I'm taking what the bishop calls a *sabbatical*. In his wisdom, he's told me I'm not quite "up to par" lately.'

'Oh? Is this after you said you wanted to speak out about the strike then?'

'Maybe! Still, who am I to argue with the powers-that-be?'

Bradley glanced across at him. Was it a trick of the light or did Tom look smaller and greyer than usual? While he continued talking about his plans, Bradley began to regret being so preoccupied with his own problems – perhaps he had taken his old friend a bit for granted.

'It'll do you good to get away, Tom,' he said. 'You can tell them back in Ireland all about the stupid mess we've got ourselves into here. Wish I was goin' with you, to be honest.'

'Ah, they're not new to conflict at home, Brad, they've had their fair share of hardship too I can tell you. They're all for love and peace one minute and murdering each other the next! They're all mad, so they are!'

Bradley smiled. 'How long will you be away?'

'Not too long, I hope – two or three months at most. I need to wait for the bishop to send a replacement. He's probably got some bright young curate up his sleeve. Wheels in the Vatican turn very slowly, mind, and I'm not in the bishop's best books at the moment so he'll probably let me sweat for a bit.'

Presently the chimes of Big Ben on the car radio caught their attention and Tom reached out and turned the volume up in time to catch the newsreader's announcement:

'This is the ten o'clock news from the BBC read by John Sergeant. Another dock strike is set to go ahead next week. A crucial cargo of coal supplying Ravenscraig's Coke Works is still stranded on board the bulk carrier 'Ostia' moored up in Belfast Lough. . . .'

'Heh,' chuckled Tom, 'even when they've got the stuff out the ground they can't agree!'

'That's the cheap coal from abroad he's talkin' about,' Bradley said. 'Companies won't be hangin' round for our coal for long when they're shippin' in stuff like that. Stands to reason if it's cheaper buyin' it from abroad they won't wait for us lot to get back to work. Why should they?'

'Thought the dockers were supporting the strike and refusing to unload it?'

'They are, but they don't need the dockers! The steel workers'll shift it themselves. Too much money to lose – they're not stupid like us, starvin' ourselves for the sake of a few principles! It makes me sick, Tom, it does really!'

'What, them bringing in the foreign coal, you mean?'

'No, puttin' our heads on the block to stop 'em shutting the pits down – we've shot ourselves in the foot. Loyalty to the unions! What about loyalty to our families? Why should we break our necks over it? They don't care about us!' He flicked the radio knob. 'Hope you don't mind, Tom, but I'm sick o' hearin' the news.' Pop music flooded the car with a new mood.

'*I just called to say, I love you,*' sang Stevie Wonder. '*I just called to say I care. . . .*'

'Not long now. We'll hit the curfew soon,' said Bradley.

'Oh, don't worry, they won't stop a priest out on an important mission.'

Bradley glanced at him, raised his eyebrows and carried on driving.

'How much was that cash donation?' Tom asked after a while.

'Don't know, I didn't count it. Quite a bundle there though.'

'They're generous people, so they are. They didn't have to do all that for us, did they?'

'No.' Bradley accelerated, overtaking a lorry. 'On strike themselves an' givin' money away? It's beyond me what they're up to. We're all like rats scrabblin' around in a hole tryin' to fill our bellies an' they're givin' it away!'

'What, you think it's bribery and corruption?' said Tom, with an impish smile. 'That would please the bishop to be sure!' The idea amused him and he began to nod his head in time to the music.

'Seriously, though, they could be tryin' to get us on their side.'

'You're tired,' said Tom gently. 'Let's just get home and thank God it's not been a wasted journey.'

'Yeah, you're right, I'm dead tired.'

'Shall I take over the driving for a bit, Brad?'

'You're all right, Tom. Won't be long now.' He switched off the radio and put his foot down. Adrenalin was powering up inside his head and as the speedometer climbed, rain began to fall. The only sound was the roar of tyres on tarmac, the rise and fall of the engine and the monotonous 'swish-swish' of the windscreen wipers. Lorries sent up spray as they sped up the motorway. Tom, dazzled by the headlights, closed his eyes. Presently they turned off and, reducing speed, drove quietly through dark winding lanes.

Out of nowhere, a figure loomed in front of the car.

'Bloody hell!' Bradley swore, braking hard. He brought the car to an abrupt halt and shielded his eyes.

'What the devil's going on?' asked Tom. Torches were shone straight into their eyes.

'Police! Open your door and step out!'

Bradley wound down his window instead.

'Turn your ignition off, sir, if you please, and step out of the vehicle,' commanded the policeman.

'Has there been an accident or somethin'?' Bradley asked. As he climbed out, he was grabbed by both arms and held in a bruising vice.

'Don't move till we say you can.'

'Easy, Officer, that's my friend you've got there!' Tom protested, but he too was grabbed and thrust against the car bonnet. He wished for once he had worn his dog collar. 'Jesus, Mary and Joseph, what's going on?' he muttered.

'And where are you two off to at this time of night, if you don't mind me asking?'

'Thought this might 'appen,' Bradley whispered to Tom. The policeman jerked his arms, almost dislocating his shoulder.

'No talking, sir! Plenty of time for that later.'

'We're on our way home, Officer. What's happened?' asked Tom.

'What's the heavy load, sir?' asked the policeman, ignoring his question. 'Any more passengers in there? Carrying any offensive weapons are we at all? Would you mind opening the boot of your car, sir? You seem to be carrying rather a lot of luggage if I might say so. Been on our holidays, have we?'

'I'm a priest,' Tom declared. 'We're on our way back from the Midlands picking up food – donations for the miners' soup kitchen, and clothes for the kiddies.'

'So it's a priest on a mercy mission!' He looked Tom up and down doubtfully. 'And where's "home", if I may be so bold to ask?' Turning to Bradley, 'And you, sir! If this one's a priest, suppose you're the Angel Gabriel? Let me see your driver's licence please?'

Bradley took out his wallet.

'Are you aware, sir,' said the officer, 'that there's a curfew in force? No one's permitted to cross this line without permission at this time of night.'

'Since when have we 'ad to ask permission to go 'ome?' asked Bradley.

The police were searching the car, ripping open boxes and spilling the contents. Not a stranger to curfews, Tom tried again:

'I'm the Roman Catholic priest of this parish, Officer – Father Thomas McNeice. We've just driven a hundred miles to fetch these things.'

'Want to bring in the dogs?' The officers muttered to each other, ignoring him. Evidently deciding against it, the officer raised his voice and shouted, 'Nothin' doin' here – waste of time. Let 'em go, boys!'

They climbed back in the car and drove off in silence, both stunned. However, on entering Silt Edge, they were even more amazed to see a huge crowd of police. Their riot shields flashed, reflecting the headlights as they stood shoulder to shoulder, lining the road ahead. It was nothing less than a war zone. Bradley and Tom drove slowly, unable to believe they were home. The wall of policemen divided in front of them and waved them through.

'Dear God in heaven!' puffed Tom. 'What on earth's going on?'

'Hey, look!' Bradley shouted, peering over the steering wheel into the darkness. 'That's never Kim and Danny's place – look at it!' he braked hard. Two policemen stood on guard, one each side of the front door. Police cars flashing their hazard warning lights lit up the property where incident tape barred entrance to the front path. Then they saw the word 'Scab' crudely daubed on the walls in letters as tall as a man. Bradley dived out of the car and made towards the gate.

'Anyone hurt in there?' he yelled.

'Stop right there, sir!' The policeman grabbed Bradley's arm. 'Don't go over that line or I'll have to take you in.'

'But my sister lives there!' he shouted. 'Let me go!'

'No one's in there, fortunately. Your sister, you say?'

Tom got out of the car and immediately a policeman recognized him.

'Good evening, Father! No offence, but keep your lively friend back, would you?'

'What's going on, Pete?' asked Tom. 'Has there been an accident or what?'

'It's been ransacked – seems the jokers tried to set it on fire. The lads have been right through and had a good look – pretty mess in there, but no one's in there. Perhaps they saw what was coming and did a runner. Lucky for them I'd say.'

'Who d'you think did this?' asked Bradley.

'Who d'you think did it, the bloody fairies?'

Bradley turned away, his eyes scanning the damaged windows, the slogans and graffiti daubed all over the walls. He couldn't believe that miners, such as those who had been so generous to them earlier that day, could turn round and destroy Kim's home.

Chapter 8

Winnie was taking her evening stroll. She was tired; it was late summer and the fast-approaching dusk had snatched the warmth away from the churchyard. Mosquitoes buzzed in the half-light and Ben struggled for breath.

'Poor old thing, you don't know whether you're coming or going do you, old boy?' She had a hunger for the old days. In the apple orchard, beyond the churchyard, trees had been torn down and building work on the apartments was well underway. Winnie was a creature of habit; she liked her routine. Enjoying cooking and mundane tasks, she went about her chores with a sense of love and purpose. Her devotion to Edith was unshakeable. Recently, though, Winnie had felt left out. The new building dominated her once-peaceful view from the kitchen window and workmen with noisy machinery had invaded her quiet world. 'Oh dear, Ben,' she murmured, 'it's all change now.'

Meanwhile, on the veranda, Edith was pouring her guests their after-dinner drinks. With much grandeur, she announced:

'Well, my dears, I would like to propose a toast: the new apartments should be completed soon after Christmas and our residents will be able to move in by the spring. So, to that hard-working team – the builders!' She raised her glass.

'Cheers!' came the resounding chorus all round.

Her face glowed and her eyes melted into pools of sublime joy. Offering a plate of mints with almost girlish dizziness, she said, 'I don't know what these things are, Major, but would you care to try one?'

'Ah! Thank you,' he replied, popping one under his moustache with one eye fixed on her. 'I must say, your building project is a truly commendable gesture, Edith. It must be quite disruptive for you personally, I imagine?'

'Goodness knows, yes. I have had to endure endless noise and mess,' she said, raising a hand to her forehead. 'I've had to sacrifice one of the few joys I had left: the fragrance of apple blossom wafting through my bedroom window! I do miss it so! But my dears' – she paused, gathering momentum – 'to offer a place of sanctuary and renewal to my dear friends in the twilight of their years is of the utmost importance to me.'

'Hear, hear!' chimed the major, raising his glass of port. To Edith's satisfaction, the guests congratulated her on having such a forthright and inspired idea. Sister Ruth raised her puppy eyes and pleaded:

'Lady Ashby, please would you put my name down for a flat?'

'I doubt your convent would let you go, Ruth darling, but I will bear you in mind, of course.' The nun blushed and sipped her orange juice; her woollen hair hung in a fringe over her eyes, replacing the veil which once concealed all but her very round face. Unlike Ruth's solemn stare, another guest – Isobel Pentley – never kept her eyes still. With a haughty, somewhat amused expression, she held her glass balanced, an elbow on her hip, smiling expectantly.

As the heady scent of wine and perfume mingled with the major's pipe tobacco, the evening sun was setting into a molten lava pool of orange and crimson. Suddenly, to everyone's surprise, Isobel slammed down her glass and, standing up, lifted her arms to embrace the sky.

'Look! Just look at that sky!' she cried in rapture. 'Oh, my darlings, you haven't *lived* until you've seen the skies in Africa!' Her eyes flashed like quartz crystal. This outburst was all Ruth needed to spark her inflammable curiosity: she had an insatiable thirst for news of the outside world.

'Do tell us about Africa, Mrs Pentley!' she pleaded. 'What was it like? Did you really live there all on your own?'

A thin sparrow of a lady, Isobel was one of Edith's oldest and dearest friends. She had recently returned from Africa, where she had been a landowner for many years. The major, being a regular visitor to Chalkfield Hall and anticipating the conversation to follow, opened his newspaper.

Taking the stage, Isobel took a gulp of gin and began:

'Not always alone, my darling. Now listen,' she began in a conspiratorial tone, 'my bedroom on the farm had french doors opening out onto a veranda, not dissimilar to this,' she said, glancing about as if sizing up the plot for comparison.

The major shook his paper irritably and winked at Edith; she pretended not to notice, gave a small cough, and turned aside.

'We had quite a few men working for us on the farm at the beginning. Good men, black, of course,' she interjected, 'and we had dogs, two beautiful Great Danes.' She clasped her tiny hands together and gazed over her knuckles into the blood-red sunset as though they had all sprung to life before her eyes.

'It was a good farm, we were very successful, my husband and I, perhaps too successful for some people.' She swallowed. 'Unfortunately my dear husband passed away – heart attack, of course – but I carried on alone. My staff were hardworking, devoted. It wasn't long after that, the trouble started. My neighbouring farmers were being driven off their land, their wonderful horses slaughtered, and people murdered in their beds! And then' – she drew a sharp breath – 'one by one my staff were killed too, or they ran away.' She shrugged her shoulders. 'In fear for their lives and for their families, until there was no one left except my two most faithful and wonderful servants.' She embraced her servants' memory with outstretched arms. 'Archibald and Tobias! They would sleep on my veranda at night, stretched out across the double doors, just to protect me.' A shadow crossed her face. 'One morning I awoke as usual, pulled the blinds across and, to my surprise, my men weren't there! I called them and called them but nothing. I went to fetch my spectacles and looked outside – there I had the fright of my life! A mob of blacks were coming across the paddock towards my house! They were waving machetes, fence posts, shovels, I don't know what! And making the most horrible noise!' She took a gulp of gin, and slammed the glass down again. 'I thought to myself, Are they coming to *murder* me? Where are my dogs? Where is everybody?' Her eyes were glassy now, crazy looking. The guests started looking uncomfortable and exchanged glances.

'I've always kept a rifle in my room,' she whispered. 'You have to, you know, in Africa. It was my father's – a beautiful weapon. Although I'd never actually fired the blessed thing, I had always kept it cleaned and loaded. I still do even now – you can never be too sure, can you? Anyway, so I took this rifle out, this big gun.' She extended her bony arms to illustrate the size of it. 'And then I saw my poor men right in the path of the mob. Old Tobias had a broom and my dear Archie, he was running, running straight towards the mob with nothing in his hand but a white shirt, waving it! Like this! Like this!' and she demonstrated vigorously, waving her handkerchief wildly. 'But the blacks just kept on coming!'

The guests shifted miserably, not quite believing her story perhaps, or not trusting her sanity. The nun was holding a hand to her mouth in horror.

'They were coming towards me like a herd of elephants! They knocked my men down and ran over them like stampeding cattle, and headed straight for me. They were making such a dreadful noise I just knew they were going to kill me!' She gave a little gasp. 'I lifted my rifle – I thought that if I fired over their heads they might. . . . So I aimed, closed my eyes, and pulled the trigger. Oh, the bang! It nearly blew my head off!' She shrieked with hideous laughter. 'It blew me backwards onto the veranda, flat on my back!'

'Oh, my dear, you were so brave,' interjected Ruth, laying a hand on her arm.

'Wait! I lay perfectly still and listened. Nothing! Then very cautiously I sat up and took a peek to see where they were and I could just see them, right in the distance, running away like frightened little rabbits!' And she clapped her hands in childish glee.

'I say!' applauded the major. 'Well done!'

Ruth, overcome with awe, looked towards Edith for commiseration but Edith, already familiar with the story, just gave a benign smile. Enjoying the attention, Isobel let the drama in her story take effect before resuming.

'Then I saw two figures lying in the paddock,' came her voice again, 'their faces in the dirt. They were quite still. And my dogs were standing full-square over their bodies – not moving or barking – like statues.' Isobel looked round now at her audience, appearing exhausted. Slowly, returning in mind and body to the company present, the verandah, and the chill night air, she sighed, letting herself down gently. 'They were both good men, good loyal friends.'

'Ah, yes.' The major gave an impressive cough and knocked out his pipe on the wooden ledge below his seat. 'I've lost good men too; hard to replace. Good trusted servicemen, yes, indeed!'

Ruth was concerned. 'But you were all right, dear? Thank God you weren't hurt!' Easing her weight closer to Isobel's tiny frame, she slipped a podgy arm around her shoulders protectively.

'My dogs,' Isobel croaked, 'you know, my darlings, my dogs in the end were all I had left.' She had a distracted look in her eyes now, as she stared away from them into some distant African sunset, trailing the tatters of her memories behind her.

'And your farm?' Ruth persisted, unwilling to let it go. 'All your land? Did you sell it?'

'I lost it all,' replied Isobel. 'I had to get out, of course – it wasn't safe. I ran away like a thief in the night, left it all, my house, my land, my belongings, all my clothes, even my beloved dogs. I had them shot. I had no choice. I left it all and within twenty-four hours I fled the country.' Making a wide gesture in the air with her arms, she concluded her story: 'And here I am, my darlings, with nothing left but my life!' Her regal smile embraced them all. She picked up her gin and raised her glass. 'Let's drink, my dear friends, to freedom!'

'Freedom!' echoed her audience and as their glasses chinked, their voices were snatched away into the night.

Edith, having been forced out of the limelight long enough, was looking disgruntled, annoyed even. She had heard the story before, more than once, and she wasn't in the mood to talk about *'that place of savages'* as she called it. She looked over her shoulder in a gesture of impatience, to see if Winnie was bringing more drinks or just to escape the company for a moment. Then a thought occurred to her:

'Should I put your name down for an apartment, my dear Isobel?' she asked.

'I don't expect I could afford it, Edith darling, but thank you for the kind thought. No, I really don't know where I shall settle at all. It'll be the workhouse for me,' she giggled, 'if there are such establishments still in England. . . . What do you think, Major?'

'I think what we all need is another drink,' he proclaimed. 'Shall I go and jolly it along?' And rising from his seat clumsily, he made his way indoors.

Chapter 9

'I'll have a small loaf, please,' said Kim.

'They're sold, sorry.'

Kim cast her eyes hungrily at several fragrant loaves on the counter.

'OK, I'll just take some biscuits an' a pint o' milk then, please.'

'Sorry, I'm closed now, so if you don't mind—' Coming from behind the counter, the shop assistant held the door open.

Cast out into the bright sunshine empty handed, Kim saw other customers outside, talking in a huddle. One of them looked over her shoulder.

'You've got a cheek, lass. You ought to know you're not welcome round here any more.'

Kim's throat closed against any reply. Holding her purse tightly, she hurried away. A trembling began in her knees and crept upwards, inducing the nausea that had racked her thin frame since early that morning. On her right, she noticed the church path offered a reprieve and, turning in, she entered the dim interior and slipped into one of the pews at the back. Here she sat hunched with her eyes fixed on the comforting flicker of the candles before a statue of the Virgin Mary and child. Two women who were arranging flowers near the altar raised a hand to her and continued working.

Presently, Kim heard footsteps behind her. 'Heh! Well, if it's not our Kim!' came Tom's voice. 'Here, come with me to the house now and we'll have some coffee, eh?' She followed him meekly.

Ten minutes later, she sat at the table in his sitting room clutching a hot drink and began feeling more herself.

'I don't know what's the matter wi' me really,' she complained to Tom, who was busy in the adjoining room searching for something on his desk, which was piled high with paperwork. 'I should've shouted back at 'em, I suppose.' The wooden surface of the table felt so cold to her bare arms. The room looked even more empty in daylight; there were no photographs or ornaments on the mantelpiece, in fact nothing to make the place look homely.

'Probably wouldn't have got you anywhere,' he called. 'No point in entering into an argument with these people, is there? Excuse me a moment while I find this thing, and then I'll be with you. I'd like to give them a piece of my mind, those women,' he said, picking up books and flinging them down again. 'If I knew who they were, I'd go and have it out with them, God forgive me.'

Kim found his haphazard activity a comforting distraction. The sweet coffee flowed through her bloodstream and her trembling ceased.

'Ah, here it is!' he exclaimed. 'Heh! I knew it was here all along!' Holding up a letter, he came through and gave her a secretive look. 'Between you and me, Kim, I'd like to give the bishop a piece of my mind as well, so I would! I'd say: "Put that in your pipe and smoke it, my dear bishop!" Wouldn't that be just grand!' he added with a mischievous smile.

Amusement flickered across her face, 'Will you then?'

'No, I wouldn't have the nerve. You know, Kim, if it makes you feel any better, you're not the only one caught like a pig in the middle.'

She stared at him; he seemed to be speaking in riddles.

'So, have you heard from Danny lately?' he asked, realizing she wasn't following his train of thought.

'No, I don't know where he is neither. He must have 'eard about our place bein' all trashed up but. . . .'

'You're all right staying with your brother though, aren't you, Kim? You have told Helen, haven't you, about your baby, I mean?'

She shook her head. 'No!' she protested. 'I can't! You ain't told 'em, have you? You promised you wouldn't, Father!'

'No, of course not. I gave you my word, for what it's worth. That's about the only thing I have left which has any value at all. Helen would help you, you know – women know about these things. And your brother – he's a good man, he'll see you're all right.' He studied her face but she remained mute. 'You'll have to tell them sooner or later,' he added, 'or they'll work it out for themselves, you know.'

Kim blushed. 'I know, but I can't tell 'em yet,' she said. 'I will one day.'

'That's my girl!' said Tom. 'Right, now, more coffee?'

It was later that evening when Tom knocked on the Shepstones' door. Kim was curled up in an armchair with her head buried in a magazine. Helen welcomed the priest inside and went to make some tea. Bradley, clearing the toys from the sofa with one sweep of his arm, said, 'Here, Tom, sit yourself down!'

'And how are you all keeping? Any news of Danny at all?' Tom directed this question to Kim, who shook her head.

'No, Tom, he's gone to ground,' replied Bradley. 'We've not seen nor heard from him. Good job an' all, I reckon.'

'Oh! I've brought you a fruit cake, look,' said Tom, retrieving a large round package from his bag. 'My dear mother bakes these cakes for me, bless her, and I can't eat them all.' Helen thanked him and immediately set about cutting them all a slice. 'I've been to see Lady Ashby at Chalkfield Hall this evening – she's had a bit of a tumble. Some young lunatic knocked her down at the Royal Show, would you believe!'

'Shouldn't she be in hospital?' asked Helen.

'It wasn't a vehicle, Helen. Some boisterous youngster running past knocked her flying. She's a bit bruised, that's all; lucky she didn't break a hip. It's her pride that's hurt more than anything, but her housekeeper's clucking over her like a broody hen, so she is.' He munched on his cake with a satisfied air. 'I'm very fond of the old girl myself.' He smiled. 'Not that I would tell her to her face, you understand. Yes, Edith's got a heart of gold, even if she is a bit old-fashioned,' he said, puffing out his cheeks in contemplation.

'She sounds just like someone out of *Pride and Prejudice* – don't you think so, Brad?' sighed Helen. 'I wish we lived in the olden days!'

Bradley raised his eyebrows at her, the flame of anger always ready to ignite.

'I thought we were goin' backwards enough already,' he sighed, standing up and beginning to pace the floor with his hands thrust in his pockets. 'Isn't life hard enough for you already, Helen?'

Kim looked up anxiously. A silence of several seconds loaded the air with ammunition.

'How are things with you two?' ventured Tom.

'I dunno, Father,' Bradley replied. 'I keep waitin' an' hopin' an' prayin' for somethin' to happen. The union says one thing an' the bosses say another, an' all the while we're stuck with no money an' the bills mountin' up. It's enough to drive a man crazy!'

Helen held Tom's gaze for several moments, both acknowledging the fact that Bradley had ducked the question.

'Something will turn up, Brad, you'll see,' Tom said. 'The strike won't go on for ever.'

'But when the strike ends, what then?' Bradley challenged him. 'The pits are floodin'. God knows what state the place will be in when we get back. There's talk that they'll turn the pumps off – it's gettin' too expensive to keep 'em runnin'. Then the whole pit will go underwater. Well, it's what that lot want anyhow! They won't be happy till they've shut us down. See if I care, serve 'em right.'

Helen glared at him, her colour rising. 'They won't shut the pit down,' she said. 'Not while we're here fighting for it, there's too much at stake!'

'It's all right for you, with all your cookin' an' organizing. Seems to me you're almost enjoyin' it.'

'Brad!' Helen retaliated. 'How can you say that?'

Tom noticed Kim tearing at her fingernails with tiny white teeth. 'Come, come now, don't go upsetting yourselves,' he interrupted and stood up to leave. 'It's getting late and we're all dog-tired. I'd better let you good people get to your beds.' But as he reached the front door, he paused.

'Do you mind if I ask your sister something before I go, Bradley?' Retracing his steps he said, 'Lady Ashby has asked me to look out for a girl to help in the house, cooking and cleaning and that. I thought you might like to give the job a try, Kim. It would be full-time and live-in. What do you think?'

'A job? What, you mean a proper job, with pay an' that?'

'Yes, you would have your own room and meals too, as part of your wages.'

Kim's eyes grew wide in astonishment. 'I don't know,' she said, glancing quickly at her brother. 'I dunno if I'd be any good at cookin' an' that.'

'Winnie's the cook, poor old soul,' Tom explained. 'It would help her just to have another pair of hands, to be honest, especially since Lady Ashby's had her fall.'

'Sounds a good idea to me,' said Helen. 'You're used to the hotel work aren't you? Go for it. I wouldn't mind a job like that myself.' Bradley flashed her a look.

'But what about Danny though?'

'What about him? As if he cares! He's left you to fend for yourself, hasn't he? You don't even know where he is! Do it, Kim! Brad, you tell her!'

'It's OK by me,' he replied. 'You can't be sleepin' on the sofa all your life.' He looked downcast. 'Tom, I'm not ready for bed yet – got time to come up the club for a drink?'

'Sounds like a good idea, yes, I'll join you for a quick one. Well, Kim, I'll leave you to think about it, shall I? Thanks for the tea, Helen.' He opened the door and made to leave. Kim was instantly on her feet.

'Where did yer say she lives, this old woman?'

'Chalkfield Hall. You must know it, Kim, the big house next to the church in Ebbingsfield. I'll take you to meet her if you like, to see what you think.' Adding that he would pick her up at eleven the next day, he bid them good night and stepped out into the night air, where Bradley was already waiting for him at the gate.

'Pint o' bitter, please, Jean! Tom, what are yer 'avin'?'

'I'll have the same. Make that two, please. I'll get these,' he added, placing a note on the counter. Bradley thanked him and glanced around to see who was there. Jean, pulling their pints, placed them on the bar.

'Seen our Danny about anywhere, have you?' Bradley called to some miners having a game of cards. They all froze – none of the men responded to his voice but neither did they move or speak. The delay became so odd that Bradley met Tom's gaze and they both started to feel awkward. He was just about to try again when one of the group stood up and faced him; a cigarette hung from his lower lip and a malicious glint was in his eye.

'We don't know anyone by that name, do we, lads?' he said, turning to gain the approval of the others, who all stared. Bradley's mouth felt dry. He dare not take his eyes away. He kept looking, spellbound by that stare. All the years' hard toil on his father's back ached in his own bones at that moment; all the dust and phlegm in his father's lungs came back to choke him. But still they stared. Minutes ticked away, and the silence threatened to engulf him. Gradually he became aware of a warm hand on his forearm.

'Forget it, Brad, let it be, there's a lad, eh?' said Jean, giving his arm a squeeze. His stare shifted away from the miners into the warm pools of the barmaid's eyes. He relaxed, took a gulp of beer and watched the cream froth fizz down the side of his glass. Losing interest, they turned back to their table and their card game resumed.

Simultaneously a crowd came crashing through the doors, calling their orders for drinks and scraping chairs into a huddle. They provided a welcome distraction. Jean went over to the card players, collecting empty glasses; any words they might have exchanged were lost in the background noise. When she returned to the bar, Bradley called to her:

'Same again over here, love, please.'

'Listen, he's barred – that Danny Stuart,' she said under her breath, reaching under the counter to pick up a glass. 'Those lads are out to get him. They'll fix him for good if he dares to show his face round here, so don't ask after him – and don't say I didn't warn you. OK?'

Their bedroom was crowded with sacks of second-hand clothes; donations for the campaign's 'swap-shop' had spilled over from the Welfare Hall due to lack of storage space. The clutter seemed to sap the air from the room. Bradley couldn't sleep. Hadn't he worked alongside those men for years? Now, just because he had asked after

Danny, they treated him like a stranger. He tossed and turned until Helen began to complain so he got up. Stumbling over several sacks, he pulled on his jeans and crept downstairs, careful not to wake the baby.

It was the early hours of the morning. He sat by the kitchen window lost in thought. The faces of those miners up at the club drifted into his mind – the tone of their voices, the look of suspicion – but he felt they were like brothers to him. Hadn't they grown up together? Sharing such dangerous physical labour deep underground mingled not only their sweat but their blood – they were his blood brothers, they would give their lives for each other. But now they treated him like an enemy.

It was a quarter to five. The first luminous hint of light was swelling up the clouds across the back gardens, casting eerie shadows and causing him to feel a strange fear and anticipation.

Picketing was on his mind. Should he be going up to the picket line? It wasn't an easy decision and he was afraid of his own feelings, torn between what was right and wrong. Should he try and stop the scabs? Should he go and block the brutish determination of men going into work? Those men who were oblivious of their loyalty to their fellow miners. Could he bring himself to fight them? He felt anxiety drain the blood from his hands and they felt so cold he stood up in the kitchen and shoved them tightly into his pockets. He had no will to go and fight. But then a word came into his mind, as a hint of light shot through the asphalt sky – courage! Hadn't his father said: '*When all else fails you – and it will at some time or other, life's like that, son – then remember what your old dad told you. Have courage, lad!*'

He stood up and put on his jacket, pulled on his pit boots and laced them up, took his gloves and hard hat and turning up his collar slipped out into the chill dawn air. It was time he showed a bit of solidarity to his fellow man – he was going to join the picket line. No-one was going to call him a 'scab sympathizer'. He knew who his friends were and he needed to be with them more than ever before in his life.

*

The pit gates soon loomed up ahead and Bradley could see the list of scabs' names written there. Momentarily he wondered why they had used white paint but then he realized: white was for surrender. Were they weak though? Were they cowards? He was still contemplating this when the shrill dawn chorus was punctuated by voices. As he drew close, he could smell the picketers' fires burning. Several dark figures were huddled round an oil drum, flames lighting up their faces. As he approached, a rush of adrenalin surged through his veins.

'Hello there, Brad!' One of the men beckoned and a cheer went up. He joined them, holding out his hands to the warmth.

'Good on yer, Shepstone!' they shouted, coming up and thumping him good-naturedly on the back. 'There'll be a lot more coming to support us today, so they say. Here's some more now, look!' They turned to see several stragglers emerging out of the darkness, wearing donkey jackets with fluorescent shoulder strips, hard hats and balaclavas.

'Gather round, lads!' came a loud voice. Bradley didn't recognize the newcomer but someone next to him said:

'He's one of them flying pickets come down from up north.'

'When the time comes,' the man said in a broad Yorkshire accent, 'don't wait for instructions from me, just dive in there and do all you can to stop that bloody bus, all right, mates?'

A loud cheer went up. Bradley geared himself up for the fight. This could turn nasty, very nasty. What chance have we got, he thought, of stopping a coach travelling at forty miles an hour? But the miners were joking and laughing – some were used to it, they had been there every morning, some at night too. You have to admire these chaps, he thought, risking everything for what they believe to be right. He began to wonder what his dad would have done. Would he be there alongside them? Or would he be one of the scabs on the bus, still working and slamming the strike for being a waste of time?

They were grouped about a quarter of a mile from the pit head itself. Before them were the colliery gates, barricaded with corrugated iron and tangled rolls of barbed wire. To Bradley's amazement he saw a long line of policemen – military in their stature – and as motionless as lead soldiers.

'Are those coppers usually out here, mate?'

'Too right they are! Some ain't even coppers – they're army lads in coppers' uniforms, so they say! Don't wanna get on the wrong side of them, Brad. Keep out their way, stick by me an' you'll be OK!'

'Thanks,' replied Bradley, wondering if Helen had woken up yet, and whether she would worry where he was. Be a surprise for her, telling her he had been out picketing, he thought. She might actually be pleased for once.

They were preparing themselves for battle now, picking up fence posts, poles, spades and placards that were hidden in the long grass. 'Save our Pits!' proclaimed one and 'Coal not Dole!' another. They were also arming themselves with bricks, flour bombs and eggs, which magically appeared out of pockets and bags. Gradually he realized the distant sound of a vehicle was approaching. Simultaneously, a growl went up from the men.

'Here they come!' they yelled, raising their assortment of weapons. Bradley picked up a steel pole and along with the crowd surged forward in a tribal assault as the coach came hurtling into view. Shoulder to shoulder, they were moving as one, chanting 'Scab! Scab! Scab! Scab!' louder and louder, stabbing the air with their fists. The coach bristled with barbed wire. Steel mesh and filthy urban dust obscured the faces inside. His first instinct was to step back – one brush from those sharp steel edges and his flesh would be ripped. It looked ugly, like a war-dog, a ravaged grey vehicle smeared with grease, grime and graffiti, and bearing the nature of its cargo in red paint: 'Scabs!' How he hated that word! A wound that never healed but festered skin deep, poisoning the blood for generations to come.

Forgetting themselves, spurred on by a mutual hunger for justice, they threw themselves at the coach as it hurtled past, roaring their frustration. Bradley thought he saw the miners inside, smug-faced in their warm seats, riding high with toffee-nosed union leaders and Coal Board officials. He imagined the fat wallets in their pockets and their bellies full of fried breakfast. Hatred for the injustice of it all rose up inside him and he threw himself headlong at the body of the coach. The noise, the clash of steel against steel was deafening. But it was like trying to stop a charging elephant. The coach accelerated, oblivious of boots and legs and missiles, it became a massive weapon. Bradley lunged forward, yelling at the top of his voice, hitting out blindly with his pole – and he lost control. He didn't care. Hatred spurred him on. Above the overwhelming tide of violence came a man's scream, penetrating the innocent dawn like a stricken hare. . . .

Bradley didn't know what had hit him. In an instant something had made such an impact on his head that it sent his hard hat flying. He was reeling backwards into a swirling well of black water that engulfed him in flashing lights; sinking into a swamp, he was gagging on the dense water and blood that filled his mouth.

The heat of battle died down; the men inspected their cuts and bruises, rubbed their injuries, laughed and swore, lit cigarettes and collected their bits together. It was only then that they noticed him.

'You all right Bradley, lad?' one of them asked, peering down at him from a great height.

Everything was spinning. He put his hand to his forehead and felt a slippery wetness.

'Think I'm bleedin' a bit,' said Bradley, surprised at the sound of his own voice. Strong arms hauled him up, one on each side.

'You'll be OK in a tick!' they said. 'Here, have a fag!'

Dizzy and sick, he attempted to make out the direction of home. Their voices were like echoes from the past. There was a loud ringing in his ears. He tried to walk but each foot was a leaden weight as though he was in quicksand.

'I'm off home,' he said, and dragged himself away.

The sun was just beginning to rise in the sky. His teeth chattered. He felt as though he was dragging his shadow along like a heavy sack; it tugged at his heels and tripped him, hung over his forehead like a dust-laden cobweb, obscuring his vision. Trying to brush it away, he thought the darkness of the night had somehow got into his head and it was hanging like a blanket at the back of his eyes. He couldn't see properly. The weight of his body began to pull him down into the ground and he struggled, trying to stay upright, but every step he took seemed to be a mile long. Each foot seemed to be embedded in cement.

'Right!' he cried. 'Left!' He forced himself to march, just knowing he had to get home.

Kim found him sunk on his knees on the kitchen floor.

'What happened to you? Brad? Look at you!'

'I feel a bit rough, Kim – where's Helen?' Somehow he managed to stand up.

'She's gone up the Welfare. You been fightin'? They never set on yer, like they did Danny, did they?'

'No, I've been picketin', that's all.'

'You're jokin'!'

Moving carefully, he walked through to the toilet, a small closet by the back door. A stabbing pain shot across his forehead and slamming the door to, he vomited from the pit of his stomach.

Kim started banging on the door. 'Brad! Open the door! Shall I go an' fetch the doctor? Shall I get Helen?'

'No, no, I'm all right.' Recovering himself, he caught his reflection in the mirror above the sink. It looked so unlike his old face he felt almost amused. After splashing his face with cold water, he emerged to find her waiting for him.

'Fetch me a nice hot cuppa, will yer, Kim?'

While she was making tea, a knock came on the front door. He tried to get out of sight but, swaying, he hung on to a chair.

'That'll be Father, come to take me to see that old lady,' she said, glancing at him before opening the door.

'Mornin' to you!' cried Tom breezily. Kim offered him tea.

'Thanks, but I think we'd best be on our way. Edith will be expecting us.' He paused, seeing Bradley. 'Well, look at you! Have you been in a fight, Brad?'

'Could call it that. I'm OK though.'

'Heh, tis a pretty black eye you have there! So you're ready, my girl? Right, we'll be off.' He studied Bradley again. 'Are you sure you don't need that looking at?'

'No, I'll be fine, honest, just need to rest a bit.' Longing for sleep, he wished they would just leave him alone.

Watching them go down the path, a soft drowsiness descended

over him and at last he let himself crumple onto the floor where he fell into a delicious sleep.

Chapter 10

'He looks in a bit of a mess, your brother,' said Tom as they drove out of Silt Edge. 'Not like him to get in a fight.'

Kim smiled. 'He's been out picketin' – the idiot!'

'So that's how he got a black eye!' Tom gave a quick shake of his head. ''Tis rough up there. I've been up to the picket line myself a few times; just to give the lads a bit of support, you know, seeing as how—' Glancing across at Kim, he saw she wasn't listening. She was watching out of the car window like an excited child. 'I hope you'll like it at Chalkfield Hall, Kim. It'll give you a new start in life. We all need a helping hand sometimes. I've been through a sticky patch or two myself in the past.'

'What, you have?' She turned to him in surprise.

'Oh, with us Catholic priests, y'know, it's not all a bed of roses. I've been strapped for cash myself more than once. We don't get paid wages or anything, not like the Church of England. No, I'm in the wrong job, that's for sure. When the Sunday collection's a bit thin – folks can't afford to give much nowadays – Lady Ashby's been very generous. Any scraps from the kitchen she'll pop into my doggy bag and to be honest her leftovers are something else!' He smacked his lips in satisfaction. 'She's a good soul, bless her. At least you won't go hungry living there.'

Kim was thoughtful. 'I didn't know priests had to—' She stopped.

'Beg, were you going to say?' he chuckled. 'Oh, that's not such a bad thing. Buddhist monks – they only have what people put in their begging bowls. Seems I don't do too badly, judging by the size of me!'

His joke was lost on her as she continued peering through the windscreen for sight of their destination.

September was a busy month in the kitchen at Chalkfield Hall. Preparations for Christmas began with the wrapping of apples and pears in newspaper for storing, although fruit wasn't plentiful since half the orchard was given over to the new building. Winnie liked to get the Christmas puddings boiled, and the tempting fragrance of cinnamon and nutmeg filled the house. Making chutney was one job Winnie disliked but worst of all was pickling the onions – how they made her eyes sting, and how the odour permeated the house! Edith always complained about the smell too and she went about filling vases with lavender and rosemary cut from the garden, but the alternative of purchasing such items ready-made from a shop was, in Edith's opinion, a step too far.

Winnie, being arthritic, was having difficulty reaching the glass pickling jars from the top shelf of the dresser and she failed to hear the doorbell. Edith, aided by a walking stick, answered the door and led the visitors straight into the kitchen.

'Oh, my word, Father!' exclaimed Winnie, flushing as pink as a schoolgirl.

'This is Kim,' Edith announced. 'She's thinking of coming to help us for a while, aren't you, dear?' She inclined her head gracefully in Kim's direction, waiting for confirmation. The girl smiled but said nothing. 'Kim, this is my loyal housekeeper, Winifred.'

Winnie beamed. 'Hello, my dear,' she said and began to make excuses for the untidiness of the kitchen. When she began describing the numerous chores entailed in the preserving of fruit and vegetables, Kim stood looking bewildered. Ben got up and laboured across to greet them, pressing his nose into Tom's hand.

'Kim, my dear.' Edith drew Kim aside to consult her on a more personal note. 'Tell me, would you like to have your own room here? Your board and lodging will be included in your wages, with all your meals provided, of course. Your hours will start at seven-thirty prompt and finish at five – Monday to Friday, and some weekends as necessary. Would that suit you?' She inclined her head, again waiting for a response.

Kim stood gazing about her, unable to speak, while Edith remained passive, with pencilled eyebrows raised expectantly.

Tom intervened: 'It's OK, Kim, you needn't decide now. You go home and think about it, heh. Tis a lot to take on board all at once, is it not?' He patted her arm affectionately and simultaneously caught Edith's eye, who understood him perfectly.

'Come along, Ben – you shouldn't be in the kitchen anyway, naughty boy!' she scolded. Leaning on her walking stick, she withdrew, the dog's long claws making scratching noises on the tiles as he followed her. Tom also turned to leave.

'Father, before you go,' Winnie called, 'would you mind lifting down those kilner jars from the dresser? If you would put them there on the table, they'll be ready to be washed and warmed in the oven tomorrow.'

Kim watched him climb the stepladder as she absentmindedly stroked the dog who had padded straight back into the kitchen and sat leaning his weight against her thigh. 'Oh, he's a lazy boy, aren't you, old fella?' called Winnie.

'You're not talking about me, I hope, Winnie?' Tom teased as he brought down the jars, passing them to Winnie one by one.

Kim felt the heavy warmth of the dog and instantly relaxed. Sensing this, Winnie said, 'It'll soon be time for his walk, poor old thing. He can't go far these days, but then, neither can I. If you'd like to, once you're settled in, you can take him out for me sometimes, give my old legs a rest. Would you like that?'

Kim nodded. 'OK,' she replied.

She was quiet in the car going back. Tom guessed there was a bit of a battle going on in her mind. Finally she said, 'It's nice there, bit like an old film on the telly.'

Tom smiled at her idea. 'Yes, I suppose it is,' he said. 'Would you like to give it a try?'

'Yeah, but I don't know what Danny'll say,' she added, glancing up at Tom quickly as he drove, 'wherever he is.'

'Is he still working?'

'I dunno,' she answered. 'Anyway, I dunno what he'd say to me livin' in a big 'ouse like that.'

'There's not just Danny to consider now though, is there?'

'Oh, my brother! No, he ain't bothered, he's fed up wi' me already, sleepin' on the sofa.'

'I didn't mean Brad.'

'Oh that!' Kim said, biting her lip. 'I suppose when that Lady What's-her-name finds out I'm pregnant, she won't want me there anyhow.'

'The lady's name is Lady Ashby,' Tom corrected, smiling. 'Edith already knows you're expecting a baby, Kim.'

'Oh, did you 'ave to tell 'er!' she protested loudly. 'I mean I could've worked without her knowin' for ages yet!' She surprised Tom with her sudden reproach.

'I didn't tell her, she guessed. I don't know how, but she's a clever woman.'

Kim was astonished. 'Does it show already? Blimey!' she cried, feeling her stomach and looking dismayed.

'No,' he laughed. 'Call it female intuition! She liked you, I could tell, so don't worry. Edith has helped a lot of people in her time, even me, you know,' he added. 'I told you I've been through a sticky patch or two myself. Once when I was away, back home in Tipperary with my dear parents, squatters moved into the presbytery.'

Kim looked at his profile curiously. 'What, an' lived there, y'mean?'

'They had some notion that I wouldn't mind – me being a priest, I suppose. Homeless people, seven of them! Seems they weren't used to living in a house at all because they used the corner of my living room as a toilet, so they did.' He clicked his tongue. 'I was probably wrong, may the Lord forgive me, but when I got back and found all the mess I threw them out on the street.' He shook his head. 'They'd got dogs with them too, Kim; they'd trashed all my papers and goodness knows what. The kitchen was . . . ugh! Some of my books were burnt in the grate, trying to keep themselves warm apparently, although there was plenty of coal in the shed outside. T'was a cold spring, just before Easter, five, six years ago now.'

Kim was staring at him with her eyes wide open.

'Well, it was then Lady Ashby took me in. The place was in such a state it took me weeks to clear it up and get rid of the smell of urine. She was very kind to me, Kim, very sympathetic. She has a heart of gold.' He sighed. 'But to think I threw those people out into the cold, heh!' He shook his head at the thought. 'Call myself a Christian!'

'I don't blame yer, Father, not fair them doin' that – didn't the police catch 'em then?'

'I didn't report them.' He pursed his lips. 'I told the bishop though! Your brother helped me clean the place up. He's a good man. And Helen helped too. They scrubbed it all down, put up new wallpaper, painted the place out for me. It was grand in the end, just grand!'

They pulled up outside the Welfare Hall where Tom had planned to drop her off.

'I'll call by tomorrow, shall I, to see what you've decided? You'll need some help with transport if you're going to move into Chalkfield Hall.' He paused. 'Kim – Edith will see you're all right, you can trust her. Don't worry.'

'Thanks, Father,' she replied, closing the car door and with it, her face – closing herself down protectively and bringing up the barrier again. Tom watched her thoughtfully for a few moments before finally driving off.

Kim walked into the Welfare Hall and the hubbub of noise instantly put her on her guard; she had been hoping to find Helen alone. Women's voices rang above the clatter of cutlery, and the aroma of boiled potatoes mingled with the tang of sausages frying.

'Have you come to help?' Helen called.

Kim shook her head. Drying her hands, Helen left the sink.

'What's up? You OK?'

'I'm fine, it's just I wanted to, you know. . . .' She trailed off, her eyes resting on the other two women.

'Let's go outside. Won't be a minute,' she called back. 'Keep an eye on Sam for me, will you?'

'So how did it go at Chalkfield Hall?' she asked, as they stepped into the sunlight.

'It was OK,' said Kim, adding a brief description of the curious chores Winnie had described to her.

'I think you should take it. It'll be great and it'll get you out of Danny's— Well, what I mean is you're best off without—' She stopped herself. 'Sorry, Kim, I know it's hard.'

'I ain't seen 'im, nor heard from 'im – not since he got beat up,' she sniffed. 'I can't stop on your sofa for the rest o' my life, can I, an' his place is all in a mess. You won't tell Danny where I've gone, will yer? I don't want 'im goin' down there makin' a scene in front o' that nice old lady.'

'No, of course not, and Brad won't say anything – no one need even know.' Helen kept her voice low; the door stood ajar and the distant rattle from the kitchen reminded her they were not alone.

'Helen? I'm . . . that is. I'm. . . .' A terrible urgency gripped her.

'You'll be all right, Kim, don't worry. They won't eat you alive down there, you know!' Helen put an arm around her shoulders.

'I hate Danny now though, an' I don't want him comin' near me.' She stumbled on, trying to put her thoughts into words. 'The thing is. . . .'

'What? You don't have to ever see him again if you don't want to!'

'But Helen!' She turned away as her nerve failed her. 'When he finds out he'll come after me.'

'Nothing needs to happen, Kim. You've got a new job and it'll be great. Why are you worried? Tell him to get lost – he's history! You don't want to get back with him, do you?'

'Oh no, it's just—'

'Just what? Come on, Kim, it's over!' exclaimed Helen, going back towards the doorway.

Kim stood still. Letting her sad eyes rest on Helen, she stared helplessly. In those eyes were secrets too ripe for keeping; they shed from her lips like cherries on a summer's day. Realization dawned on Helen then, and instinctively her eyes travelled down to where Kim's hands were now clasped together anxiously across her abdomen. Suddenly she knew.

'You're sure?' she murmured. The wind caught the door of the Welfare Hall and slammed it shut, sending dust and litter into a swirl.

'You can't be, can you? I mean, surely you and Danny took

precautions or something?'

'Suppose we didn't. I dunno about all that though, do I? It's never 'appened before!' She giggled nervously. 'We was brought up good Catholics, sort of, anyway.' Suddenly she remembered something which she thought might be in her favour and brightened.

'Oh, yeah, I told Tom – y'know, about the baby like.' She paused for Helen's approval. 'He was really nice about it so that's good.'

Helen gaped at her incredulously. 'But Kim! How could you? He's just gone and found you this job!'

'Yeah, I know. He said it'd be all right though.'

Helen looked at her in disbelief. 'What *did* you tell him exactly?'

'I said' – she took a deep breath as if reciting something off by heart – 'if there was a girl gonna have a baby, right, and—'

'But you *did* tell Tom it was you though, didn't you?' asked Helen, desperate now.

'Oh yeah, I said that right, an' I said, "Is there a place I could go an' have it, like, cos I wouldn't want the doctor to get rid of it for me or anythin' cos that's horrible that is. . . ." '

'But Lady Ashby will go mad when she finds out you're pregnant! Anyway, it's wrong not telling her and starting a new job when you know you're preg—'

'It doesn't matter, honest!' retaliated Kim. 'Tom said she already knows; he said she could tell, I don't know how.' Stroking her stomach curiously, it only emphasized how her clothes hung from her thin frame, showing no sign of her growing womb. 'It doesn't show already, does it, Helen?' she asked meekly. Helen shook her head, her face stricken with worry.

'He was really nice to me, Tom was, an' he was nice to Danny, when he got beat up. He sorts everythin' out for me, he does.'

'Yes, you're very lucky that he's helping you,' said Helen, but her eyes became dark. 'Watch yourself, Kim, that's all I'm saying.'

'How d'you mean?'

'If folks round here get to hear, y'know, that it's a scab's baby you're carrying, well – they won't take kindly to it, you know.'

'I ain't tellin' no one, an' you won't go and tell 'em will yer?'

'What about Brad? Does he know yet?' asked Helen. It had

occurred to her that the way things stood between them, it wouldn't have surprised her if Bradley knew and had kept this from her.

'No way! Brad will go mad, you know what he's like. You won't go an' tell 'im, will yer?' Kim pleaded. 'I wouldn't have told you otherwise.'

'He's got to know sooner or later, Kim. But Brad's in no mood for talking at the moment.' Immediately, the thought of going home filled Helen with anxiety. To bear this secret alone was a lot to ask of her and yet when she looked at the girl she found it impossible not to consent. Why hadn't she foretold this happening? Anyone could have guessed Kim would get herself into trouble.

Seeing her standing there, looking so immature and undernourished, she couldn't think of a less likely candidate for motherhood. Kim was hardly able to look after herself, let alone a baby.

'So when is it due?'

Kim shrugged. 'After Christmas. You won't tell! Promise?'

Reluctantly, Helen agreed. And finding the truth had brought a chill to the air, they both went inside.

Kim started to play with Sam, who was on a blanket surrounded by toys. Helen rejoined the others. The kitchen was a fair size which opened out onto the main part of the Welfare Hall with a large serving hatch. On the counter, cutlery and condiments were placed in readiness for the arrival of the miners and their families.

Raising a questioning eyebrow, Jean asked, 'Everything all right?' and glanced across at Kim's forlorn figure.

Helen nodded. 'She's fine; she's got the chance of a new job, lucky girl.'

'Thought she'd have had plenty of cash already, seein' as her fella's gone back to work.' Jean scowled. 'The scum, he's be earnin' a pretty penny I shouldn't wonder.'

Helen looked up at her quickly. 'She's finished with Danny Stuart. It's over.'

'Good job! Wouldn't like to be in her shoes if she hadn't,' Jean sneered. 'I wouldn't have had anythin' to do with that scab in the first place if it was me – wouldn't give him the time o' day, let alone let him into my bed. After all we've been through,' she said under her breath, 'that Danny Stuart thinks he can waltz back in to work as if nothin's happened! Pass me that bag of sugar there, love, will you?' Jean sprinkled the apples and taking the pastry up with floured hands, she continued: 'You know her trouble, don't you?' she said, nodding in Kim's direction. 'She needs to stand up for herself a bit more. She's like a flippin' church mouse, that girl. Where is this new job she's got herself anyway?'

Helen told her.

'Oh, very posh! Now, these pies are just about ready to go in. D'you want the custard making now or shall we leave it till later?'

The clatter of plates signalled that the meal was ready. Seeing Kim still playing with Sam on the floor, Helen's anxiety increased. Being associated with Danny was bad news – if she was recognized when the miners arrived there might be trouble. But something stopped her from going over and asking Kim to leave. The rare smile she saw on Kim's face as she sat dangling a fluffy toy above Sam's head touched her so deeply she couldn't bring herself to send the girl away. Presently a few miners started arriving. Kim, no more than a child herself, was still sitting cross-legged on the play mat in the corner. To Helen's relief she remained unnoticed. How can I ever tell Brad that his sister's expecting a scab's baby? she asked herself while starting to dish out hot potatoes to a growing queue of noisy people.

When the lunchtime meal was finished and cleared away, Helen arrived home. She was alone and carried Sam on her hip. The sight of Bradley's body on the floor shot all anxieties about Kim straight out of her mind. Panic gripped her. She froze, immobilized in fear. The weird hump of his shape on the floor was unreal. She tried to speak as she rushed over to him. 'Bradley! Bradley?' she screamed, but her voice fell uselessly into the quiet room. He didn't stir.

'Ambulance!' she yelled down the phone. Stifling sobs, she clung to the reassuring voice on the other end of the line. All kinds of possibilities raced through her mind. While waiting for the ambulance, she knelt down and put her lips to his face, feeling with a rush of relief the quivering warmth of his cheek and the shallow rise of his breath. How she loved him! Gazing at his unconscious face, she felt shut out and afraid.

If only he would wake up, speak to her! Covering him in a blanket, and holding Sam close in her arms, they stayed huddled together on the floor – the three of them. Sam gurgled happily, seemingly unaware of their dilemma, while Helen's tears surged into her throat. She couldn't, wouldn't cry, not yet – not now. Reaching for the phone again, she rang her mother.

Every day, police sirens tore through the streets of Silt Edge. Hearing emergency vehicles had become an everyday experience for the residents. At one time, such a sight would cause terror among the miners' wives. They would drop whatever they were doing and converge on the pit head, waiting for news of their men as the restless ground rumbled beneath their feet. Now, Helen longed to hear that sound. Minutes later, it came screaming through the village, its blue lights illuminating the walls of their sitting room.

'All right love, where's the casualty then?' they called. To her relief, Bradley stirred as the paramedics descended on him.

'It's OK, mate,' they said as they examined him, all the while asking Helen questions which she was unable to answer.

Bradley felt the ambulance men lift him. He felt the strength of the stretcher rise and bear him away and it came to him that he was on the sea again. The tide swelled beneath him, and the great roaring of the ocean's boiling foam filled his ears. When the fresh air struck him, he became aware of Helen's presence and lifted a leaden arm out towards her.

'Helen?' he called and grasped her hand as he slipped away again beneath the waves. Purple-coloured shapes of trees and houses began to flash past the ambulance window. With head pounding, he thought he could hear the jeers of the men at the picket line. Their voices were echoing: 'Scab! Scab! Scab! Scab!' Were they really outside or inside his head? He was on the scabs' coach, hurtling through a mob towards the colliery gates while the picketers stabbed at him. Now he could see their faces pressed up against the glass – even his friend Gavin was there, with his eyes full of malice. Loathing and menace poisoned the men's features; their skin was bloated and their eyes blood red. How they must all hate him! And now the sea: now the sea was inside his head again, crashing its freezing waves down on him and he began shivering uncontrollably.

In the hospital some time later, he awoke to find Helen beside him.

'Brad? My love!' she cried. As soon as he opened his eyes she started kissing his sore face. 'Are you all right? What happened to you?'

Looking around in confusion, he saw a long white room, and her urgent face – wanting something, needing him. But he couldn't respond, he felt so weak and detached from everything; it all seemed like a dream. He grasped hold of her hand but a dark shadow came across his eyes and he struggled to see. In sudden claustrophobia, he sat up, shouting,

'Helen! Helen!' he cried desperately, struggling against the weight of the sheets as though he was being buried alive. A nurse came swiftly, checked his pulse, and returning, gave him an injection. Drowsiness lifted him on the ebb tide and he drifted on a small fishing craft, away from the rocks and safely out to sea . . . Within minutes, he was asleep.

When dawn broke, Helen was slumped in the armchair at his bedside; a nurse had covered her with a hospital blanket. Bradley was weak but he felt himself again. For a long while he lay watching her sleeping face and thought how beautiful she was, how time had changed them both, how things had come between them, and a great sadness filled his heart. The hospital ward was already stirring in the half-light, the figure of a nurse tending to someone at the far end, the distant sound of a vacuum cleaner, and cups chinking. His gaze came to rest on Helen's face again, abandoned in the depth of exhaustion, and he realized just how much he loved her, how much he longed for everything to be right.

Finally she stirred. 'Oh, I wondered where I was!' She smiled, reaching out to place her hand tenderly on the side of his face. 'Are you feeling any better?'

'I am, an' thanks for waitin' with me.'

'Oh, thank God! What happened – who did this to you?'

'It were my own fault,' he relented. 'I went picketin' – just wanted to help the lads out a bit. I'm OK now, a bit tired that's all.'

'You went up on the picket line? Oh, that's brilliant!' She jumped up and kissed him. 'I'm so proud of you, Brad!'

'I shouldn't have gone, Helen, it was crazy up there,' he said soberly, wincing as he tried to sit up.

'I'm glad you went. Look, don't try to move yet; just stay there and rest while I pop home and see Mum's all right with Sam. If she'll stop with him a bit I'll come straight back.'

He felt her kiss, saw a warmth in her eyes which he hadn't seen for a long time and watched her walk down the ward happily, throwing her shoulders back and smiling. A sense of betrayal crept up on him because he could see how thrilled she was and yet what sense did it all make? He struggled to feel the excitement she felt; memories of the picket line haunted him like a nightmare. It was madness. Did he really have to risk being killed by a coach just to stop his mates going in to work? They were simply doing what he had been doing himself for years! It was crazy!

This strike meant everything to Helen. Picketing had won him that love in her eyes which he had craved to see for so long. The tragic reality came home to him: now he was certain he couldn't give her, or the strike, his support. He felt as though he was embarking on a long journey alone and it was only just beginning. Loneliness crept up on him like a stray dog. He was on his own. All Helen wanted him to be – and he could see it so clearly in her face – all she desired of him, he knew was impossible to give her. When she came back to see him later, with her face full of love, he didn't know if he would be able to bear it.

When Bradley was discharged from hospital, his face still showed bruising and a dressing covered his head wound. Yet he refused to be petted. Memories of his injury only fuelled his enthusiasm to think back to his original plan: to take on a smallholding, to get away. He was convinced of the utter futility of the strike. Far from being proud of his achievement, as Helen was, he withdrew into himself. The anger hadn't left him; the smell of blood was in his nostrils and he felt empowered by it. He sat in his armchair, gazing through the window to where he could see the slag heaps towering in their glistening steely peaks. They were no more than looming shadows, ghosts that threatened to block the sun and steal his freedom. In his weakness, he began to feel that the pit was creeping like a cancer through his entire body, turning his bones to dust.

There must be a way to escape this vicious circle, he thought, as he watched Sam playing on the sitting-room carpet at his feet. A shaft of sunlight piercing through the window caught the baby's hair and turned it into strands of gold. At eight months old, he was able to sit up unaided and, now teething, his rosy cheeks only emphasized his winning smile. Just as his father before him had vowed, Bradley knew he must stop the inevitable tide of destiny, break the link that enslaves young men to the pit and save his son from the fate of years underground.

While Helen cleaned and tidied, he rested, dozing for what may have been minutes, may have been hours. He drank some water, sipped the sweet tea she brought him, and finally he slept. But he was tormented by dreams: men screamed in the dark, torch-lights blinded him, and the grating metallic sounds of steel pit gates being dragged across concrete deafened him. Oil cans rolled with flames spinning from them like Catherine wheels. Miners were screaming, trapped in a steel cage that was falling vertically down the shaft, hundreds of feet, past smooth water-soaked rocks black as jet, down into hell itself.

'No!' He jerked awake, shocked by the sound of his own voice; it was cold and dark in the room. He shivered and realized he must have been asleep for hours. Wondering if Helen might be putting the baby to bed, he rose stiffly from the armchair and called out but there was no reply. Going upstairs, he found Sam's cot was empty. But making himself a coffee a few minutes later, he realized that in spite of everything his head was clearing and he felt stronger. Also, he realized, he was ravenously hungry.

*

When Helen arrived home carrying Sam, she exclaimed, 'I thought you'd still be asleep! Are you feeling better?' She seemed excited and flushed. Again he had the feeling that he couldn't match her mood.

'Bit better, yeah. Where've you been, to your mother's?' he asked, taking Sam from her. 'Hello, little fella, what have you been doin' then – all this time with your mummy?' Sam wriggled and began to whimper.

'Put him down,' she said. 'You're scaring him, looking like that with your black eye!'

'You're not frightened of Daddy, are you, little man?' he asked, giving the baby a kiss and putting him down. 'So, where've you been then?' he repeated.

Helen busied herself putting things away while she answered, 'I've been to that meeting, up at the Welfare; Jean had Sam for me.'

'What meeting's this? What do you want to be goin' to meetings now for?'

'Well, seeing as you weren't well enough, I thought I'd better go and see what was going on.' She looked uncomfortable. 'The girls are all talking about going up to London soon, so I want to know what we're up against.'

'London? Who's goin' up to London? What for?' His head began to ache again. Sam began to cry.

'Look, just let me get the baby fed and I'll tell you all about it.'

He felt desolate. Had she forgotten he hadn't eaten either? Turning away from her, he started to rake the ashes in the grate, fighting the weakness. He pulled out the ash pan and took it outside. Doing that small task seemed such an effort it shocked him. Emptying the ashes into the tin by the shed, he looked across the gardens; lights twinkled from kitchen windows and he could see the movement of figures inside. There was a warmth about each house, the way it contained a unit of family life with its focus on the kitchen, the television, and the children. He turned and looked back to his own house. It was unlit and cold. He had to brush away the feeling that he was a stranger, like a lodger in his own home. Shovelling some coal and taking the kindling from a stack he had chopped days before, he went back indoors.

113

When Helen joined him in the sitting room, he was kneeling on the floor by the hearth laying newspaper and sticks to start the fire.

'Do you want something to eat, Brad?'

'Yes please, I'm starvin'. Hope there's some food in the house,' he said, striking a match and holding it to the paper.

'I'll do you some egg and chips, shall I?'

'Sounds good to me. You havin' some?'

'No, I've eaten already, up the Welfare,' she said and hung back from the kitchen. The flames rapidly licked at the dry wood and they began to leap and crackle into life.

'Brad?' He looked up at her change of tone. 'You wouldn't mind, would you, if I went up to Downing Street with the girls? We've got an appointment with Mrs Thatcher.'

He stopped what he was doing. 'You think you women can bring the strike to an end, do you?' he replied. 'You think she'll listen to a few women, when she won't take notice of thousands of us miners?'

'I don't know. I'm interested in going, that's all. It might be worth a try. The strike affects me too, you know.'

'It affects us – that's what you should've said. That's how you think now though – it's not us any more, is it? You're always sayin' how you can do this and how you can do that. It seems like you're really enjoyin' this strike – with all your lists and letters and organizin'. What did you find to do before you had all this? You must've been so bored.'

'That's not fair! You know I've been happy enough looking after the baby and the house and everything. It's just that now—'

He stared at her, dreading what she might say next.

'Now' – she took a deep breath – 'for the first time in my life I've been able to do things, write to important people, and they reply as if I was important too. I know that sounds pathetic but is that so wrong?'

'Isn't Sam important? Aren't I important enough for you?'

She looked alarmed. 'Of course you are, but—'

'But what?' He looked at her.

She turned away and went into the kitchen. Presently he could hear her frying the eggs but his appetite was gone. Something inside him was changing, he could feel it. This was a fight for survival. It wasn't just a fight for jobs to keep Silt Edge Colliery going. The strike had driven a lethal wedge between them. But he still had his dream. It occurred to him that his dream was opposite to hers: he craved the open countryside, the fresh sea air, for time on his hands to sow seeds, cultivate plants, and keep a few animals, for peace and quiet. He longed to be a million miles away from speeches and letters and talks and deadlines. He wouldn't care if he never saw the pit head ever again in his life.

It was more than about earning a wage; he had been down the pit, down in the darkness of the mine for too long. It was time to come up for air, time to recapture his boyhood dreams. He could see the glimmer of daylight at the top of the shaft and he didn't want the dirty muck of coal on his face any more; he didn't want Sam to grow up and be a prisoner to the same fate. He owed it to his father to get out. Helen might not understand him, but he had to escape or he was a lost man.

When she came through with his hot meal, it was dark in the room and all the light they had was the glow from the fire.

'I'm sorry, Helen,' he said. 'I'm not interested in politics, you know that. I never have been. If I could get back to work and earn some wages again, at least then we could see a future ahead of us, put some money by for a better way of life than this. At least it would get us something to live on – now the winter's coming.' He sighed, afraid now.

She didn't reply. Instinct took over perhaps, but he began eating his dinner ravenously. Finishing his meal, he lay back in the armchair with his eyes closed. The warmth of the fire permeated the room, his stomach was full and at last he felt rested and satisfied.

Helen got up, saying she was going to bed. She paused and kissed the top of his head; reaching up he held her hand tightly, wanting so much to get through to her, to pull her down into his arms, kiss her and hold her. 'Stay here wi' me a bit, love,' he said. But she pulled away from him.

'I'm going to check on Sam. I'm tired and it's getting late.'

He remained where he was for a long time, seeing pictures in the fire: he could see fields, a barn that needed a bit of work, and chickens. He began to plan the smallholding that one day he hoped he would have. When Helen came downstairs again half an hour later, he was sound asleep in the chair.

Chapter 11

Tom carried the suitcase up to the front door of Chalkfield Hall trailed by Kim holding a carrier bag bursting with things Helen had given her. As the bell sounded through the house, Tom pulled out a handkerchief and was mopping his brow when the door opened.

'Come on inside, my dears,' called Winnie. 'I'll go and tell Lady Ashby you're here.'

A door into a nearby room stood ajar, revealing lavish but ageing furniture, a faded gold velvet sofa, and worn carpets scattered with Chinese rugs. There was a chaise-longue under the window upholstered in tapestry and finished with carved wooden scrolls. Looking up the stairwell to the high ceiling, Kim, who until now had not spoken a word, stared at the elaborate ornamental cornices, crowned in the centre with a crystal chandelier.

'It's like a palace in 'ere!' she whispered.

Whistling through his teeth and as nervous as a schoolboy, Tom replied, ''Tis grand enough, Kim, to be sure!'

There was the sound of uneven footsteps and Edith came, descending the staircase with difficulty and leaning heavily on a walking-stick.

'Good afternoon, Father, Kim,' she called. 'Welcome to Chalkfield Hall!'

Holding out a jewelled hand expecting it to be kissed, Tom obliged clumsily. Kim perched on the sofa in the lounge while Tom sat stiffly on a regency chair. Dominating the room was a huge fireplace with sawn logs stacked beside it. On the marble mantelpiece stood some photographs – of horses, mostly, and a soldier in uniform. In the corner was a television half-covered by a velvet cloth.

'Kim, my dear,' began Edith, 'I expect this will all be strange to you at first but I hope you'll be comfortable here. Winnie has prepared your room.' She peered over her glasses at the girl. 'I want you to make yourself at home as best you can. You may want to bring some of your own pictures or trinkets, to make your room feel more like home.' She smiled and if she appeared condescending it was lost on Kim, who replied that she hardly had anything she could call her own.

'I've got one photo – of me mum,' she said, gazing around as if to get her bearings. 'Me dad's dead. I ain't got a photo of 'im.'

'I'm sorry to hear that, Kim.' Edith sounded truly sympathetic. 'How long since he passed away?'

Kim shrugged her shoulders. 'Dunno, ages, I remember me mum though; she was pretty, not like me. Don't see her now though, haven't done, not since I was small. We don't know where she is neither.' She glanced at Tom as though for confirmation.

'No, no indeed!' replied Tom, shaking his head.

'Never mind, dear, it's your future we're to think of now!' said Edith, patting her arm. The cold touch surprised Kim and she noticed the raised blue veins and the weighty diamond rings that adorned every finger. At her suggestion, Kim got up and went into the kitchen to find Winnie. Tom brought her suitcase to the foot of the stairs, and stood eyeing up the long climb dubiously.

Once home again, Tom made himself a cup of tea and sat down to open his mail. Curiously he noticed there was a letter from the diocese.

'Oh, what's the bishop got to say this time?' he asked himself. As he read it, a look of disbelief crossed his face. '*Openly sympathizing with the striking miners . . . seen on the picket line using violent and abusive behaviour.*'

'Dear God in heaven!' he exclaimed. 'Has the bishop gone mad? Of course I've sympathized with the lads, but "*violent and abusive behaviour!*" ' He almost laughed but then fear gripped him and a prickly sensation started on the palms of his hands. He scrubbed them on his thighs and, sinking into a chair, felt close to despair.

'He refuses to offer me any help and now this!' he muttered. 'What does the man expect me to do?'

Throwing the letter down, he got up and looked out at the streets that had tested his vocation and sapped his strength – he didn't know which way to turn. Steel shutters blocked out the windows of the local shop, graffiti adorned every blank wall, car tyres littered the streets. Police cars and riot-control fences were a constant reminder that everyday life in Silt Edge had completely changed.

'I need a drink!' he mumbled and with a reply to the bishop already forming itself in his head, he set off on foot up to the working men's club.

Bradley was also on his way there. When he arrived, he saw a group of his mates in the bar and, taking his pint, joined them in the window seat. Still sporting a black eye, his injury at the picket line had renewed their bond of friendship. The door opened and Tom appeared, going straight to the bar and leaning heavily against it.

'Hey, Father, join us over 'ere if you like,' one of the lads called out, but Tom didn't respond. The men looked at each other and raised their eyebrows.

'Just a minute,' Bradley said and went over. 'Are you all right, Tom? Hey, let me get you a drink, you go and sit down.'

'No, no, I'll pay,' replied Tom, recovering himself. 'Thanks, I'll be all right in a minute.' He handed Jean a ten-pound note. 'Scotch please, double,' he said. 'Oh, and one for yourself and a round for the lads, that should see to it.'

'Somethin's happened – they haven't trashed your house have they?'

'No, nothing like that, Brad. I'm OK, just had a bit of a shock. I'll be fine in a minute. Cheers!' He took a gulp of scotch, sighed and smacked his lips. 'Ah, that's better. No, I just received a rap over the knuckles from the boss, that's all.'

'The boss? Not him up—' Bradley raised his eyes skywards.

Tom gave a wry smile. 'No, no, not Him! My earthly boss, the almighty bishop! I shouldn't be telling you really, it's between him and me, so it is.'

119

'So what 'ave you been up to Tom, you old rogue?'

'Oh, whatever I do is wrong apparently, according to the powers-that-be.'

Bradley looked mystified.

'Changing the subject,' Tom began, 'Kim's ex-boyfriend – I don't suppose you know where he's hanging out, do you? He wouldn't still be roughing it inside that wreck of a house, would he?'

Surprised, Bradley glanced furtively over to his friends and shook his head.

'Doubt it. We could go an' have a look if you like. I don't fancy it though,' he muttered under his breath.

Joining the group by the window, talk turned to the latest news of the strike. Not wanting to delay any longer, they made their excuses and were soon walking together up the road.

'When I took Kim down to Chalkfield Hall she gave me her front-door key,' explained Tom, 'and asked me to fetch something out of there for her.'

'Danny won't be in there, I'm almost sure of it.'

'To tell you the truth I hope to God he's not. All she wants is a photo – a picture of your mother apparently.'

'Of Mum?' Bradley was shocked. 'Is that all she wants bringin'? No clothes or nothin'?'

'No, that's all.'

'D'you think she knows where Danny is, an' she's not sayin'?'

'No, Brad, she's got her head full of new things at the moment and she seems happier, I'm glad to say.'

'She'll be gettin' too posh to talk to us lot soon, livin' there like a flippin' lady,' said Bradley but instantly regretted it when he caught Tom's eye.

'Don't be too hard on the girl. She's had her fair share of trouble and her heart's in the right place, that's for sure. I've got a hunch she might still care for Danny a bit. You know, when he was beaten up she was beside herself with worry, poor girl. They might be good for each other in the long run, Brad. It's a lonely old world, this life, being on your own. You're a lucky man having Helen and the baby.'

Bradley didn't feel lucky; the rift between himself and Helen left him with a hollow feeling that nothing seemed to fill.

Approaching the boarded-up house, they knocked on the front-door, just for appearances' sake more than anything, but there was no reply. They went round the back, stepping over some rubbish; graffiti was scrawled across the walls of the house. A neighbour peered over the fence at them.

'What are you after?' she asked. 'There's no one home, y'know.'

'Haven't seen the lad who lives here lately, have you?' called Tom.

She shook her head. 'I keep myself to myself, Father, don't do to get too involved,' she said. 'He's a bad sort. Other folks have been banging on the door too – he owes them money no doubt.' She went back to hanging out her washing.

Tom took the key from his pocket. 'You go in and look round, Brad – I'll wait here. Make sure he's not lying dead somewhere in there, eh?'

'Thanks,' said Bradley glumly. He set off round the front to let himself in and the first thing to hit him when he opened the door was the musty smell.

'Danny! Danny, are you there?' he shouted, sincerely hoping he wouldn't appear. Junk mail littered the hall floor. Downstairs generally was in a sorry state, the sitting room was wrecked. Sifting through the broken glass, Bradley found the photo of his mother, thankfully still intact, and tucked it into his pocket. He recalled the evening he had spent with Kim, when she had peered out of the window like a prisoner, and bracing himself, he climbed the stairs. In the semi-darkness of the bedroom, he saw the shadowy shapes of crumpled clothes which were strewn across the floor; the place reeked of stale beer. But all was quiet; with relief he realized no one was there and anxious now to get away, he retraced his steps and went down to find Tom.

'It made me a bit jumpy, being in there!' Tom puffed.

Bradley patted his jacket. 'I've got the photo for 'er anyway.'

'Any idea who Danny might be working with?' asked Tom. 'You know some of the lads who have gone back in, do you?'

'I know 'em all right, but they're no friends of mine, Tom. I'm not gonna ask 'em, if that's what you're saying.'

'No, I'll speak to them, Brad, just give me a name, a phone number, anything. Say where I can find them – I'll do the rest.' And handing him a notebook and pen from his pocket, Bradley scrawled on it and handed it back.

'Won't make any promises they'll talk to yer. I'll be off now.' He took the photo from his pocket. 'Give this to Kim next time you see her, eh?'

Tom found himself alone, holding the small silver-framed photograph of a pretty young woman with a shy smile who looked surprisingly like Kim herself.

It wasn't often that Bradley drank a lot; he couldn't afford it for one thing. On this particular night, however, he went a bit overboard and he had chalked up several pints 'on the slate' before saying goodbye to Tom, who was setting off for Ireland to catch the morning ferry from Holyhead. The prospect of a break had cheered the priest up and brought the colour back to his cheeks.

Having seen him off on the train, it was very late when Bradley returned home. Helen was still awake, fired up by her trip out to London that day with the other miners' wives for their meeting with Margaret Thatcher. Silt Edge had welcomed them back with something resembling a carnival atmosphere in the streets, but this excitement was lost on Bradley. One thing he knew: he and Helen had to talk. Their paths were taking different directions and communication between them was breaking down to a hopeless, exhausted silence.

Helen didn't look him in the eye when he arrived home. She was sitting surrounded by paperwork with the television news blaring. 'You've been drinking,' she stated, switching it off.

'So I have,' he replied, slumping heavily into his armchair. 'There's only one way out o' this mess, an' that's to have another drink an' forget all about it.'

'And where would we be if we all did that, Brad?' She held a letter suspended in her hand while she looked at him over her reading glasses.

He wished he felt more drunk. The tension in the room brought the adrenalin coursing through his veins; he felt horribly sober. It was time, he knew. It was time to say something, but he couldn't face having another row. How could he talk to her without it all exploding in his face?

'I'm not drunk, love, don't worry, I'm just tired,' he said gently.

'Well, you smell drunk,' she retorted, dismissing him and turning back to her paperwork.

'Helen, can we talk for a bit? I've been meanin' to talk to you for a while now.'

'We can talk, Brad,' she replied smartly. 'We can talk all right – I often try to talk to you reasonably, but you just won't listen.'

'Look, you've worked so hard for the strike. I know you've done well and you deserve all the credit you get, I don't deny it. The men think the world of you – they never stop talkin' about you up the club an' I feel proud of you, of course I do but—'

'But you don't think I should be doing it, is that it?' She was watching him, on the defensive.

'I want to talk about me for a bit, not the strike, or the union or anythin' else. What you're doin', it's fine, it's just that what I want is somethin' else altogether. I'm sorry, Helen, we've been going down different paths for a long while now. I just can't keep this show on the road any longer – I'm not on the same wavelength as you and we both know it.'

He had her full attention at last. 'You're not tellin' me you've got another woman?'

He was almost knocked off balance by her remark. 'You what! Of course not!' He was so amazed that she had interpreted his attempt to reason with her in this way that he almost laughed.

'Words!' he sighed loudly. 'How can words be so meaningless? I give up! Look, love,' he said, fumbling in his pocket. Taking out his wallet, he produced the crumpled advert from the newspaper that he had shown Gavin weeks before. He handed it to her tentatively, feeling naked and defenceless under her scrutiny. This was his only lifeline with sanity. Such a tiny creased-up photo, such a poor little place – but its stone walls and sloping barn, its overgrown paddock and broken gate had become a part of him. He loved every inch of it.

Showing her the picture of the smallholding seemed the only way to explain what he meant. She glanced down at it carelessly and looked baffled.

'What's this then?' she asked.

'It's my dream, Helen, that's all.' A shudder of emotion caught his throat and he was afraid.

'Your dream? Have you gone out of your tiny mind? We're in a crisis here, Brad, if you haven't noticed. We're in for the fight of our lives to save the pit and now, at last, now we're *that close* to a breakthrough' – she held her index finger and thumb up to show a pinch of air – 'all you can say is you're having daydreams about some stupid farm! Are you completely out of your head?'

'It's only a smallholdin'. It's right by the sea, in Wales, an' it's the lease that's for sale. If we could get enough money together, save it up, or if I take voluntary redundancy, we could get us a place like that one. Just imagine! Being able to walk down on the beach with Sam an' fillin' your lungs with the fresh sea air! There's lots o' places like that – a cottage with a big garden would do – just enough to grow food for us to live on an' keep some chickens. . . .'

Helen stared at him as if he was speaking another language. 'We'd need some money, of course,' he persevered, 'but in Wales or Cornwall there's plenty of outdoor jobs I could do part-time. We could sell some fruit an' veg by the side o' the road too, an' some eggs. It would be great for our little Sam to grow up in the country . . .' He faltered. 'In the fresh air.'

'What planet are you living on, Bradley Shepstone? Here am I fighting for our livelihood, working my guts out cooking and feeding half the flipping village and here's you daydreaming away about some stupid half-baked idea stuck out in the middle of nowhere!' She screwed the advert up and flung it into the fire. 'You really think you're capable of running a farm? You can't even keep the front lawn mowed! Just because you've got a few cabbages growing on your daft allotment you seem to think. . . .'

He stopped listening. He watched the precious piece of paper burn, bursting the dying fire into life. That tiny advert had been in his possession for weeks. In one brief flame of glory it was gone. He watched the fire until every trace of the burning paper had disappeared. Desperately he tried to resurrect the image in his mind's eye. Quickly it came back into focus. Now he could see the little cottage again with its creeper-covered walls made as though built out of pebbles from the beach. He could see the line of the roof, sinking in the middle like a pit pony's broken back and the crumbling outbuildings, falling like a sandcastle into the waves of gorse and thistledown. He loved that place. He almost felt the cold metal of its front-door key in his hand. He would turn the key in its rusty lock, open the door and chase chickens out of the kitchen, fling open the windows, breaking years of cobwebs that hung on them like net curtains. Outside in the barn, he would find some old tools abandoned under rusted cartwheels and mildewy straw. Pigeons would be roosting in the rafters, and strands of horse hair stuck to the stable door. It was a timeless, magical place that would wait for him, thirsty for his hard-working hands to bring it back to life. He belonged there. He didn't belong here – not any more.

Suddenly he felt a new kind of strength growing within him, a fresh spring of confidence. There would be other adverts. There were often acres of land up for auction, derelict barns, dilapidated cottages or even caravans – it didn't matter, there would be somewhere.

'It's not a daydream,' he said, getting up quickly and seeing her eyes flash with red darts of anger as she too rose from her seat. Facing him, she bore down on him with all her crushing words, trying to drive every hope out of his head. But he wasn't going to be beaten that easily. His imagination set him free – there a shaft of sunlight came stealing through yellow beech trees and the jewels of raindrops bulged on waxy cabbage leaves. It was all there in his mind's eye – she couldn't destroy that.

Armed with this new spirit, he said, 'Do you really believe all that political stuff you tell 'em at your rallies? That us miners want jobs for life, job security, no matter what they throw at us? You don't really believe all that, do you?'

'After all I've said and done, you dare to ask me that!' She spat the words like a cat.

He refused to raise his voice, believing in his dream more than he had ever believed in anything. Calm inside, knowing that what he said was right and true, he replied, 'You want me to keep workin' down that pit for the next thirty-five years, do you? Workin' till I'm good for nothing, coughin' my heart up like old Jack Partridge, like my poor dad? Is that what you're sayin'?' She didn't answer back, but there was no stopping him now. 'Is that the job you want for our little Sam when he's grown into a young man, is it? Get him some filthy lungs or even pneumoconiosis before he's thirty, eh? Or d'you want him buried alive under ten tons o' rock like I was when the roof caved in? Is that what you want? You make me wonder, Helen, you really do. Don't you see?' He reached out and took her shoulders gently. 'I want to try and get us away from all this – get us away to another place where there's fresh country air for Sam to breathe and where it's safe.'

'It's not so dangerous now,' she said, dismissing him. 'They've modernized it a lot.' Picking up one of her letters, she replaced her reading glasses.

But he couldn't let it go now. 'You think you know about it, do you? You've been down there for an eight-hour shift, in that stifling heat – you've done that, 'ave you?' He saw her put the letter down again. He had her now.

'It's not like it was in your dad's time though, is it?' she said. 'I know you had the accident and your friend was killed but—' She paused, sounding slightly unsure of herself. He saw colour flush her cheeks before her textbook response came: 'Safety is one of the union's priorities,' she announced. 'Better working conditions, shorter hours. We're negotiating about all these things right now.'

'So it doesn't matter that it's still one of the most dangerous jobs in Britain? So that's OK then? You really think it's going to change that much overnight?'

She was mute. Bradley's head was crystal clear. At last he felt he was on a firm footing, he knew the arguments like the back of his hand. Life underground wasn't fit for a mangy dog, let alone a man.

'Anyway—' He seized the chance to appeal to her family loyalty. 'I heard your parents thought you were above these things, that bein' a coal-miner's wife wasn't good enough for you cos you're *different*, you're *educated* and you could've *been somethin'* if it weren't for me. You could 'ave gone on to *higher things*. They said I was holdin' you back. Well, OK, I admit it, I probably was. But things are all changin' now.' His voice became warmer and hopeful. 'Life's changin' all around us, Helen, can't you feel it? The pits are finished! We want to get out there in the daylight, and breathe the fresh air! That's what young Sam will want to look forward to when he's a growin' lad. He might have the chances you had, he might even go to university! Think o' that! We've got to give 'im that choice, haven't we? Please, Helen, I don't need any bit of advert from the newspaper any more – it's all up here!' He tapped his forehead. 'I've got plans – plans for all three of us – that will get us away from Silt Edge for good. You an' me an' Sam, we'll go an' find us a little place somewhere with a bit o' land. We can both work hard – you've proved you've got a lot of go in yer—'

'And where do you intend getting all this money for a *little place* as you call it?' she broke in. 'Seeing as how we can't even afford to pay the electric bill? Tell me that.'

'I'll put in for voluntary redundancy, Helen. I'll have to go back in to work first, of course, just to qualify for it, but as soon as I start back I'll go an' see the foreman and he'll put my name down.'

'Start back at work?' Helen cried in disbelief. 'Start back? You mean break the strike, Bradley, become a scab? You can't mean it?' Exasperated, her face was turning livid red as she stared at him in horror.

'It'll be worth it, for the sake of gettin' out of this mess. It'll be worth it in the end,' he pleaded. 'Think about it! Of course it won't be easy for us, I know that, but—'

She took a deep breath. 'If you return to work, Brad,' she said, restrained now, like a snake about to strike, 'do you realize what it'll be like for me? Have you thought of that? My own husband – a scab! I'll be a laughing stock!'

'Not as much as I will, love. I'll be in for it, I realize that. The lads will slaughter me, but it won't be for long. Once I've got my name down, and I'm earnin' money again as well, the redundancy might come through quickly and then we can be out of here. It'll be worth it, won't it, to start a new life!'

She wasn't crying. She was strangely calm as she stood up and walked away. Then she turned back and stared at him. In an alien voice she said, 'Whatever happens, I've got a duty now to carry on the fight, to stick together with the girls and see it through till the strike's over. They need me. If you go back in and break the strike, you needn't bother coming home. You'll not be welcome here any more. I won't have a scab living under my roof. I'm not having you force me into that position. You'll put our house, even our lives, in danger, d'you realize that? You'll be on your own. Do you understand me, Brad? Do you understand what I'm saying?'

He was silent for several moments. He knew what she said was true but he couldn't make sense of it and exhaustion overwhelmed him.

'You're tired now,' he said gently. 'We're both dead tired. Think about it, think about what I've said an' sleep on it, eh?' He reached out and touched her arm gently with his fingertips. He held wide his arms and made to hold her, but she turned away from him and walked quickly out of the room. As she went she turned out the light, leaving him standing there in the dark, with only the dying fire for company. He heard her switch the hall light off and slowly, deliberately climb the stairs.

Sitting there in the dark for a long time, he watched the faint glow of the embers until they gradually disappeared altogether. He felt as if his world was falling apart. It took him back to when he had lain in bed in that back bedroom all those years ago, listening for the footstep of his mother on the stairs, waiting for her perfume to envelop him in its sweetness, straining his ears to hear the soft reassuring humming sound she made to herself.

At first he thought Helen might come back down straightaway. She might say she was sorry and that he was right – for the sake of their son's future if not for their own. He imagined her undressing, putting on her faded nightdress, brushing her hair. There would be no hot water without her having to come down to boil the kettle; she would be washing her face, perhaps washing away her tears, in cold water. She might turn towards the bedroom door and listen, perhaps wondering if he was coming up. Turning sadly towards the bed, as she turned back the sheets she might smell the musky fragrance that would remind her of their lovemaking – how passions rise and fall in timeless consuming desire. She might remember how their bodies once dissolved into each other, and in their coming together, remember how they had vowed that they would never be parted. Before the pit, and after it had gone, they had believed they would always be as one.

He waited. He longed for her to come back down to him. The house was quiet. Not a sound. He heard the resisting creak of the old bed. Alone, she would feel cold without his body to warm her. It might kindle in her some sympathy and love for him. She might rise and descend the stairs. '*Come to bed, my love,*' she might say, '*I love you, I'm sorry, come to bed.*' He waited, and the room grew colder and colder. She didn't come.

All night he sat alone in the chair in that dark room. He didn't stir. He didn't sleep. Then, when the first glimmer of dawn found itself running in a silver ribbon along the bottom edge of the curtains, he stood up stiffly. Taking his jacket from its hook in the kitchen, he opened the door silently and slipped out.

Chapter 12

It was a cold October morning in Ebbingsfield. Winnie was up early as guests were due to arrive that day and she had their rooms to make ready.

'Come along, Ben,' she called, coaxing the old dog out of his basket. She put on her shabby overcoat, which she reserved for the purpose, and picked up the dog's lead. Winnie's walk with Ben took her through the side gate and past the church. Building work was well underway and it was very noisy. Her early-morning peace had been shattered once again by the clanging of scaffolding being erected.

Ben stopped to sniff at the roof tiles stored under tarpaulin sheets and lifted his leg in acknowledgement. They walked on, up the church path, which was shrouded in mist and softly carpeted with fallen leaves. Cobwebs, perfectly spun, hung white with dew on the hedges. Slowly they ventured further into the cold fog, pausing only once while Winnie checked the church door. Her legs felt particularly heavy in the chill morning air and once or twice she winced with pain. After walking for twenty minutes or so, she turned round and together they made their way back to the house.

Glad to shut the door on the noise, they entered the kitchen by the back door. Ben was padding breathlessly around her feet, his broad tail thumping the furniture as Winnie dried him with a rough towel. Suddenly she stopped and told the dog to be quiet, listening intently.

'Well, I never!' she said. It was unusual to hear the television.

'What's happened, dear?' she called, entering the room where Edith sat hunched in her silk dressing gown. Edith waved her question away and put her finger to her lips.

'*The bomb went off at 2.54 a.m.*,' announced the newsreader, '*ripping through the Grand Hotel in Brighton, and bringing down the three top storeys of the building. Many people attending the Conservative Party Conference were known to be staying at the hotel including the prime minister, Mrs Margaret Thatcher. There are believed to be casualties, and some are said to be still trapped in the rubble.*'

'It's a confounded bomb at the Grand Hotel in Brighton!' Edith cried, turning to appeal to her in disbelief.

'My goodness! Anyone hurt, dear?' Winnie replied, craning her neck forward to look at the screen.

'Yes, I must get in touch with Reggie,' said Edith, and reached for her address book. Thumbing through it, a tremor thwarted her attempts to find the right page. 'What's the number of his private secretary? Darling, please would you be so kind as to fetch my glasses?'

Returning with them, Winnie retreated to make some coffee. 'What a day, what a day,' she muttered to herself, 'and guests arriving too!'

The newsreader's voice followed her: '*Prime minister Mrs Margaret Thatcher, who was with her husband at the time, has suffered a narrow escape in the bomb blast. She has insisted that the conference should go ahead as normal. Apparently Mrs Thatcher was still up, making the finishing touches to her speech, when the bomb ripped through the building.*'

'Thank goodness! Maggie's unhurt!' called Edith. 'It's business as usual! Good old Maggie!'

Winnie paused. 'Who would have wanted to blow them up, dear? Surely the coal miners wouldn't go that far?'

'Oh, no, I'm afraid we can't blame the miners for everything, much as I'd like to – it will be terrorists no doubt. It's a miracle our prime minister escaped injury, a miracle!'

Unaware of the commotion downstairs, Kim was watching the builders from her bedroom window. Her room was at the back of the house, upstairs under the eaves. Grasping the edge of the curtain, her breath misted the glass. She wiped it away, attempting to see the faces of the men, but peering down, all she could see were pots of unruly plants tinged with the first frost, trailing across the verandah. A stone bird bath stood smothered in ivy and fading ornamental grasses; seed heads and cobwebs reminded Kim of the fairy-story book she had had as a child. She glanced at the photo of her mother in its silver frame on her dressing table. Kim had never had a dressing table before. It stood with its tall mirror set against the window so that to peer out, she had to squeeze in between the heavy curtain and the wall. It was a cosy room; she liked to look at the flowered wallpaper when she lay in bed and feel the coolness of the starched white sheets which were so unfamiliar and yet so comforting. All her life she had longed for a pretty room like this to call her own.

As she twisted her body to try and see more of the builders, her hand instinctively went to rest on the soft ledge of her unborn child; it gave a tiny kick, causing her to turn away from the window and think about the future. Whatever the future held, she no longer felt so apprehensive. In the few weeks that she had lived at Chalkfield Hall, a sense of security had manifested itself in her mind. Under the care of Winnie, a new response had been born in her which, coupled with the growing baby in her womb, was sending sensations through her body which were different and vibrant. It was almost as though she had left her old self behind, up at Silt Edge.

A quarter of an hour later Kim descended the stairs. It was the first time she had heard the television blaring out in the morning. But drawn into the warmth of the kitchen, she was pleased to find Winnie cooking the breakfast.

'Oh, there you are, my dear!' Winnie smiled, her cheeks pink with excitement. 'It's all go this morning! Lady Ashby's watching the news – there's been a bomb in Brighton at the party conference, would you believe!'

'Oh,' replied Kim. She was unsure what to say. 'Why?'

'Goodness knows why, dear, there are a lot of madmen about. Could you see if there are any biscuits in the tin? The builders have already been to the back door twice looking for their cuppa!'

Kim smiled at her. 'Do you want me to get the mugs out from the top of the cupboard as well?'

'Thank you, dear, but do be careful. We don't want you climbing on steps in your condition.'

'I'm OK. Them builders aren't half makin' a noise aren't they!' She put three mugs down on the table and went to get some more. 'How many do we want?'

'There's seven men this morning, six for coffee and one for tea. Builders always take sugar and we'll need more biscuits from the pantry.' Taking the opportunity, Kim peeked through the kitchen window to see if she could see any more but the mist obscured most of the view. A loud drilling noise was now permeating the house, its vibrations causing the teaspoons to rattle on the tray.

Kim carried the tray laden with steaming mugs and biscuits out of the back door. She placed it on a low wall for the men. The air was cold and, receiving a thumbs up from the foreman, she hurried back indoors. Winnie, by this time, was busy at the kitchen sink. 'I've taken Lady Ashby her coffee and I'm just rinsing through my smalls,' she said. 'She's so upset about this bomb going off.'

'Why do people drop bombs like that?'

'They plant them, dear, they don't drop them from aeroplanes. But don't ask me why – nutcases all of them. They were trying to sabotage the Tory party conference.'

'You know that old lady,' Kim began thoughtfully, 'the guest who talks to herself – do you think she's a bit, you know, nutty?' She made a swirling gesture towards her forehead.

'If you mean Mrs Pentley, you should say so, dear, and not *old lady*,' Winnie corrected her mildly. 'You could do a bit of sewing for me, Kim, when you've had your breakfast, if you've nothing else to do.'

'I can't sew,' Kim replied, not appearing surprised at all by Winnie's change of subject.

'There's no such word as *can't*, that's what my mother used to say. If you fetch me my work-box, you know the one, dear, the wicker box down by the mantelpiece in the drawing room, I'll show you if you like.'

'Why does she though? Mrs Pentley, I mean,' asked Kim when she was seated again, licking the cotton and attempting to thread a needle. 'Why does she say things, you know, when no one's there?'

'If no one's there, dear, how do you know she says things?' Winnie asked, her eyes dancing with amusement.

'Because I've heard her an' anyway, when I walk in she doesn't even try an' hide it – like there really *is* someone there.' Kim was looking puzzled. 'She's a bit weird though, ain't she?'

'You shouldn't say that, dear, it's not polite, and we really shouldn't be speaking behind people's backs.'

'But—' Kim began and then seemed to change her mind.

'Now,' Winnie said, 'the pocket in my apron is working loose; it could do with a stitch in it. If you pass me the needle and thread, I'll start you off.' Kim gave it to her and waited patiently. 'Sometimes,' Winnie said, starting to sew, 'when people are old, very old, a bit like me, they have so many memories, words and conversations all stored up in their heads, that some of them tend to spill out sometimes when they're not supposed to.'

'But *you* don't talk to yourself Winnie.'

'I'm pleased you said that, dear.' She smiled. 'Watch carefully – the stitch I'm doing is called chain-stitch.' Winnie's big hands were red and rough with hard work yet she made the dainty stitches effortlessly. 'Now, begin by holding the needle and thread like this. . . .'

It was warm in the kitchen beside the Aga. The dog dozed in his basket, snoring occasionally. They spent the next half hour in studious effort, with the work changing hands several times, while in the background the noise that the builders were making rumbled through the house. Eventually, Winnie was quite pleased with Kim's progress; she took it from her and held it up for inspection.

'Not bad, dear, for a first attempt – not bad at all.' She snapped off the thread and to confirm completion, put the apron on and announced that she was going to collect Edith's breakfast tray.

When Winnie entered the lounge, she found Edith in a worse state of agitation. 'All the phone lines are either engaged or drowned out by the noise of those wretched builders!' she complained.

134

'Leave the phone calls until the noise is over, dear!' Winnie suggested.

But Edith would not relent. 'I really must make sure our Reggie isn't hurt – it's always the old faithful who suffer – one can't trust anybody these days.' And re-dialling, she flicked the telephone receiver impatiently. Out of her depth, Winnie retreated to the kitchen.

'I'm afraid Lady Ashby seems to be suffering from a headache; we'll probably all have one before the day is out. By the time those flats are finished, Kim, I wouldn't be surprised if we're all at each other's throats. I hope you won't regret moving in here, with all this commotion!'

'No, I like all the goin's on,' Kim replied. 'It's excitin', ain't it, things happening.'

Winnie eased herself back into her chair painfully. 'Oh, things are happening all right, although whether my old bones will stand it I don't know!'

Kim shot her a glance, wondering if she was seriously complaining. 'Shall I take Ben out for you later?' she offered.

'Oh, would you, dear? Thank you. We must make the guestrooms ready, and I really don't think I'm up to much today.'

Kim set off on the same route Winnie had followed earlier, wearing Winnie's old gardening coat, which was several sizes too big for her. 'Come on, old boy!' she coaxed, giving a futile tug on Ben's lead as he sat down stubbornly on the church path, his chest heaving and his breath hanging in clouds of vapour around him. The deafening sound of a drill splintered the frosty air, drowning out any attempt she made to coax him further. The noise enveloped them both and almost in unison, girl and dog turned back towards the house.

'It's no use, Winnie, he won't budge!' sighed Kim as soon as she was indoors again.

'It's not you, dear, it's all that racket!' chuckled Winnie. 'You don't understand what's going on, do you, old thing!' she said. The dog thumped his tail apologetically. 'Take him out the front door and down the road to the village; it won't be so noisy that way. Change into your good coat first though – we can't have you going out dressed like a tramp, can we!'

Delighted to be out, with the dog walking laboriously beside her, Kim felt a rush of excitement. She couldn't believe her good fortune: to be trusted with Lady Ashby's dog! To be wearing a new coat! Edith herself had given it to her and it was such a good coat! Kim turned up the collar and felt the luxury of the warm wool against her skin. It fitted her perfectly, except that due to her growing baby, the lower buttons had to be left undone.

Gradually, as they made their way down the hill through a tree-lined avenue carpeted with leaves and pine needles, the builders' noise receded. Birds sang ecstatically from branches high up above her head and sunshine filtered through, causing drifts of steam to waft up from the road.

An elderly gentleman raised his hat to her and called out a greeting: 'Good morning, my dear!'

'G'morning!' she replied and smiled. Walking a dog in a posh coat, in a posh village like a real lady, she thought. Simultaneously, a stirring in her womb made her pause in her step to catch her breath. The dog looked up at her quizzically and sat down on the pavement, panting; she wondered, when her child was born, whether she would dare to walk out pushing her baby in a pram. Would they think she was a proper mother, who had a husband and a nice house? They wouldn't know, would they, she mused, that she was just some penniless girl from the mining village. They might think she was a real lady!

Coming to the crossroads in the village of Ebbingsfield, there stood a postbox, a telephone kiosk and a signpost: Silt Edge, three miles in one direction – Dover eight miles in the other.

Ahead of her was a level crossing and passing trains to London came through quite frequently. Beyond, there were two shops, a post office and a grocery store. Her experience with the shop in Silt Edge immediately caused her to stop in her tracks – she didn't want to risk spoiling the morning by encountering some difficulty with the locals. For the time being it was enough to be able to pretend that she was a proper lady, walking a dog that belonged to the owner of Chalkfield Hall.

136

'I think we've come far enough for today, Ben. Let's go back to the house.' The dog looked up at her and, with a good-natured grunt, turned round obligingly and followed her back the way they had come.

Chapter 13

As Bradley stepped out into the dawn, from somewhere across the rooftops, a cock crowed. The half-light magnified his feeling of alienation. Once out in the chill morning air, he buttoned up his jacket, turned up his collar, thrust his hands deep into his pockets and walked quickly away from the house. It was time to move on. He was heading towards an isolated row of farm cottages which lay on the road between Silt Edge and Canterbury. It was a good half-hour's walk but he hoped he would be in time. Within the hour, he guessed his foreman would be leaving for the pit. Mick had never supported the strike and to the disgust of all the men, had continued working throughout. Bradley had one purpose in mind: he intended to break the strike and return to work.

As he walked on, the faces of his friends began to haunt him: he saw them in the clouds, the cracks in the pavement, the shadows under the trees. Miners who had worked alongside him for years were watching his return to work; good men who he knew would have risked their lives to save him. These were the very men he was betraying – those miners on the picket line, his mates – his blood brothers. The thought that he was letting them all down stung his eyes and he felt the pain of it almost physically punch him in the stomach. It stopped his breath. There was no way he could rid himself of the thought that he knew they wouldn't believe it – that he could stab them in the back and become a scab. Yet still he walked on, feeling as though he was breaking every strand of friendship he ever had, but he was beyond any possible inclination to change his mind. It was too late; already he knew there was no other way.

His thoughts turned to the picket line where honest, hard-working men, blinded by desperation, had thrown themselves in the paths of vehicles. He considered how gentle folk had changed into monsters who spat and punched and bit. It was like hell itself. How could he ever expect his friends to forgive him for breaking the strike? He had been through so much with them, starved with them, got into debt with them, picketed alongside them. How could he bear to tell his mates that he had been up to the gaffer's house and had offered himself available for work? The tragedy of his situation formed a choking knot in his throat and tears sprung from his eyes like warm blood and ran down his cheeks. He was walking through a sheet of tears, sobbing to the empty country road, the birds and the hedgerows, as though appealing to any living thing to help him.

Bradley wasn't a religious man. In spite of his Catholic upbringing, his faith had long since deserted him, but he prayed now. He prayed to the vast open sky, he begged the swaying trees to hear him, he searched for God in the hedges and ditches, and looked to the horizon. 'God, help me!' he moaned under his breath, while his stomach churned with anxiety, and his fists bore into his ribs. As he ploughed on, he found himself gazing longingly at the grassy banks, wishing he could just throw himself down there to sleep, never to wake up. Sobs racked through his body in torturous spasms. A man can cry aloud, freely, when he's alone, when there's no one there to laugh at him. He cried until his tears were exhausted, but still he walked on, one step in front of the other, with deliberation and purpose. Now he was truly alone. Now he had nothing but his own conscience for company.

Later that day, having declared himself ready to return to work, Bradley returned home almost as if he was sleepwalking. With relief, he discovered Helen was out. Hastily, he took some clothes from the bedroom, some papers from the sideboard drawer and a few items from the bathroom and pushed these into his rucksack. Having made his decision, he had managed to switch off his thoughts as if there weren't any more thoughts there – only pain. As he passed through the kitchen on his way out, there on the floor lay a blue baby's sock, one of Sam's. He picked it up, looked at it sadly and slipped it into his pocket, putting it into that vacant spot where the advert for the smallholding had been. Going out of the back door, he left a letter for Helen on the table, and closed the door behind him without a second glance.

'Just think what I would say to the girls if they found out I had a scab for a husband living in my house! It's ridiculous, Mum!'

'You say he's really gone for good though, dear?' Beatrice was unusually quiet. Brewing some tea, she began cutting some sandwiches, while Helen related the row between her and Bradley. Beatrice made sympathetic noises, clicking her tongue disapprovingly at times, but she knew her daughter well; she knew inevitably that sooner or later the anger would subside and give way to tears.

'Look at it this way, love,' she said. 'Maybe he's just thinking of you? He's done you a favour in a way. As you said, life would have been hell for you. You certainly couldn't have kept working on the campaign once he'd returned to work! He must have realized that, so he cares about you; he wouldn't want you to be victimized. The house could be vandalized – he knows what they're like. Look what happened to Kim's place!'

'I made sure everyone knew I wasn't behind Brad going back in, Mum, I made that quite clear. I told them he hadn't better show his face back in my house or I'll fetch the police to him.'

'There's no need to exaggerate, dear,' Beatrice said. 'I'm sure he realized he would be putting you in a difficult position and that's why he left. Now, let's have our lunch. Do you think Sam would like some scrambled egg?'

'He'll chew on a bit of toast, Mum.' She picked the baby up from the floor and put him into the highchair.

'How's his sister getting on? Can't be long before she's due.'

'After Christmas sometime – she must be seven months gone by now I should think. We haven't seen her, not since she went to work at Chalkfield Hall. That'll be a surprise for Bradley, won't it, when he finds out his sister's pregnant!'

'You mean he doesn't know?' exclaimed Beatrice. 'Why, I thought he must know. You didn't think to tell him, dear?'

'No, Kim said not to tell him, just in case Danny got to hear. Anyway, I don't think anyone's set eyes on Danny since he went back in.'

'You could go and visit her at Chalkfield Hall. I'll come with you if you'd like me to? You ought to tell her how Bradley's walked out on you and everything.'

Helen's brow darkened. 'What, tell her that her flipping brother's turned scab? I don't think so, Mum!'

'You needn't put it like that, dear. Don't you think it's only fair to warn her, seeing as he's her brother?'

Helen fell silent. She had a conflict of interests. They ate for a minute or two, interrupted only by Sam wriggling and grizzling and asking to be taken down from his chair. When she finally met her daughter's eye, Beatrice knew her suggestion had hit home.

'So? Shall I come with you?'

'No thanks, but if you'll have Sam for me – he can be having his nap this afternoon and I'll walk up there I suppose.' Drawing back her chair, she added, 'It was my fault Brad walked out really. I said if he went back to work he needn't bother coming home again.'

'But you didn't mean it, dear, of course you didn't! You were upset, that's all.'

'I did mean it, Mum! Oh, I don't know what I meant really,' sighed Helen suddenly, burying her face in her hands. 'Oh, what a mess. I don't know what to do now!'

Putting her arms around her, Beatrice whispered into her hair, 'You go to Chalkfield Hall and talk to Kim. Let time take care of the rest.'

When Bradley started work again that morning, he didn't recognize many of the men who worked with him; they had been ferried in from other pits just to keep things ticking over. They walked in silence mostly, no cheerful voices raised him a greeting. The pit yard itself was looking derelict. Ragwort had grown through the tarmac in the summer but was dying back now, dusty and tarnished by frost. It was a momentous day: he had started back but also he had submitted his application for voluntary redundancy. The wheels were now in motion.

He was heading for the steel cage, its shutters open in readiness to take them down underground. He took a deep breath and filled his lungs with the morning air like a diver preparing to plunge into icy waters. His eyes lingered lovingly on the softly swaying silver birch trees, the trace of smoke from a nearby chimney, and the strands of ivy climbing up the wheel of a cart. These would be here waiting for him when he came up again in eight hours' time. He would cherish these images, trusting them to carry his dream into the daytime as dawn turned into day, as traffic started building up and children went to school. Normal life would continue above ground, while men laboured invisibly underground − fathers, sons, husbands and brothers, who risked their lives cutting into coal seams to gather chunks of black gold. They were, he felt, hidden from view and conveniently forgotten underneath the humdrum of everyday life.

Bradley was tired; he had been back at work several weeks. At the coal face, above the relentless grind of machinery, the whistle signalled a tea break. Unrecognizable now with a layer of coal dust coating their faces like a second skin, men threw down their tools with aching shoulders, wiped their mouths on their sleeves and went to fetch their snap-tins and flasks.

Bradley looked up and was surprised to recognize a face − it was Danny Stuart. They exchanged nods, neither interested in talking as they hunkered down in the tunnel with a group of others. The lights on their hard hats flickered like moths around a candle as the men communicated with the whites of their eyes.

'This coffee tastes like shit,' Danny growled, glaring at his flask.

Bradley sipped his tea in silence. Finally he commented to no one in particular: 'Mick's workin' right through tonight, double shift, so I hear.'

'It's up to 'im, ain't it,' Danny sniffed, wiping his nose with the cuff of his jacket and turning his eyes directly onto Bradley for the first time. 'Seen your missus lately then, 'ave yer?'

'No, as it happens − why?' Bradley stared at the black fingerprints he had just made on his cheese sandwich before biting into it savagely. 'Too busy, ain't she,' he added. His lips seemed to have lost their proper function; they felt like cloth mittens on his face and his food tasted of wool. He washed it down carelessly with another slurp of tea.

'You're not kiddin' me she's busy,' said Danny.

Bradley shot him a look.

A black face with a white stripe on the forehead, like a clown's face, appeared. 'You heard the good news, chaps? Our Christmas bonus has come through!' He stuck up two pink thumbs and gave a wide toothy grin, rolling his eyeballs. 'We're quids in! The boss said so just now – it'll be in our pay packet next week!'

Several of the men cheered, punching the air.

'Fantastic!' they choroused.

'Hallelujah,' grunted Danny morbidly. 'Hally-bloody-lujah.' His eyes shifted towards Bradley again, as though reminding him his comment was still standing.

Bradley too looked apathetic about the news, staring at his sandwich as though he was about to choke. If things were different he'd have been over the moon – some extra money for Christmas – Helen would've been delighted. He collected his thoughts and addressed his attention to what Danny had said.

'What if I have seen my missus? I've not, as it 'appens, nor my sister neither come to that, not since I started back.' He watched Danny for any reaction, and went on: 'I've not seen Kim since she got a job at the big house, have you?'

'I don't go out the pit, mate. I'm stoppin' up in Gerry's caravan up in the yard. Get me a shower, somethin' to eat an' that's it – bit of kip and I'm back to work. There's no point in me doin' anythin' else, too much hassle. I soon gave up on getting the bus into work – if it's not the bloody pickets beatin' yer up it's the cops themselves.' He slurped his coffee, staring over the edge of his mug moodily. 'You'll see, you'll soon get tired of that shit.'

'I don't think about it,' lied Bradley. He felt he was more than tired of it already. Usually he was lucky enough not to have to catch the bus. He got a lift in to work with Mick, but they still had to run the gauntlet of the picket line. Often as not Mick told him to keep his head down out of sight while they drove through. Going into work made Bradley feel like a leper. But then, everything about his life had begun to feel odd, as though he was cut off from reality.

One morning when he set off for his allotment at dawn, frost had set in and the ground was as hard as iron. Black ice cast a steel sheet in the shadows of the country lane. It was a fair walk from Mick's house to the allotments in Silt Edge. Conscious that his presence there might be unwelcome, Bradley usually went when others were unlikely to be around – sometimes he did a bit of digging or tidying up in the pitch dark, or he just sat there in the doorway of his shed, on an old chair, oblivious to the cold, watching the lights in the houses. Occasionally, the headlights from a car turning the corner sent an arc of light flashing across the fields. He knew the men hated him; he almost hated himself. They believed he had betrayed everyone. It was only his long-term plan to escape which kept him sane, and helped him carry on.

When he came within sight of his allotment that morning, there wasn't a soul about. But to his horror it looked as though a hurricane had ripped through it: his vegetables were torn out of the soil by their roots, his cabbages were crushed, and the shed was upended and smashed, its contents strewn everywhere. The other plots were untouched – his was completely destroyed.

Nearby, a song-thrush gave out a crystal-clear volley of notes, declaring to the world that Nature takes back into itself all that it has so generously given. *Ashes to ashes, dust to dust.* A memory flashed into Bradley's mind: Ash Wednesday. Kim, aged about five, was fidgeting beside him when the priest said, '*Remember, that thou art dust and unto dust thou shalt return,*' and he felt the priest's thumb crunch a wad of charcoal ash onto his forehead. He had scrubbed it off with his sleeve before the other kids saw it. Involuntarily, he raised his arm now and scraped it across his brow in shame, before sinking down on his knees.

Was he dreaming? He reached out to touch the splintered shed but his fingers found blood-red paint. It was dripping wet from the freshly daubed word – scab, painted on the shed door. The wounds on his allotment trailed off to a tin spouting arterial gloss paint that was running in rivulets down the splintered sides of his shed. It was splattering the ground, its lacerations glistening on the white hearts of cauliflowers, ruined now after weeks of tending. He traced its murderous trail back towards the footpath that had once been his route home into Silt Edge.

All his plans for the future had been nurtured on this plot, from the tiny germ of an idea to have his own smallholding, to the bitter decision to leave all that he loved and return to work in pursuit of his goal. He imagined it was his own blood that was spilt across the land; he felt it draining out of him as surely as though he had opened his own veins. The faces of his dear friends came into his mind – it was his dream that had alienated him from everyone.

A twig snapped like a rifle shot. Out of the mist, a figure emerged, coming along the footpath. It was a retired miner, he knew him well.

'Hey!' shouted Bradley. 'Charlie! What's been goin' on 'ere?'

The old man stopped and stared at Bradley for several minutes before making his way straight towards him.

'There's only me 'ere to tell yer, or I wouldn't be sayin' nowt, but you had it comin' to yer, y'know. Not my doing, mind, but take a look yonder,' he said. Shielding his eyes with a gnarled hand, the man's eyes became slits against the breaking light. 'Them ain't touched, see, it's only yours. Them that knows what you are – how you betrayed 'em – them that did it could've done a lot worse, I'm tellin' you straight.' His eyes returned to Bradley and fixed him with a tragic stare. 'You ain't better show your face near 'ere again – it ain't worth causin' folks more grief.' He moved off, deadpan, severing the cord with a few parting words: 'Sorry, mate, but that's how it is.'

Chapter 14

The train drew into the station at Ebbingsfield and Tom stepped down onto the platform. He hailed a taxi.

'Been away for long, Tom? Don't seem to 'ave seen you about,' the taxi driver said, taking his suitcase.

'Longer than I intended,' said Tom, climbing in. 'I've been on my sick bed for weeks in fact.'

'Sorry to hear that, Father,' the driver replied, with a sideways glance as if looking for signs of disease. They pulled away from the station. 'In hospital, were you?'

'No, I've been at home – Tipperary – with my parents.' He was breathless and a sweat stood on his brow. 'I didn't mean to stop away so long, but it really knocked me back – pneumonia, you know.' He thumped his chest as though to confirm the diagnosis. 'How have things been here? 'Tis a bit of a mess, I believe.'

'You're tellin' me! I tell you what, Father, you're better off out of it. I'd get away too if I had half a chance.' He clenched his teeth defiantly as he stared at the road ahead. 'My missus is sick an' tired of all the talk, an' all the bullyin' and back-bitin'. Them and all their slogans and principles! The rest of us have to go on bloody workin' for our livin' while they just go off an' talk about it! Sorry, Tom, excuse my French but they get up my bloody nose some of them miners, they really do!'

Tom was smiling to himself and surveying the countryside with a warm tenderness. He was back all right! They drew up at the presbytery. Once Tom had paid and retrieved his suitcase, he gave a thumbs up to the driver. Alone, the extraordinary silence hit him. He looked about as he searched his pockets for keys. Then he saw it: the cross. Leaning against his front door was the lifesize wooden crucifix which was usually attached to the main wall of the church.

'How in God's name did that get there?' he said aloud. It had been thrust there with such force it had damaged the door. Leaving his case, he went to check the church, but everything else seemed normal. He wondered where the curate was who was supposed to have been minding the place. With trepidation he went round and let himself in through the back door. Once inside, he found a note from the curate who had left the previous day – 'thank you and regards', nothing more. The house was clean and tidy. Whatever joker had shifted the cross, it must have been done overnight – the insult must have been intended for him personally.

The huge cross cast a dark shadow in the hall. Tom guessed, judging by the size and weight of the cross, the prank would have had to involve several men. He filled the kettle, sat down in the armchair and closed his eyes. The kettle in the kitchen boiled and switched itself off, but Tom continued to sit there, trying to recapture the atmosphere of the warm kitchen at home in Tipperary. He was missing it already.

Half an hour later, Tom's appearance at the working men's club caused a curious hush.

'All right lads?' he called out, ordering a whisky, but his greeting failed to raise a single response.

'Scotch, please, Jean?' The barmaid gave him a studied look as she poured his drink.

'What's up?' he asked. 'Someone died?'

'Could say that,' she replied. 'If you're looking for your friend, that is.'

The colour drained from his face. 'Bradley?'

'He's as good as dead, Tom, you mark my words,' she said, tossing her head. 'You know he's gone back to work, don't you?'

'No, I didn't know,' he muttered. 'I've been away. Are you sure he's gone back in, Jean?'

'Would that lot be actin' like that if he hadn't?' she asked, nodding at the gang in the window and wiping the counter with several angry strokes of a cloth.

'But that's not half of it,' she added in lowered tones. 'He's walked out on Helen, upped an' left her and the kid high an' dry.'

This news was more than Tom could believe, knowing Bradley to be a trustworthy man. How long have I been away, he asked himself, and the world's turned upside-down? Taking his scotch, he approached the men sitting in the window.

'Hello, lads!' he said. 'How is everyone? Have you missed your old priest then? I've been at home on my sick bed for weeks. . . .' He drew up a chair but didn't sit down. Those staring into their beer sighed, those apparently absorbed in the view through the window clenched their jaws. Tom watched their eyeballs as a cat watches holes. 'Mind filling me in?' he asked finally.

Silence. He was looking from one face to the next. 'I hear our Bradley's gone back in – is that true?'

One of the men began shuffling cards. Over and over again he shuffled them, while the others watched his moving hands in silence.

Suddenly one of them stood up.

'Father, look! Stay out of things you don't know nothin' about, will yer? Do us all a favour, eh?'

'I'm not here to judge anyone,' mumbled Tom, jumping at this whisker of a response. The miners relaxed a little, occupying themselves with taking long draughts of beer, adjusting their chairs, doing anything to avoid meeting his gaze.

'Look, lads, whatever Bradley Shepstone's done, he must have had a pretty good reason, right?'

Nothing.

'Look—' he tried again. 'I've just arrived back this afternoon. I've still to find out what's going on but, to tell you the truth, lads, I'm in a spot of bother up at the presbytery. Some joker's gone and ripped the big crucifix down off the side of the church and shoved it up against my front door. I can't open it, and I can't shift it on my own. What d'you say, lads? Could you see your way to doing your priest a favour and help me move it, eh?'

He waited. They eyed each other under their heavy brows. As no reply came, he lowered himself onto the chair and sat down. Tiredness crept up on him so easily these days.

'I'm not asking how it got there, or who did it,' he added. 'All I want is to see it back where it belongs, lads – just to be able to open my front door.'

He was about to give up when one of them scraped his chair back and stood up. 'Lead the way, then, Father,' the miner said. 'Come on, lads, let's be havin' yer!' To Tom's amazement they all followed suit, shifted their chairs back, finished their beers and stood up. Tom bounced into action, thanking them profusely and making for the door. They all trooped after him – stocky, defiant and swaggering in their shirt-sleeves.

Jean stood watching them all leave with her hands on her hips. Just as they all disappeared outside, the last miner turned back and gave her a wink.

'Men!' she sighed, raising her eyebrows.

As Tom approached Chalkfield Hall he was surprised to see how much progress had been made on the new apartment building.

'It's you, Father!' said Winnie as she opened the front door. 'Such a long time since we've seen you! Come in, come in!' She called him inside as though he were a wayward child. 'I thought you were the taxi driver. I'm off to take Ben to the vets. His back legs are playing him up – he can hardly walk, the poor old thing!'

Tom grunted sympathetically, patting the dog that limped across the tiles to greet him. He found Edith sitting by the window reading several letters which were spread out across the chaise longue.

'Tom! How good to see you!' she said. 'Come in and sit down.' At that moment the doorbell went again, causing the dog to give another half-hearted bark.

'That will be the taxi now! Kim will see to everything, so don't worry.' In a flourish of coats and voices and slamming of doors, they were left alone. It struck Tom that it was unusually disorganized for the household he knew to be quiet and dignified.

Settling himself down in an easy chair he sighed, ''Tis good to be back, ma'am. How have you been keeping? Have you recovered from the fall?'

'Oh, almost forgotten! What with the building work and everything, I haven't had time to notice a few aches and pains. What about you? You know the parish had almost given up on you? You do look a trifle pale, Tom, if you don't mind me saying so,' she added.

'I'm well now, thank you. I had a nasty spell when I was at home. Took to my bed for weeks – pneumonia, the doctor said. I'm over it now, thank goodness.'

Edith regarded him over the top of her glasses. 'You look peaky, Tom, and you've lost weight. You ought to take vitamins, you know. Winnie and I swear by them.'

'Edith,' he asked, 'how are you finding young Kim? Tell me, is she settling in well? Has she been a help?'

'You know, Tom, that girl's been a godsend to me, and to Winnie too, I hasten to add. With these builders traipsing in and out every five minutes asking for water or tea or goodness knows what . . . I don't know how we're going to manage without her!'

'Without her? You mean she's leaving?'

'No, I mean – when you see the size of the girl – her confinement can't be far off, can it? She will have her hands full and where will we be with Christmas upon us and the guests to see to? Oh well, I suppose we'll battle through somehow – we usually do!'

'Yes, of course, the child!' He had almost forgotten. 'Edith, with respect, would you mind if I had a few words with Kim – in private, I mean?'

In a flourish of exaggerated courtesy, Edith confirmed that his request was only to be expected and reaching forward she rang a small brass bell on the table before her. Within moments Kim appeared wearing a rather large apron over her ample form. Agreeing to her suggestion to talk in the kitchen, Tom followed her through. In the absence of Winnie, he could tell immediately that Kim was holding her own. She was in the middle of making mince pies and the warm spicy aroma enveloped them.

'So how have you been, Kim? You're looking very well, if I might say so! Blooming, in fact! I can see you're being well looked after.'

'I love it 'ere, I do,' said Kim, patting the pastry mixture. 'Don't know that they'll let me stay 'ere though,' she said, matter of factly, 'when the baby comes. I could easily put it under the kitchen table in a box or summat and carry on doin' what I do now, but I don't think Lady Ashby will let me. It won't be no trouble; they sleep most o' the time, don't they, babies?'

'Have you spoken to Lady Ashby about the baby, Kim?' Tom asked rather sternly, trying to avoid the picture conjured up in his mind of a baby asleep under the table like a puppy. 'She speaks very highly of your work, Kim, very highly.'

'Winnie's kind to me an' shows me how to do things. She's always givin' me things as well, biscuits an' chocolate an' that.' She was rolling the pastry out as she spoke, dusting it with flour.

'Kim, I'm certain that they're both very pleased with you,' Tom said, 'and they do want you to stay, when you've had the baby, I mean. You must try and talk to Lady Ashby, tell her you intend to stay on.'

'Well, I ain't got nowhere else to go,' she replied, selecting a pastry cutter from a drawer, pushing it neatly into the pastry and producing a row of tidy shapes. 'No way I'm goin' back into Danny's place! It's a right dump now! I ain't seen 'im anyway.'

'Did you happen to tell him you're expecting his child?'

Kim looked up in astonishment. 'No way! Never got a chance to anyhow; he went off to the pit an' I never saw him after that. He weren't bothered about me anyway, so I'm well out of it.'

'Kim?' Tom began again with a change of tone. 'Have you heard from your brother lately? Or seen him?'

She continued making the mince-pies, picking up each small circle and carefully placing each one into the pie tin. She made several before she spoke again.

'Don't see Bradley, haven't, not for ages. Helen came to see me,' she said, wiping her floury hands on her apron and taking a jar of mincemeat from the dresser. 'She said he's gone an' walked out on her.' Now she gained confidence and began spooning the mincemeat into the pie cases. 'She said he's turned "scab" just like Danny an' she ain't havin' nothin' more to do wi' 'im cos he's broke the strike! She were right angry with him, she were!' Smiling, she glanced up at Tom, but her smile quickly faded. 'I dunno.' She shrugged. 'It might not be true, but that's what Helen said.'

'You haven't tried to contact him then, to see if he's all right or anything?'

'See if he's all right?' She gave an odd laugh. 'He's gonna look after himself ain't he, specially if he's back at work. Ain't many of 'em would dare do that!'

'Do you think he's done the right thing, Kim?'

'I dunno, do I!' She laughed again, a nervous humourless laugh which left Tom feeling cold. He felt as if he was getting nowhere, but more than anything, he knew he had to speak to Bradley directly – and soon.

'Kim, I must be going now but listen, remember what I said and speak to Lady Ashby about the baby. Tell her you want to keep working here; tell her you're happy to stay on. You'll do that for me, won't you? I'm sure she'll be only too pleased to help – you and your baby.' With these words he left her.

Thanking Edith briefly, he let himself out.

'It's a hard world that child's being born into,' he mumbled to himself as he started the car. 'Poor little beggar!'

Taking the road out of Ebbingsfield, he came across a rather humble row of farm cottages. The end one, which bore the number he was looking for, was defended by barking dogs. The small terriers were loose in the front. While Tom stood at the gate wondering whether to take his life in his hands and enter, a man appeared and shouted at the dogs, who obeyed instantly.

'Come along in, they won't eat you,' he said and, opening the gate for Tom, he extended a hand. 'Mick's the name. What can I do for you, Father? It's not often I see a priest out in this neck o' the woods.'

'My name's Father McNeice, but call me Tom. It's a friend of mine I'm looking for: Bradley Shepstone. I've been told he's staying here and I've dropped by to see if I might have a word with him, if he's at home.'

'Who told you that?' asked Mick guardedly, dropping his hand.

'It was his sister Kim, she lives in Ebbingsfield. She hasn't seen him, mind.'

'Ah, right. I can't be too careful at the moment, that's all. There are folks about who don't appreciate a bit o' kindness.' He stared into the distance, his eyes squinting at some unseen danger.

'I'm not here to cause trouble, Mick, to you or Bradley, believe me, I just thought I might—'

'You're all right, Tom,' Mick relaxed, thumping one of the dogs affectionately who was sitting on the path at his feet. 'Just keep it to yourself that he's here, would you? Just until things get smoothed over a bit, eh?'

'To be sure I will, Mick. Ah, tis a bit cold up here in the wind today.'

'It's always fresh up here, but I like it, suits me, an' the dogs. They don't breed 'em any better than this: Border Terriers,' he said, squatting down and tugging at one of the dog's ears affectionately. 'See this coarse top coat?' He held the bristles of brown fur up from the dog's back for Tom to appreciate. 'They're bred for the hills, rough weather and moorland, and see these feet?' He took one of the dog's paws and showed Tom the thick pads. 'Tight feet they are, cover any kind of ground. And dig? They'll dig you out any fox or badger, no problem!'

Tom was nodding and smiling, stroking the smooth nut-brown head of the terrier tentatively as if it might change its mind at any moment and take his hand off.

Mick took a slim hand-rolled cigarette from behind his ear and, popping it between thin lips, lit it with a lighter from his trouser pocket. 'Sorry I can't offer you one, Father. I'll fetch some baccy from indoors if you want to join me?'

'No thanks, Mick, I don't smoke.'

The man nodded. 'I'm Bradley's foreman,' he said, exhaling smoke. 'Follow me then, Tom, I reckon our man will be indoors; we got back from work half an hour ago.' Tom followed him up the path to the back door which he noticed was scuffed all down one side by the dogs' claws. 'I'm on my own so the kitchen's nothin' to look at,' said Mick as they passed a counter stacked with washing up, bowls of dog biscuits, spanners and jam jars full of nuts and bolts.

Reaching the foot of the stairs Mick shouted, 'Bradley? You've got a visitor!' There was a response and the sound of creaking floorboards.

'Look, Tom, I've got things to do outside,' said Mick. 'I'll leave you two to talk if that's all right. Make yourself at home.'

Tom sat down on a threadbare sofa. Next to him on a sideboard stood some framed photographs of dogs. There was a pile of pigeon-fancier magazines on the floor, and a newspaper crossword, half finished.

'Ah! The man himself!' exclaimed Tom, standing up as Bradley came into the room. 'So this is where you've been hiding yourself.'

'I heard you were ill, Tom. It's good to see you back at last – are you better?' He gave his hand a firm shake.

'Much better, thanks, but I'm feeling my age a bit, I think,' he said. 'And you? I had trouble tracking you down.'

'Sorry, Tom, I thought I might be here for just a night or two but. . . .'

'Ah, t'was unforgivable of me not to have kept in touch.' Tom shook his head gravely. 'I do apologize, Brad; the pneumonia struck me down so fast. Heh, so many changes back here, I can hardly believe it. So—' He paused. 'How are things really?'

Bradley shrugged. 'Here, sit yourself down. I'm OK. You have to keep goin', don't you – whatever 'appens.'

'And Helen?' Tom asked. He parted with the question reluctantly but it had to be asked.

Bradley gave a gasp as though someone had just driven a nail through his hand. 'Oh Tom, it's hopeless!'

'I'm sorry, truly. Did she throw you out or what? It's not like her – I can hardly believe it.'

'No, it was me who left – I had to leave for her sake. You heard how it happened?'

'No; t'was unforgivable of me not to have phoned,' muttered Tom, shaking his head sadly.

'You're all right. Anyway, not much you could've done, eh! You know I've gone back to work? Well, that ruffled her, I knew it would. She won't have me back now, she's got too much to lose, with her campaign and everythin'. She don't want a scab in her 'ouse while

154

she's doin' all she can to keep the strike goin' – it wouldn't make sense, even I can see that!' He chuckled, but a lump rose in his throat.

'But you're her husband, Brad!' Tom retaliated. 'She won't give you up just for the sake of the strike surely?'

'I left her the same mornin' I went back in,' he explained. 'It was my choice. She could've got reprisals, the house trashed or somethin'. Anyway I couldn't run that risk – not with little Sam there – I'd be puttin' them both in danger. It wouldn't be right.'

'But they're your family. The strike won't last forever.'

'I don't know, Tom. Seems it's all she cares about now, the strike I mean. She thinks of nothin' else. If only Helen knew what it was *really* like down there then she might change her tune. Does she really want our littl'un to start workin' down the pit when he's sixteen? He could be doin' somethin' with his life instead of throwin' it away like I have mine.'

Tom could see the hours of lost sleep in Bradley's face, how working underground again had already coloured his skin grey with fatigue, and he could see, under each fingernail, the telltale signs of coal dust. 'Have you talked to Helen? Have you tried to make her see reason?'

'It's safer I don't try an' see her now. There's no point anyway. She's told everyone I've dumped her, told everyone I'm a scab an' she won't have me back. They'll buy it as well – at least she won't be a target, so it's best that way.'

Tom lay a firm hand on his shoulder. 'My dear friend,' he said, 'something will turn up; I pray to God things will take a turn for the better.'

'Tom!' appealed Bradley, facing him with a sudden passion. 'You know how I hate that pit! I wish they *would* close the damn pit down and fill it in, the hell hole that it is. Look how men have died just trying to do their job o' work an' the roof comin' down on 'em. It's no way to go, not when you're young an' got a life ahead of you. One o' my mates, he had a wife an' baby not a month old. He was out in the mornin' with his snap an' flask o' tea an' by midday he was dead.' Bradley's throat closed up on him and he struggled to continue. 'When my dad was alive, Tom, he says to me: "*Soon as you can, son, you get out o' this pit and get yourself a farm or a fishin' boat. It's no life for a man to give himself up to, no life at all." '*

Tom shook his head. 'Hey, tis a sorry old business,' he said. 'Does Helen know how strongly you feel? Surely she'll understand, knowing how your father died; she's a good woman at heart.'

'She's lost her head to the politics, Tom, it's like she's gone mad with it. She can't think of anythin' else except fundraisin' an' picketin'. She'll keep the strike goin' on, no matter what.'

Tom sighed. He couldn't comprehend how the situation had become so final, so unredeemable. 'What do you plan to do now then?' he asked. 'You're going to stay on here with Mick?'

'I can manage here an' I don't need much – I've been workin' his garden for him a bit. You should see what they did to my allotment!'

'I saw it, Brad, tis a right mess – shameful!'

'I need to work the land, Tom!' He brightened, seeing pictures in his mind that Tom could only guess at. 'I'm gonna get me a smallholdin' in Wales or the West Country, miles away from this place! I wanna be able to get up of a mornin' an' walk up the hill to collect some warm new-laid eggs from out the chicken coop an' have a bit o' fried bacon an' egg before I. . . . Oh, I'm dreamin' again.'

'No, sounds just grand, Brad. My poor old dad, he loves the outdoors; he won't admit it, mind. He'll work and work till the sun goes down, bring a basket full of veg home but not say much about it. My dear mother' – Tom smiled – 'she'll not thank him, just scold him for bringing mud into the house – there's no pleasing some women!' He chuckled, throwing Bradley a quick glance. 'So what did Helen say about your plans for a smallholding?'

'I told her it was my dream – told her I was plannin' to get a smallholdin' for us when I get my redundancy through but she wouldn't listen.'

'So you're going for redundancy then? Do you think you'll get it?'

'I'm hopin' so, I'm on the list. That's why I had to go back to work or they wouldn't put my name down. It's only a matter of time, and while I wait I'm workin' an' earnin' a bit so I can pay the bills and save up. Helen don't want me to pay her bills, I know that, but I'm payin' them for her anyway, and I've paid her rent. I'll make sure I do that, whatever she says.'

'You're a good man, Brad, and you mean well. I'll go to her, I'll try and talk to her, make her see sense.' He stood up to leave.

'No, Tom,' Bradley said, catching his sleeve. 'Let her be for now, let her think on it for a bit. Be safer that way.' He paused. 'Have you heard how my sister's gettin' on in the big house? I've not seen nor 'eard from her for ages now.'

Tom's face brightened. 'I saw her this morning – she's just fine! She's doing really well, I'm pleased to say.' He was moving towards the door now. 'She hasn't seen nor heard from Danny apparently – shame really, considering.'

'Considerin'?' asked Bradley. 'Considerin' what?'

'Well, you know with the baby coming and. . . .'

'Baby coming?' The shock ran like a bolt of electricity through his body. 'Baby!' he gasped. 'What? Kim's never havin' his baby?'

He turned away from Tom and walked towards the window. Outside the trees were beginning to sway as though a storm was brewing up. He could see Mick in the distance, mending the fence with the dogs at his side. Time stood still. He stood staring out of the window in utter silence, seeming to have forgotten Tom was still there.

'You didn't know, did you, Brad?' said Tom finally. 'I'm sorry, I didn't think. I just assumed they would have told you. I've been away such a while, I—'

'They? So who else knows? Suppose Danny knows and didn't even mention it, the bastard!'

'No, no, Brad,' protested Tom hastily. 'Kim said this morning she hasn't told him, she doesn't want him to know. She seems afraid of him. I gave her my word I wouldn't say anything.'

'Does Helen know about this?'

Tom nodded.

'You're kiddin' me! So Helen knew all along and never even bothered to tell me!' His eyes were shot through with glistening coals of anger. He started pacing the floor in agitation, repeatedly punching the palm of his left hand.

'It's not Helen's fault; Kim didn't want anyone to know. Actually it's me who is to blame. I should have told you myself, but I gave Kim my word I wouldn't tell anyone and as her priest I had to. . . .' Tom seemed to give up on the explanation, as if he didn't have the heart to continue. 'What a mess I've made of things,' he mumbled to himself.

Deep inside, Bradley's anger subsided; he began to feel calmer. Nothing else, he knew, could hurt him now. It was finished. The pain, the loneliness, it had all become a part of him. He turned and saw Tom's head bowed in shame.

'Don't blame yourself, Tom. If you hadn't said anything I'd still be in the dark. Women. Honestly, I'll never understand women for as long as I live. How far gone is she?'

'Well, let's see, where are we? I'd say she's got another month, six weeks or so at the most.'

'Is that all? All this time an' I never had a clue . . .' he murmured to himself, reflecting on the news with bewilderment. 'They must take me for a complete idiot. I bet they're laughin' their socks off at me. I don't even get to see Sam any more, you know.'

Tom attempted to muster up some pastoral strength. 'God's with you, Bradley, remember that; you have strength, you know, deep down. You'll get through this, I know you will. You're a good honest man; I'll pray for you.'

'Ah, I don't know, Tom, sometimes I feel like sayin' to hell with the lot of 'em.'

They heard the stamping of feet in the kitchen; it was Mick coming in from the garden. 'Didn't you get the man a cup of tea, Brad?' came his voice from the kitchen. 'This kettle's stone cold!' His rugged face appeared in the doorway.

'I'll tell you what,' said Bradley, 'we could do with a beer, never mind tea.'

'A beer?' said Mick, giving Tom a wink. 'Where d'you think you are, mate, the Queen's Head? There's a strike on, remember!'

Chapter 15

One morning, Kim came downstairs to find a note addressed to her in Lady Ashby's flamboyant handwriting. It filled her with apprehension.

'This were on the table,' she said, as soon as Winnie came into the kitchen.

'Worrying won't help – go up and see what she wants, dear,' said Winnie, ushering her off with the breakfast tray. 'Can you manage to carry that all right?' Kim nodded, biting her lip.

'Smile! She won't bite you!' she added, pinching her cheek.

Kim took the tray and began to climb the stairs. Days before, they had been out in the grounds of Chalkfield Hall collecting evergreen foliage, and the staircase was now entwined with garlands of holly and ivy cascading around the banisters. An aroma of pine needles rose from the Christmas tree in the hall.

Reaching the top, Kim knocked on the old oak door.

'Come in, my dear, don't be shy,' called Edith. 'Put the tray down and come and sit near me. I'd like to speak to you for a moment.'

She obeyed, grasping her tiny hands together in anguish. The room was draped in grey silk, the curtains were long, flowing onto the carpet and fastened loosely with swags. A shrouded winter sunlight streamed through the window. Edith sat like a queen at her dressing table.

'Kimberley, it hasn't escaped my notice that your time must surely be due soon. Tell me, my dear' – Reaching forward, she put a shockingly cold hand onto Kim's own – 'have you made any preparations for the child?'

Kim stared at her in dismay.

'Don't look so frightened!' she chuckled. 'Anyone would think I was going to eat you alive!'

Kim smiled nervously. 'I know . . . that is, I know it's gonna come soon, ma'am.'

'Exactly! Well, I don't expect you've had much time to put together a layette, have you?'

'A what, ma'am?'

'Little clothes for the newborn baby, my dear. Don't look so terrified – we were all born once, you know, even me!'

Kim relaxed, smiling faintly. 'I don't have nothin' for it, ma'am. I know babies have them lovely pretty things an' that but I ain't got nothing.'

'Well, you've been very busy helping poor Winnie out with all the Christmas preparations, haven't you, and I'm very grateful. My word, I don't know how she would have managed without your help – that's just between you and me, you understand?' Kim looked at her. Any moment, she was expecting the bad news to come. She made shallow bird-like gasps for breath, not knowing how she was going to bear being sent away.

'So, my dear,' came Edith's voice again, 'I would like to give you one or two things to put by, for when the baby comes.'

She opened a drawer in her dressing table, took out a package wrapped in tissue paper and placed it in her lap.

'Open it up, my dear,' she said, sitting back in rapt anticipation. Kim was lost. Her experience of unwrapping presents was minimal – memories of such things were submerged in years of bewilderment since losing her mother.

'Is it for me?' she asked.

Edith nodded, her excitement melting into unmistakable joy as she waited for Kim to unwrap it. The only sound in the room was the rustle of paper and when Kim glimpsed what was inside, it was like the first sight of her own baby – a tiny white knitted baby's jacket, bound with white satin ribbons. Opening it further, she found a bonnet and the tiniest pair of socks in white angora. They were exquisitely made, fluffy and light as a dove's wing. She held the soft woollen garments against her cheek and looked up at Edith in awe.

'You mean these are for my baby? But they're so small, ma'am.'

'Your baby *will* be small, Kim. Not for long, but it will be small, believe me!' Edith's happiness was complete.

'Kim,' she said, 'keep them safe. I had a woman knit them for you in the village. They're very good round here, you know, clever with their hands. Oh, and I thought this might come in useful too. I hope you will have the little mite baptised?' She produced a long white baby's gown from an oak chest at the end of her bed. It was tinged cream with age, but delicately edged with broderie anglaise. It seemed slightly brittle. Kim was afraid it might fall to pieces if she touched it.

'I'd like you to have this,' said Edith. 'I sewed it myself when I was even younger than you are, my dear.' She smiled sadly as a silent longing to voice the fragile memories of her little Georgina overwhelmed her.

Her daughter! She remembered dressing her in that delicate christening gown and watching the priest pour the holy water over her forehead. Her tiny face had looked so like a miniature of her own dear lover, George, with his eyebrows and his thoughtful frown. The painful recollection of the baby being dragged out of her arms ripped Edith's heart wide open and suddenly she clasped the garment to herself, pressing it against her chest and closing her eyes.

Edith's intensity affected Kim; when the gown was put into her lap she was speechless, touching the parchment-like material in awe.

'Kim, now,' said Edith, sitting down again and taking an envelope from her dressing-table drawer, 'as I've said, you've worked very hard in the time you have been with us. How many months is it now?'

'But ma'am,' Kim responded in fright, 'this don't mean I've gotta go now, does it?' She began to whimper. 'I don't know where I could go, I ain't got no one I could—'

'Kim, darling! I didn't mean anything of the kind! This is your Christmas bonus – a little something to spend on yourself for Christmas! A present, that's all! I have no intention of asking you to leave! I hope you will be staying with us for a long time, you and your child, of course – all of us.'

'Oh, ma'am!' cried Kim, flinging herself at Edith and accidentally letting the baby clothes slide from her lap.

'Come, come,' said Edith, 'let's not be silly now.' Unaccustomed to physical contact and instantly flustered, she withdrew slightly but, still smiling, pressed the money into Kim's hand.

A few minutes later, Kim left the room clutching the tiny packages as carefully as though she was already carrying her newborn baby in her arms. Edith watched her go and she continued to stare at the door long after Kim had left, her thoughts locked in the past.

As Bradley approached Chalkfield Hall nervously that evening, he cringed as his pit boots rattled on the gravelled drive, setting off the dog inside. Through a space in the curtains, he could see a chandelier hanging from the ceiling. Without knowing what to say, he rang the bell. He had nothing left to lose: his sister, like his wife, was almost a stranger to him now. On each side of the porch stood a large stone urn, trailing dead geraniums. The steps were cracked and covered in moss and the house, he thought, looked surprisingly neglected.

'Yes?' said Winnie, peering round the door.

'Good evenin',' he said. 'Could you tell me if my sister's at home please?'

'Well, young man, that depends on who your sister is, doesn't it?' she suggested, peering at him mischievously.

'Her name's Kimberley, sorry, ma'am,' he said, feeling foolish.

'Ah, so you're Kim's brother? She didn't say she was expecting you, or perhaps she did and I've forgotten – I do tend to forget things a little these days.'

'She didn't know. I've come straight from work.'

'That's all right, young man. Step inside; I'll go and see where she is.' As the door closed behind him, he began looking around him in much the same way his sister had done months before. His gaze instantly fell on the Christmas tree which dominated the hall, resplendent in tinsel and fairy lights. Evergreen foliage bristled from every corner; he had quite forgotten it was Christmas.

Close by, he could hear someone playing the piano. Catching sight of his reflection in the mirror, he regretted not changing his shirt and ran his fingers through his thick hair. Footsteps approached and Kim came into view.

'I'll let you two talk in the kitchen,' said Winnie. 'It's warm in there. Ben's in his basket but you don't mind dogs, do you, dear? He won't hurt you, he's too old to jump up, poor thing.'

Bradley was stunned by his sister's appearance. Obviously in the later stages of pregnancy, she looked rosy-cheeked and cleanly dressed, even bonny. Gone were the frayed sleeves, the haunted expression, the traces of grime under a pale translucent complexion.

Feeling his eyes upon her, Kim blushed. 'How did you get here then?' she asked. 'Did you walk all the way?' and without waiting for his reply: 'D'you want a cup o' tea? I can make you one if you like.' He followed her into the kitchen, nodding thanks to Winnie.

'OK, yeah, thanks,' he said. 'I walked over. I had to come the long way round. I live up at Mick's, my foreman's place. Suppose you know that though?'

'Helen told me.' She moved the kettle across the Aga to boil. 'You've gone back to work then, like Helen said you had?'

'Yeah, I went back in. I couldn't keep up the strike – not payin' the bills an' no food for the littl'un nor nothin'. I told Helen it was for the best but—' He looked away, feeling drained of any explanation he might give; somehow it all seemed irrelevant. 'You're lookin' well. You goin' to have it soon then?'

'Could be any day now, doctor says. Hope it's not Christmas Day – we've got dinner to cook an' all the people here. Some are comin' to see the new flats too.'

'You didn't tell me you was goin' to have a kid, did yer! Why didn't yer tell me, like, last time I saw yer?' He was finding it difficult to keep his voice on an even keel.

She shrugged. 'Could have been a false alarm. Anyway, I didn't want Danny findin' out – that's why I didn't tell no one. Well, I only told Tom.'

'Yeah, an' Helen too. Why did you go an' tell them and not me? I'm your brother an' all,' he said reproachfully.

'I only told Tom so he could help me. The doctor said I should ask Tom. He said priests have these places where you can go. . . .'

He stared at her. 'You could've asked me for help, y'know. I would 'ave tried to do something.'

'You 'ad the strike; you were all worked up over that. I thought you'd have gone mad if I'd told you I was havin' a baby.' She sighed and glanced sideways at him. ''Specially a scab's baby. Anyway, if Danny had found out he'd have murdered me.'

'He might not 'ave done,' suggested Bradley, watching her.

'Oh, yeah, right!' She half-smiled at him; at last he recognized the old Kim he knew.

'Can I have that cuppa then, sis?' he asked. 'Seein' as you're in charge now,' he added, teasing her. While she poured the tea, he looked around the kitchen, taking in the vast array of jars, decorative plates, shiny copper pans and the large saucepan bubbling away on top of the Aga, which was filling the kitchen with the delicious aroma of chicken broth.

Bradley took his mug of tea, squatted down on the floor and stroked theold dog's head.

'You're a poor ol' boy, aren't you, Ben!' Kim called, and the dog raised his head wearily to look at her and thumped his tail. 'He can't walk far now. Winnie said the vet's gonna put 'im down if he don't get better soon, with the tablets. . . .'

'So Danny still doesn't know about the baby then?'

Kim shook her head. 'Be all right if he weren't such a pig,' she reflected. 'Anyhow, he won't be interested; he ain't even tried to see me, not since he went back to work, and that were ages ago.'

'What if he finds out though?'

Kim shrugged and a shadow passed across her face. 'He hates kids. I'm better off here, he was 'orrible to me. I ain't goin' back with 'im – never.' She looked at Bradley sheepishly. 'So now you're workin' again too. You're askin' for trouble, aren't yer?'

'I told Helen I want to get some money behind us and get a smallholdin' or rent a farm or summat. I told her I could put in for voluntary redundancy an' get the money that way. Well, when I said that, she went flamin' mad!'

'Not surprised!' Kim giggled. 'Helen's all for the strike. Look at all that stuff she's doing.'

'You're tellin' me! She went bananas! She said if I broke the strike I needn't bother goin' home no more.' He left off patting the dog, stood up and finished his tea.

'Is that really what she said? She's got a point though – if you're a scab then, well, she'd be right in the shit.' Glancing guiltily at the door, she corrected herself. 'She'd be in right trouble, wouldn't she, Brad?'

He nodded. 'I'm best out of it, for her sake. But I don't get to see Sam any more. I can't go up the club for a drink neither, cos I'm barred – we're all barred, us lot that have gone back in, I mean,' he added.

'What, all you scabs, you mean?'

'Yeah,' Bradley admitted, his face breaking into a smile. 'All us scabs!'

He was relieved to feel she was still his little sister after all. 'I'd best be going,' he added, 'before you get a brick through the window!'

'They wouldn't, would they?' she asked, wide-eyed.

'No, only jokin'! I think you're safe as houses 'ere, and I'm glad. I wish I was you.' He looked her up and down and said, 'Well, perhaps not!'

Kim flicked the tea towel at him and, laughing, led him through to the hall.

Edith had just finished playing the piano and was carrying her sherry through to the lounge. She stood still, her glass poised, with an expression of expectancy on her face as she encountered Kim's cascade of laughter followed by Bradley's deep voice.

'Ah Kim!' said Edith. 'Aren't you going to introduce me?'

'Yes, ma'am, this is my brother. He works down the pit.'

'Bradley Shepstone, ma'am,' he said holding out his hand. Edith extended her fingertips in a regal gesture and he, unsure what to do with the jewelled hand, took it gently and found himself bowing slightly.

'A coal miner? Tell me, Bradley, on which side of the fence are you fighting from?'

The direct question took Bradley by surprise. 'I'm workin' hard, ma'am, an' I only fight from my own corner.'

Her face melted into a serene melancholy. 'Good man!' she said, and raised her glass to him. 'That's what I like to hear! Kim, go and pour your brother a stiff drink. I think he deserves one.'

It was just after eleven o'clock at night when Bradley set off carrying a heavy box. With aching arms he reached the footpath in Silt Edge that ran round the back of the allotments. Hearing a twig snap close by, he paused – hoping not to meet anyone – but it was only a fox, its eyes glowing like fireflies. Approaching Helen's from the field, he could see a light on in her kitchen but he'd quite forgotten about the fence and had to strain over the barbed wire to put the box down before leaping over.

He tapped on the back-door. Within seconds the light from the kitchen blinded him.

'Helen! I've brought you some extra bits for Christmas, an' some toys for Sam.'

'What the hell are you doing here, Bradley? Are you mad? Take it away!' She was about to slam the door on him.

'Wait! Here's some money too – it's in here.' He fumbled to pick the envelope out of the box. 'You must take it, Helen, please?'

'Get lost!' she hissed. 'Get out of here before someone sees you. You're an idiot coming here!'

'Sssh! It's OK. I was careful, no one saw me,' he whispered, as he deposited the box inside the doorway. 'Listen, I've paid your electric an' water an' that, at the post office. I'll see you're all right for the bills so you needn't worry. There's a letter I've wrote too – since I won't see you at Christmas. . . .'

She didn't reply. She stood transfixed, staring at him with dark indignant eyes. 'You'll read it, won't you?' he pleaded, feeling such a strong impulse to gather her in his arms, to drive away the raw pain of missing her that seared into his soul. But the opportunity to hold her escaped him – she retreated and started to close the door, until it jammed against the box.

'I can't take anything from you, not now. You know why,' she whispered.

'Don't worry, no one need know.'

'No! Take it away, Brad!' she said desperately, bursting into tears. The cold air amplified her voice and snatched it away greedily across the fields. But already he was going, not looking back, determined to get away without it.

'Bradley!' she wailed and started after him down the garden, wearing her dressing gown. But he was already over the fence.

'Go back indoors, Helen, you'll freeze out here!' he called.

'But why are you doing this, Brad?'

He was a distance away now but he stopped in his tracks.

'Because I love you, my darling!' he shouted desperately, oblivious now of being heard. She answered him, but the cruel landscape snatched away her reply with a sudden gust of wind, and at a loss to know what she said, he continued on his way.

It was the day before Christmas Eve. The men had just finished the last shift before the colliery shut down for the holiday. Having showered and changed, Bradley left the wash room and saw Danny Stuart leaning against a pillar, smoking. He looked rough, unshaven and his clothes were filthy. As he walked past, the whites of Danny's eyes rolled at him like a mad dog. The cigarette clung to the moisture on his bottom lip, his yellowed teeth protruded slightly but not in any way could it be interpreted as a smile.

'You all right?' he asked. The thought of him laying those dirty hands on his sister filled him with loathing.

Danny shrugged. 'Could say that.' He paused and stared back at him for a moment. 'You're not goin' home then, I take it, for a cosy little Christmas?'

Bradley ignored the sarcasm and shook his head, running a hand through his hair. 'Nope,' he replied. 'You goin' away?'

Danny flung down his cigarette and ground it into the path with his heel. 'Goin' up to Scotland maybe, mates up there of sorts, get free kip an' free drink. Don't cost me nothin'. Might get a lift up, don't know yet.'

Bradley nodded, complying, waiting like an adder in the long grass. Then he saw his chance and struck: 'Saw my sister, Kim, the other night,' he said.

'Oh yeah,' Danny drawled. He turned away and spat onto the yard. A band of miners spilled out of the washroom into the cold evening air, singing 'I'm dreaming of a white Christmas.' He eyed Bradley. Feeling in his pocket, he took out a new packet of cigarettes, removed the cellophane, threw the silver paper into the wind, put the cigarette to his lips and said: 'You saw your sister and – so what?'

'She's havin' a kid. Did you know?' snapped Bradley, watching him carefully.

Danny didn't answer at first. He lit the cigarette with a lighter, took a deep drag and blew a cloud of smoke deliberately into Bradley's face.

'Ain't she the lucky one then.' He smirked.

Waving the smoke away, Bradley said, 'Thought you might be interested, seein' as it's yours.'

Danny took the cigarette from his mouth. Keenly he brought his rugged face close up, until Bradley could see the coal dust ingrained in his complexion and the spider-red veins in his eyeballs. His breath reeked. In Danny's expression, Bradley saw the flavour of something which couldn't be interpreted as interest, or aggression – it was pure apathy. Gradually, he watched the callousness uncoil itself in Danny's cruel, calculating mind; he saw it drawing its poison up into its fangs, ready to bite.

'Mine?' He gave an ugly laugh. 'How'd you figure that one out, you bleedin' liar? Could be anybody's knowin' her, the little whore.' His sneering face transformed itself into a vicious dog that was leering at him with yellow teeth. Instantaneously Bradley leapt forward.

'You bloody bastard!' he yelled, smashing his fist into that hideous grin with all his might. He felt his knuckles bounce back like rubber hitting concrete and he hit out at him again, blindly. But Danny's steel hands closed around his neck with the strength of a python.

'You can tell your sweet sister' – Danny's words came hissing into his left ear with a painful sharpness – 'if I ever get my hands on 'er, I'll kill her, and her bastard kid, so I'm warnin' you, tell her to keep out of my way or I'll have her.'

Unable to breathe, Bradley tried desperately to think clearly. But a faraway darkness came down on him and sound receded. He felt his legs buckle underneath him and a heavy blanket of death came playing about his face, dragging its dusty wool across his mouth, filling his throat with coal dust dredged up from the pit bottom. Its suffocating weight stole his life away. . . . Slowly and silently he was sinking down into a dead sleep. 'Helen,' he murmured, as he fell.

Minutes later a crushing pain in his throat woke him. Coughing desperately, Bradley felt a horrible weight on his chest and he couldn't get the breath he craved. But men were pulling at him, men were shouting, hands were lifting his head up into the freshest most delicious air he had ever breathed: the cold salt winds that blow off the coast, that fill the sails and set a man on course for the open sea. He could breathe again! White clouds were billowing above him, like white linen sheets and pillows that were cool and soft as the sea itself – he drifted back into the water as though to float and dream for eternity.

'Break it up, lads! Break it up now!' Voices shouting, holding his arms, his shoulders, dragging him backwards, out of the ocean, away from the crashing waves to safety. He came to. Danny was being overpowered by three or four of his friends; he watched them physically pulling the man across the yard and he heard them saying, 'Leave it, Danny, let it be,' as though he was a hound being dragged off the kill.

Bradley coughed brutally as his bruised throat complained and pressed against his larynx, but he couldn't stop watching the retreat of that monstrous animal. It was glowering and showing its teeth as it loped away. Some of the men slapped Bradley on the back.

'Take it easy, old mate,' they said. 'Best not mess with him. You know he's a soddin' bastard.'

'Yeah, thanks,' he sighed, and picking up his belongings from the ground he started to make his way towards Mick's van. But he hesitated. Perhaps, he thought, I'd better just let him get clear before I go. Leaning against the wall, he took a few more deep breaths. Some miners stood around nearby, talking and chatting, and the fight was quickly forgotten. Mostly the talk was about Christmas and Bradley's mind went back to Helen; he imagined her opening her presents and as he relaxed his shoulders, he rubbed his neck where the pressure marks had caused a numb ache and started to feel better.

Just as he was about to set off for the van, a group of men came up from there. Walking across the yard, towards the old caravan over on the far side, came his opponent with two others. When he saw Bradley still standing there, he stopped abruptly. One of his mates grabbed his arm and Bradley distinctly heard him say, 'Come on, let's go an' get a beer.' But Danny threw him aside.

'So she's tellin' everyone the wee bastard's mine, is she?' came his voice, thundering across the yard.

'Take no notice, old mate,' someone said at Bradley's side. 'Come on, it's Christmas, ignore him. By the New Year he'll have forgotten all about you.'

'Yeah,' Bradley replied quietly, turning his back and walking away, 'but I won't forget about him.'

Chapter 16

Tom rose early on Christmas morning feeling in good spirits. Midnight Mass had been well attended but before celebrating Mass again at eleven, he had a few hospital visits to make. He telephoned his parents first, to wish them 'Happy Christmas'. He thought his mother sounded tired but she had been up half the night with her chest.

Driving to the cottage hospital, he was visiting parishioners mostly suffering from the lung diseases which often afflicted miners. Pneumoconiosis, silicosis and emphysema all bore the characteristic cough, sallow complexion and sometimes symptoms of kidney failure. When he entered the foyer, the uplifting sound of carols, live from St Paul's Cathedral, filtered through the corridors.

'Happy Christmas to you!' he called as he arrived in the ward. 'I come bearing gifts like the three wise men!' He chuckled loudly, laying a box of chocolates on each bed. A large Christmas tree stood in the corner and the ward looked bright and cheerful.

'I know I'm not at my best, Father,' said one man, 'and I might be seeing double half the time, but I wouldn't say there were three of you this morning!'

'You're not wrong there, Frank,' laughed Tom. 'Now, don't eat these all at once, especially if Matron's looking!'

He chatted with them for a bit and one of the nurses brought him a cup of coffee. Presently his attention was drawn to a gentleman who lay staring into space; he hadn't touched his breakfast.

'How are you doing, old friend?' Tom asked gently, approaching the man's bed slowly so as not to startle him. The miner's blue eyes came to rest on Tom's face. 'Are you having any visitors today?'

'No.'

'Oh, never mind, perhaps tomorrow, eh?'

'No, not tomorrow,' said the man in a hollow voice. 'No family,' he said, staring at him with eyes like peeled prawns. Suddenly he reached out and grasped Tom's arm.

'You know,' he said fiercely, 'they're not supposed to light up in 'ere. It's dangerous, see?'

'Of course not, you're quite right there,' said Tom, 'but they don't smoke in here, mate. Don't worry, it's not allowed.'

The old man blinked. 'It causes explosions, see,' he said. 'I kept tellin' 'em, it brings the roof down! I've seen too many o' my old chums buried.' He peered into Tom's face, gripping his arm tighter with hard fleshless fingers. 'It's the gas! You can't see it. You can't smell it till it's too late!'

'Don't worry about that now, old chap,' Tom replied. 'It's OK now, it's Christmas! You don't need to worry about things like that on Christmas Day, do you?' Before bidding him farewell, he placed a comforting hand on the old man's shoulder. 'The love of God and the peace of the Holy Spirit be with you, my dear friend,' he whispered.

Tom drove away feeling slightly perturbed. It wasn't just the old man's confusion, it was his loneliness. No visitors at Christmas, no family; it could have been his own poor father lying there. However, optimism began to flood through him again when he strode across to the church. It was still a bright morning and he had been invited out for Christmas lunch at Chalkfield Hall. He was looking forward to having a good meal, a rest and perhaps a sherry or two.

Inside the church, he greeted some parishioners and went straight to the side altar where he knelt down to pray. Before the statue of the Virgin and Child was a crib made by the children at the local school; it had been placed in the straw by grubby fingers on the last day of term. He prayed for strength to help his people, scarred over the years by the pit. Free them from ill health, release them from this awful strike and poverty! Against the bishop's wishes, he had decided to pray openly for the strike during Mass that morning. He knew his superior frowned on anything he deemed to call political, but how could he keep asking his parishioners to give money for starving children in the Third World when their own children were hungry? It was high time he said something directly. Bishop or no bishop, he had to do what he felt was right.

There was a good crowd in the church; including children clutching Christmas presents which, Tom knew, were toys donated to the Miners' Welfare Fund by well-wishers. Striking families had each been given a Christmas stocking of toys for each child: a carrier bag in reality, filled with small second-hand toys, crayons, a colouring book, and sweets. Each bag was tied at the handles with a pink ribbon for girls or a blue for boys. However, the strike breakers, the scabs, would never dare to attend Mass. They had to keep out of sight because they were outcasts, like lepers.

When the organ started up, Tom, having donned gold vestments, entered the church solemnly, followed by a line of well-scrubbed altar boys. As he made his procession down the church, he recognized the faces of many old miners – their muscular, crooked bodies crammed into ill-fitting suits, their thick necks unaccustomed to being constricted by collar and tie. Seeing their eager faces, he felt a surge of love for them. Weren't they all just like children after all, wanting nothing more than kindness, food and security?

The time eventually came for the prayers. Tom named those who were sick, after each request finishing with, 'Lord in Your mercy,' and the congregation murmured the response: 'Hear our prayer.' Taking a deep breath, Tom called out in a loud voice:

'Lord! Have mercy on all those suffering the hardship and trauma of the strike. Grant us, oh Lord, a peaceful and satisfactory end to this strike, which has caused such conflict in our community!'

The response 'Hear our prayer' rumbled around the church in unison. Tom pressed on:

'Lord, remember those on both sides of the strike, shelter those from indignity and abuse who, for whatever reason, have chosen to return to work. Help us to follow you, as you taught us to love our enemies, in loving our neighbours as ourselves. Lord, in Your mercy . . .'

He waited for the usual response, but there was silence. It was like a gaping void of sound. One or two cleared their throats, someone coughed, and then again – silence. He opened his eyes and looked up. He repeated, raising his voice even louder,

'Lord, in your mercy . . .' Their heads were no longer bowed. Every face was turned towards him. He gave the response himself, slowly and deliberately,

'Hear our prayer,' he said solemnly. Not a single parishioner joined in.

As he turned back to the altar to begin the preparations for communion, he heard a loud rumble rise from the congregation. He kept his eyes lowered, but there was much fidgeting and shuffling of feet. Finally he glanced up. Several parishioners were disappearing out of the door.

After Mass he stood outside as usual, to bid people 'a Happy Christmas', shaking their hands, joking and chatting. Some gave him gifts: a bottle of their homemade wine, jam or cake. There was no change in their manner that he could tell, and no one mentioned the interruption during prayers; in fact, he was beginning to think he had imagined it.

When everyone had gone and the women had finished clearing up after the service, they left Tom alone to lock up. He was just about to leave himself when two burly men appeared at the church door, blocking the light.

'A word, Father?' one of them said. He was a thick-set man, with balding blond hair and a fresh complexion. A local miner, and a family man – Tom recognized him immediately. His companion, though, was new to him. He was thin and wore black motorcycle gear, including a helmet which he didn't remove.

'We were at Mass just now, Father,' the blond one said, leaning forward into Tom's face. 'We thought we heard you askin' us to pray for them scabs, is that right?'

This is crunch time, Tom thought to himself. I've got to stand up and be counted sooner or later. He cleared his throat and replied, 'Yes, I prayed for God's mercy on *all* families affected by the strike,' he said, as calmly as he could.

'That's not how we heard it, is it, Paul?' he growled, glancing at his companion and then staring back into Tom's face. 'We heard you prayin' for scabs, didn't we, Paul?' he said, drawing his face even closer to Tom's in a menacing manner, his eyes glinting as sharp as glass. 'We don't want no prayers said for those scum,' he said. 'Them that stab us in the back don't deserve no prayers.'

'We have a duty to pray for all God's children, Bruce,' Tom replied. 'Love one another, isn't that what the Bible says?' He moved away, busying himself straightening the hymn books, avoiding the man's eyes. The odour of stale beer poisoned the air around them.

'Let's get locked up now, eh? It's time we were thinking about our Christmas dinner!' he suggested in as convivial a tone as he could muster. 'I hear the women are starting to carve the turkey at twelve-thirty. Best get a move on, lads, get yourselves in the queue, eh?'

'Don't wanna hear no more talk o' scabs in our church – do you understand me, Father?' the miner persisted. Lunging forward, he picked up a fist full of candles from the box and hurled them across the church.

Tom sucked his cheeks in, puffed them out, sighed thoughtfully but said nothing.

'Come on, let's get back up the club, mate,' the thin man drawled, holding the door open.

'You mention those scabs in church again an' it won't just be the bloody candles that get it. Do you understand me, Father?'

'You wouldn't be threatening your old priest now, would you, Bruce? When I first came to this parish, you were in short trousers, and up to a lot of mischief I seem to remember. Your mother was worried sick about you. I promised her I'd look out for you; I told her you were a good boy at heart and not to worry herself. Your poor mother hasn't had it easy but she's stood by you and made a man of you. Is this the way you repay her?'

'Mother ain't got no time for scabs,' he said bitterly, moving towards the door. But something must have changed his mind. Turning back, he kicked out at the collection plate viciously and it went clattering across the stone floor, spilling coins and notes as it went. 'Bloody hypocrites!' he shouted.

Tom stood frozen in shock. This might be it, he thought. Taking a deep breath, he exhaled slowly.

'Bruce, take yourself and your friend here off home now, there's a lad.'

The miner's massive frame blocked the exit. Silence. Tom could hear every breath the man took. The labour of it brought the memory of his dear mother's chesty breathing back to him so vividly he almost forgot about the man who stood before him vibrating with rage, his fists clamped like tight tattooed hams. The odour of sweat wafted across the gap between him and Tom's face. This time, prayer captured Tom's thoughts and a curious serenity melted over him.

'Come on, old chap,' he muttered. 'Let's go home, shall we?'

'Oh bloody hell!' Bruce roared, spat on the floor at Tom's feet and followed his companion out of the door.

Cast into semi-darkness, Tom stood still. It took him a while to regain his equanimity. Gently and carefully, like piecing together a spilt jigsaw, he re-ordered the things in his life and thought about other things: his mother at home beside her fireplace; the women busy dishing up the Christmas meal at the Welfare Hall; Winnie and Kim bustling about basting the turkey. Moments later the door wafted open again in the breeze, letting in a stream of light and cool December air.

Walking unsteadily across to gather up the candles, he stood with the broken wax in his hands before going back down to the altar where peace still lingered undisturbed. Wafts of incense floated in an arc of winter sunlight that shone through the window. There, at the altar rails, Tom put the broken candles into his pocket, knelt down on his knees and put his head into his trembling hands.

'Dear Lord in heaven, help me,' he murmured.

Chapter 17

Mick's house was in a row of Victorian brick terraces with long front gardens. Being the end one, it had the largest plot including a corrugated iron garage and a couple of sheds – a benefit not shared by the others. There was a concreted area near these outbuildings, and here on Boxing Day, Bradley was chopping firewood using the wooden pit-props that Mick had salvaged from the yard. It was damp and still, silent apart from rooks croaking and flapping restlessly high up in the horse-chestnut trees.

His mind often reverted back to Christmas at home with Helen. He clung to memories of ordinary things: eating dinner, watching television, bathing the baby, going to bed. Thoughts of their physical closeness made his body ache for her. Somewhere he believed, away from the business of the pit and the strike, where neither of them were held to ransom or judged by their ideas, these differences between them would dissolve away as quickly as the morning mist and they would find their love again. There had been other Christmases in his life when he had also felt sad and left out. He remembered when their mother had first left home, left him and Kim, as kids, without a word. Their father was either unable or uninterested in celebrating Christmas and it had come and gone like any other day.

His breath hung in a cloud of vapour as he warmed to his work, driving away his inward pain by swinging the axe down into the wood with a vengeance. Mick had gone to stay with relatives and taken the two terriers with him and Bradley found he missed their company, their musky warmth around the house and their alert sharp barks when anyone approached. I must try and speak to Helen again, he resolved. She won't want us to be split up like this forever – not when the strike's over and done with. She'll come round and see sense, I know she will. But the rift between them felt like a festering wound. It hurt him to think of it.

Life wouldn't be easy after the strike, he knew that. The village wouldn't accept him back. He knew what they were like towards scabs. There was one chap who had broken the strike in the seventies, he remembered; he started getting bricks through his window and dog-dirt through his letterbox. People still called out 'bloody scab!' after him in the street for years afterwards.

Harder and harder Bradley chopped, with fierce grief. Over the years the props were being replaced by steel ones to sheer up the tunnel roofs. These were safer; lives had been lost by a wooden one splitting and giving way under the weight of rock. However, some argued the ponies could hear a warning in the creak of wood, just before a tunnel collapsed, and their shying and white-eyed whinnying warned the miners to get out – giving them a few vital seconds to escape. But the ponies, like the canaries, were replaced by machines – and steel props didn't creak, they just gave way without warning.

Just as Bradley turned to pick up another prop, he heard a car draw up. Always anxious now in case it meant trouble, he looked up ready to dive out of sight. But it was a familiar car, Tom's old Ford Escort; he watched as Tom climbed out and headed down the path towards him.

'Season's greetings to you, Brad!' called Tom. 'How are you doing?' They shook hands warmly. Admiring the chopped firewood, he gazed around the garden with genuine pleasure. 'Reminds me of home,' he sighed. 'Mother busy cooking in the kitchen and Father making himself scarce in the yard. Heh! How she fusses about him getting under her feet!' He paused. 'Are you on your own here?'

'Mick's gone to stay with family. I don't mind, it's quiet and there's plenty to keep me occupied.'

'So I see; you're doing a grand job too! Oh, and I heard you took Helen some presents?'

'She told you about it then?'

Tom nodded, pursing his lips. 'That must have been tricky?'

'I hardly thought I'd get away with it, Tom, without being seen, I mean, but I managed it.'

''Twas very good of you to risk it, Brad – took some pluck I'd say.'

'She did take it in? From off the step, I mean? I was half afraid I'd be bringin' it back wi' me.'

'Oh, she did, yes! She told me how you appeared at the back door. It startled her a bit, you turning up!' He clicked his tongue and gave a rapid shake of his head as though another thought had occurred to him and he wanted to be rid of it.

Bradley noticed. 'She weren't pleased with it then?'

'Who knows? I'm sorry, would you believe she took it straight up the Welfare the next morning and gave it all away.'

'Not Sam's toys as well?'

'Seems they went too, yes. She's refusing to accept anything from you apparently. That's what she said.'

Bradley kicked a loose stone and it flew across the garden. 'She could at least have let the boy have his new toys.'

Tom watched his face glumly. 'She'll get over it, Brad. It'll take time, that's all. Women! 'Tis hard to understand their way of thinking. He's lookin' fine though, your Sam. He's a bonny lad; Helen's looking after him well. We've that to be thankful for.'

Bradley took up his axe and resumed chopping, 'Thanks, Tom, I'm grateful to you, for tellin' me.' His voice was jagged as he swung the axe and split the wood several times. Finally bringing the axe blade to rest in the chopping block once more, he went into the shed and came back with a potato sack into which he started gathering the smaller bits of firewood.

'Join me for a cuppa if you want one. Nothing stronger in the house at the moment though, I'm afraid.'

'No, I'm fine, thanks.' But Tom couldn't help but let his burden down for a moment. 'Actually I had a bit of a sticky encounter after Mass yesterday, so I did.' He pursed his lips and put his hands in his pockets thoughtfully.

'Oh yeah? They're not getting on at you as well, are they, Tom?'

'One or two of them are flexing their muscles a bit. I took it into my head to say a prayer for the strike during Mass – against the bishop's advice – I can't say he didn't warn me.'

'What's wrong with that then? Seems fair enough. Didn't I say you should be able to say what you want?'

'Would have been OK, Brad, if I'd stuck to praying for the striking families, but I included those on both sides.'

Bradley chuckled. 'You old rogue! They didn't take too kindly to that I bet!'

'No, it did get a bit sticky,' he replied, with a long face.

'Can't be easy for you, Tom. If that lot find out you've been to visit a scab like me, some folks might start gettin' ideas. Really, you'd best be careful; don't let too many know you're mixin' with the likes of me.'

'Don't worry yourself about that,' Tom replied. 'Anyway, you're not the only scab I visit, if you must use that word. I'm a priest, am I not, and supposed to be a peacemaker, eh? On both sides, that's what I am,' he added cheerfully. 'I was wondering, Brad, I've been invited down to Chalkfield Hall tonight to share a Christmas drink or two with Lady Ashby and her guests.' He began feeling in his pocket for his car keys. 'I hope you don't mind – I took the liberty of asking if I could bring you along. Will you come?'

'They won't want me there, Tom!' Bradley exclaimed. 'It was different when I went to see Kim, we just talked in the back kitchen, out the way. She won't want a miner there, showing her up in front of her posh friends!' The picture he conjured up made him smile. 'Can you see me sat in that Lady What's-her-name's parlour sippin' sherry with the high an' mighty?' He laughed out loud, probably for the first time in weeks, and his laughter rippled across the garden in a welcome bid for freedom.

Tom reassured him. 'Edith told me she would be delighted to have you, and you would be company for Kim. She's given Kim the night off specially. So what d'you say? It'll give you a chance to see your sister again and wish her Happy Christmas.'

Bradley thought for a moment. Since his talk with Kim he felt things were on an even keel again. 'I'd like that, Tom, thanks.'

'Good, that's settled then. I'll come and pick you up about seven.'

It was dark when Tom's car drew up. Bradley was already waiting at the gate. He glanced back at the house before climbing in.

'Think I locked everything up; I can't go anywhere now without thinkin' twice.'

Tom shook his head. 'That you can't,' he replied.

'Oh,' groaned Bradley, 'and I didn't think to bring a bottle or something.'

'Don't worry,' said Tom, 'the Irish whisky I've brought will do from us both. They've got more than enough down there already, so they have.'

He drove off in the direction of Ebbingsfield; their route would take them directly through Silt Edge.

'We won't drive through the village, Brad. We could do without being stopped by the police tonight, eh! I'll take the back road and save ourselves a lot of hassle.' He chuckled to himself. 'I was at Chalkfield Hall yesterday as well, for my Christmas dinner. . . . Boy, oh, boy!' he laughed, shaking his head as he recalled the plentiful scene. 'Between you and me, there was enough to feed an army and there was only eight of us!'

They had been driving for about five minutes when Bradley noticed a familiar odour permeating the car. It was the smell of mothballs and, he realized, it must be coming from Tom's suit; most likely, he thought, Tom hadn't given it an airing since last Christmas. Tom was wearing an unusual green tweed suit which had wide lapels and trousers with turn-ups. Underneath this was a red tartan waistcoat. He glanced at Tom's earnest face and for a moment imagined him as a young boy again, out on some escapade – with a hint of excitement, even mischief, in his eyes. He sighed, straightened his tie and closed his eyes for a moment, just trying to relax.

When Tom's car swung into the drive, the gravel announced their arrival and as they climbed out of the car, they heard the dog barking and saw Winnie already standing to welcome them at the open door.

'Come inside my dears!' she called.

A swarm of voices signalled a crowd of people within. Bradley nodded respectfully as he passed ladies dressed in velvet, satin, with jewels sparkling from their necks and ear lobes. He was relieved he'd put on a suit and tie. Trying to catch sight of his sister, his eyes were drawn to a table overflowing with plates of pastries, delicacies, bottles and glasses. Feeling overwhelmed, he was pleased to see Kim at last, sitting alone by the mantelpiece. She smiled and immediately rose to greet him, her pregnancy filling out a full-length blue silk dress. Her hair looked silky and braided; she was barely recognizable as the scruffy little sister he remembered.

'Happy Christmas, sis!' he said, advancing towards her and embracing her briefly. 'You all right then? You're lookin' well!'

Edith approached, extending a gracious hand. 'Good evening, Bradley!' she declared, greeting him with a radiant smile. 'Still fighting to keep the country going, young man?'

'Doin' the best I can, ma'am,' he said.

'Excellent!' She beamed at him with secret satisfaction, and cast her eyes appreciatively upon his square shoulders – from his shirt and tie, right down to his well-polished shoes. 'You're very tall, if you don't mind me saying so, Bradley.' Her eyes twinkled mischievously. 'I like to see height and strength in a man.'

'Thank you, ma'am.'

'Your sister tells me you've sacrificed a lot to keep yourself at work,' she added, gazing up into his face with intense concentration.

A flush spread on his freshly shaved cheek. 'Yes, I suppose I have, ma'am. I just had to do somethin' – with bills to pay and a family to support. It stands to reason—'

'Good for you, my man, good for you! A bit of common sense goes a long way in this poor country of ours.'

Giving him one of her warmest smiles, it suddenly occurred to Bradley that it seemed as though he had known her for years. He walked across the soft carpet inexplicably light-headed, holding the wine glass carefully in case he should crack its delicate stem in his clumsy hands. As he raised his glass, he noticed coal dust under his fingernails – this, in spite of having scrubbed them raw before he came. '*Once a miner, always a miner under the skin.*' His father's voice came back to him and it cut him to the quick.

'Let's go an' sit over there, Brad,' Kim's voice broke in. He followed her, looking around for Tom without success. They sat watching lively conversations take place like two children peering through a grand window at the party guests inside.

'Not long to go now then, sis?' he suggested, casting an eye down fleetingly.

Kim smiled. 'It's gettin' a bit impatient in there – keeps kickin'!' Her hands were folded over her bump protectively, but he noticed her nervous fidgeting had gone – she seemed placid and content. Something about her face reminded him, with a jolt, of their mother.

'You gonna manage all right, sis?'

She nodded and smiled again – self-contained, happy. He immediately felt excluded, lonely. His own family future was denied him. Love had eluded him. He looked around the room, at the animated faces engaging and understanding each other. Tom reappeared; he was in conversation with an elderly gentleman wearing military medals. Bradley knew – no matter what – that Tom would stand by him; he was a trustworthy friend, and yet . . . he couldn't help feeling so lonely. A restlessness tugged at him like the wild wind. *Let me go*, he wanted to say, *let me go out into the country where I belong, where the earth is as bitter as sloes and the air as jagged as barbed wire – I don't belong in here.*

An elderly lady began telling her life story. He watched her, an actress once, he guessed, though Kim told him she was a farmer. She certainly didn't look like a farmer to him, with her bird-like limbs and clever eyes. He began to ask Kim about her.

'Ssh, listen!' whispered Kim. 'She's crazy, that old Mrs Pentley, she talks to herself all the time and she sees things! I've heard her talkin' to people that ain't there!' Kim rolled her eyes and stifled giggles. 'She's really sweet though.'

Isobel Pentley was enlarging on her story about her escape from Africa and her sing-song voice attracted much attention. But there was no mistaking her fear; her teeth chattered and a haunted look lit her eyes that could only have arisen after witnessing experiences unspeakably cruel. He watched her, his curiosity aroused by that strange amalgam of amusement streaked with morbid terror. Her face reminded him of a cunning fox, that high cheek-boned smile tinged with greed. What was she up to? Glancing at his sister, he saw she was sitting passively listening to the story like a child. The narrative continued: farmers being murdered in their beds, farmhands slain in the fields, and crops contaminated by spilt blood.

'For every mother raped and murdered, there's a child orphaned,' she declared. 'For every father murdered, there's a family driven off the land.' She held up an instructive finger. 'To this day,' she proclaimed grandly, opening wide her arms and finishing her story with tragic poise, 'I carry that rifle with me wherever I go. It's in my room now,' she added with a curious twinkle in her eye. 'I keep it loaded, of course, under my bed. Well, you can't be too sure these days,' she said, looking around at her listeners for affirmation.

Mellowed by alcohol, rich food and Christmas goodwill, her audience applauded warmly – apart from Bradley himself and also, he noticed, Lady Ashby, who stared away from the gathering, looking bored. They were all muttering their approval, agreeing wholeheartedly, and without realizing it, giving free licence to a lethal cocktail of self-pity, resentment and insanity.

The rotund nun, Sister Ruth, sporting a large wooden cross on a cord around her neck and dressed for comfort rather than occasion, began describing her trip to paint a picture of Ayers Rock. On her breaks from missionary work, she said, she travelled the world sketching and painting. Passing around photographs, she described the Australian scenery with a bovine smile, showing square teeth under a grey square fringe.

Kim whispered at his shoulder, 'Have you seen Danny at all then, down the pit?'

He snatched a glimpse at her; the first sign of anxiety had crept into her face. 'Nope,' he lied. 'He don't seem to be on my shift – anyhow, he works over the other side. You heard from him then?'

She shook her head, biting her lip.

He sipped the bitter-sweet red wine, trying to distract himself from the vision of their fight in the pit yard. Gazing about the room, inadvertently he caught the eye of Lady Ashby, who surprised him with a warm smile, and she raised her glass to him in a private gesture of companionship.

Kim stood up and busied herself going about circulating nibbles and offering to pour drinks. He watched her, amazed at the transformation, how she blended into the household as though she had been born to it. Presently she returned to him, topped up his glass and offered him a plate of cheese straws before sitting down again.

At that precise moment, something so loud exploded outside it stopped everyone in mid-sentence.

'Good heavens!' exclaimed Edith. 'Whatever was that noise?'

Ruth was the first to look through the curtains.

'There's someone smashing up the cars!' she squealed. 'Oh dear God in heaven, look!'

A rush of people got up to join her. Bradley also got up and went to the window, cupping his hands over his eyes to see into the darkness beyond. He saw several figures out there.

'It'll be drunken thugs,' he said. 'They've probably come from the pub, with nothing better to do than cause trouble.'

Edith clicked her tongue in disgust. 'Well, whatever next!'

But what followed was unmistakable. A coarse voice bellowed in a thick Glaswegian accent: 'Kim? Kim, get yourself out here – I know you're in there!'

'Who was that?' wailed Ruth. 'He's shouting for somebody I think.'

Bradley stepped smartly over to his sister. 'Go through and sit in the kitchen, Kim, there's a girl,' he said quietly. 'Nothin' to worry about, I'll sort them out.'

'It sounded like Danny's voice,' she whispered. 'What's he doin' comin' here?' She clutched at his hand for a moment looking terrified, before rushing away to the kitchen.

'We're apparently under attack,' announced the major. 'Man the barricades, everyone!'

Ben was barking, hurling his weight unsteadily against the front door. Bradley went into the hall where Winnie was trying to calm him. Edith was standing close by, her moist eyes bulging with indignation.

'Lady Ashby,' said Bradley with restrained authority, 'I recognize that man's voice outside. It's someone who works down the pit and he's a trouble maker. I think we should telephone the police straightaway.'

'Yes, yes, of course, young man,' she replied. 'Would you be so kind? The phone's there.' She gestured to the hall table. Immediately Bradley dialled the emergency number.

'Police, please,' he said, waiting, his eyes staring. 'There's a drunken mob outside attackin' the cars and they're threatenin' us. Yes, they're right outside the house now – Chalkfield Hall, Ebbingsfield. Yes, yes . . . thank you.'

He replaced the receiver and caught Edith's eye. 'The police are on their way,' he said. 'I'll go outside and try to speak to them. Would you mind askin' everyone to stay indoors?'

He opened the front door and slipped out before anyone could stop him. Ben slipped out too, baying ferociously. There were three or four men and they began to throw handfuls of gravel at the old dog.

'I've called the police, lads,' Bradley shouted into the darkness. 'You'll go home now if you've got any sense. Get out o' here while you still can!'

Inside, Edith fanned her face. 'Well, I ask you!' she cried crossly. 'At Christmas as well! What are things coming to?' Moments later she opened the front door herself, in spite of Winnie pleading with her. Standing in the doorway, her voice boomed across the drive: 'Get off my land, you vile hooligans!' she crowed, pulling herself up to her full height and warbling in a falsetto tone. 'Do you realize you're trespassing on private property?'

The thugs jeered and mimicked her: 'Get off my land, you vile hooligans,' they croaked in exaggerated sing-song voices, falling about with laughter.

'Go on, clear off! Get out o' here!' roared Bradley. A shaft of light broke from the open door, sliced across the driveway, showing Bradley standing still and defiant, legs apart and hands in his pockets. While Edith retreated back inside, he walked on alone further up the gravel drive and disappeared into the dark shadows under the trees.

186

There was the sound of breaking glass. It was Tom's Ford Escort; the windscreen was shattered. He immediately recognized who was jumping up and down on its roof; as soon as he heard the voice and saw the stature of the man, it confirmed his worst fears – it was indeed Danny Stuart. Adrenalin surged through him and drove him forward; his heart pumped like a fist inside his chest – and with blood rising in his veins, anger thrilled his muscles with the desire for justice.

Shouting down from the car roof, Danny's slurred voice rang out:

'You! Go an' fetch your sister out 'ere, you! I wanna talk to her! Tell 'er I'm takin' her back with me. She don't belong here, the bitch!'

'Go home, Danny!' Bradley shouted back. 'Go home and take your friends with you!'

Ignoring him, Danny's drunken voice came again. 'Hey, Kim! Come out here, you bloody whore!'

'I said go home, Danny! She doesn't want to see you!'

'Who does she think she is, lady of the manor?' he roared.

Tom appeared beside Bradley, puffing breathlessly. 'Leave them be, Brad. Come back inside, man, and let the police handle it.'

'No, Tom, go back and make sure Kim stays indoors,' he growled under his breath. 'I'll try an' keep Danny talkin' till the police arrive. Quick, Tom! Go an' take care of her, this could turn nasty.'

Tom hurried back to the house, only to be met by Kim herself coming out. 'Kim! Don't! Come back indoors, girl, quickly!' he cried, but it was useless. She raced to her brother's side.

'Well! Look here, if it ain't our little madam!' roared Danny, giving out a loud whistle. 'You little bitch, come over here! I think you've got something to tell me, ain't yer? That's what I've heard – got a wee secret, haven't we?' He was swaying drunkenly on the roof of the car – a can in one hand and a pole of some sort in the other.

She clung to Bradley's arm. 'He knows, doesn't he!' she whimpered and before he could stop her, she started towards him, yelling hysterically: 'What d'you want with me, eh?' she screamed. 'What you come 'ere for, eh, Danny Stuart? Leave us alone!'

He threw the pole at her, closely followed by the beer can and, taking a crashing jump from the roof of the car, jumped heavily onto the bonnet and landed in front of her.

'You cheap cow, goin' around tellin' folks you're 'avin my kid. Told you I don't want no bloody kids, didn't I?' he shouted, towering over her, leering into her face. 'I warned you, girl, didn't I? Didn't I bloody tell you to take that stupid pill? Didn't I?' He slapped her across the face, but she stood her ground.

'I didn't mean it to 'appen, Danny,' she pleaded. 'It just, y'know, it just 'appened.'

Bradley rushed to her side. 'Come away, Kim, come back inside!'

'Just 'appened! Oh, yeah!' he roared, ignoring Bradley and gripping her by the upper arm.

She pulled back. 'I'm goin' to keep the baby, Danny, don't you see? It'll be all right!' she cried, shivering and petrified.

'No, I won't bloody see. I'll kill you first; you ain't havin' no kid o' mine if I can help it.' He hit her again, this time knocking her over onto the gravel. She fell heavily onto her side, desperately trying to protect her unborn child with her arms.

'Are you all right?' Bradley rushed to her aid, ignoring her attacker, who was still raging in the background. 'I told yer, didn't I, Kim, to stop inside!'

'Leave her be, she'll be all right. Hard as nails she is,' snarled Danny. 'Get up, girl, an' stop fussing.'

Ignoring him, Bradley lifted Kim to her feet, but she was wailing with a strange eerie cry. Suddenly she fled away from him, back to the light of the porch where Edith, Winnie and several guests were clustered. They closed in protectively around her and began helping her through the door. Hearing Danny's voice behind her, she panicked and started up the stairs crying, 'Don't let him get me, don't let 'im near me, please! He won't listen! He just won't listen!' She was still crying hysterically when she clambered up to the top floor to reach her bedroom. Winnie was following, wheezing and breathless: 'Go on up, girl, I'm right behind you!'

'Where the hell's that bitch gone runnin' to now?' Danny complained, kicking out at Tom's car in frustration.

'You lousy coward, hittin' a pregnant woman,' Bradley shouted. 'Ain't you got no sense of decency at all?'

'Shut up, you!' growled Danny and, leaping forward, he punched

Bradley hard in the chest and again in the stomach, doubling him up. 'Hey! Kim!' he roared. 'Get back out here, you fuckin' bitch, or your brother here's really goin' to get it!'

Bradley couldn't stand any more; he couldn't wait to silence that evil mouth. Forgetting his pain, he stood up and lunged at Danny, but Tom was there now, holding him back.

'Bradley, come away, he's not worth it,' Tom implored him.

'Oh, if it's not the priest as well!' Danny's face twisted into a smile as he staggered drunkenly towards them and leered right into Bradley's face.

'Where's that little whore run off to?' he sneered. 'I wanna talk to 'er! Never told me she was havin' a kid, did she, the little slut,' he snarled. 'Well, I'm takin' her back wi' me whether she likes it or not.'

Bradley felt his tie yanked tight as Danny grabbed him and pulled him up close to his own face; he could smell Danny's rancid breath as the words came, loaded with spit. 'Don't you get it, mate? I've come 'ere to take her back wi' me, right?'

'Let him go, Danny lad, come on now,' pleaded Tom. 'Break it up! We'll settle this another time, when we've all calmed down a bit, eh?'

'Keep out o' this, priest!' Danny snarled, tightening his grip.

Bradley was choking and Tom tried pulling at Danny's arm in a futile effort to stop him. In a last desperate attempt to free himself, Bradley swung his fist but it bounced like a tennis ball off Danny's jaw. Laughing, he let go of his tie, but flung him backwards, simultaneously letting fly a ham fist at his face. But the punch missed Bradley and caught Tom full force on the side of the head. The priest gasped, staggered, crumpled to the ground and lay quite still. A cheer went up in the background from the drunken mob hiding in the shrubbery.

Forgetting everything, Bradley knelt by his side. 'Tom, wake up! Tom?' Ignoring Danny, he loosened the priest's collar, put his head against his chest, and felt his pulse.

'Someone get an ambulance! Tom's hurt bad,' he yelled, staring back towards the house where several had gathered on the porch to watch.

'Get up, you idiot!' roared Danny, grabbing Bradley by the collar and hauling him to his feet.

Bradley's nightmare wouldn't end. He felt himself being punched again, heard women crying. The taste of blood seeped into his mouth, the smell of coal dust blocked his nose and something thrust him backwards. With a shock, he felt the coal face come up to meet him; it banged hard against the back of his head and sent him falling further now, as a weight falls, straight down the mine shaft. As Danny's iron fists descended on him, he felt himself falling into oblivion.

A gunshot rang out. It ricocheted around the corners of the house and left a silence so thick you could touch it. It was a unique moment, when an alchemy of confusion and fear brought about the spontaneous shift in the fate of these two very different men. The bullet left the trembling hands of a demented woman and found its target in Danny's forehead. Its echoes reverberated around the walls of the house like a firecracker, seeking destruction in its appetite for evil. There was a hush, like a prolonged intake of breath, and then nothing. Screams tore through the silence, acute, like frantic seagulls when their nests are under attack. Shadows and torch-lights circled in greedy curiosity looking for casualties. Voices came closer and then receded into the night. All became calm.

The stinging gravel had become part of Bradley's face. He strained upwards and saw a deformed shape, like a sack of coal abandoned on the path near him. Confused, he stared at it curiously. Looking up into the darkness for his snarling opponent, his eyes came to rest again on the simple sack of coal. So full and lumpy and black it was, with gleaming coal spilling out of its neck, glistening wet in the moonlight. It was the body of Danny Stuart.

Bradley twisted round to look behind him. Tom was there, quite near the sack. He too was lying as still as a corpse. People were crowded round him now; he couldn't comprehend what they were saying. Peering back towards the house, he saw the open door lit up and a tiny female figure in silhouette. This solitary person was stationary, like an actress on stage in the spotlight, but she was holding aloft not a microphone, but a rifle. The gun looked much too heavy for her thin arms and she seemed to struggle with the weight of

190

it. She was like a small tree, he thought, a sapling swaying in the wind. He gazed at the vision of her, mesmerized.

'My dogs, where are my dogs? Rufus? Gyp?' the figure called out plaintively. Isobel Pentley's fragile voice carried its unreal message out across the drive into the darkness. 'Where is everybody? Have they all gone and left me?' she asked. Lowering the rifle, she let it hang from her arm, as a hunter would do when the birds have flown.

Bradley saw another female figure walk up to her and take the rifle from her as though it was a child's toy. It was Edith; she was holding Isobel by the elbow, coaxing her gently as one would a child, urging her back indoors. As Edith passed the major, Bradley saw her hand the rifle to him matter-of-factly, as though it were nothing more than a torch. Turning round, he looked back at the sack of coal again. It lay inert as before, a black humped shape.

'Danny! Danny!' A piercing scream left the comfort of the house and made a new assault on the quiet night air. It was his sister, fleeing from the open door. He watched her curiously.

'Kim?' he called. 'I'm over here!' But she rushed straight past him and he, so weak, could do nothing to stop her.

'Danny!' she shrieked at the heap of coal. 'Danny! Wake up!'

It didn't move. It didn't stir. A wailing of sirens approached, strangely familiar in an absurd way. The police cars threw gravel up as they swerved at speed into the drive. Policemen, speaking in low tones, were in control. Radios crackling, they left their patrol-car engines running and descended on the scene with casual efficiency. One police officer took off his jacket and, strangely, placed it reverently over the sack of coal.

'Sorry, love, got to do this,' Bradley heard him say to Kim, who was kneeling on the path. Her sobs grew louder. With all the willpower he could draw upon, he pulled himself up from the gravel and stood up. As though roused from a deep sleep, he seemed to discover his voice again and said, 'I'll take care of her.' He put his arm around his sister's shoulders and they turned back together towards the house. Police officers were bent over Tom, who was still lying on the path. They were feeling for a pulse and tugging at his clothes.

'This one's still alive at least,' he heard one say.

'Still alive,' repeated Bradley. 'Thank God.' And taking hold of his sister more firmly, he brought her towards him gently and hugged her close.

'Kim,' he whispered. 'Kim, we're gonna be all right,' he said gently. He spoke to her as though she was a child again, hiding in the cupboard under the stairs. 'Come on now,' he whispered softly, 'come with me.' Coaxing her towards the house, others came out to help, murmuring comforting words and leading them both indoors. As they reached the house, the light from the doorway shone in Kim's eyes. She blinked and, as though for the first time, realized her brother was there.

'Did Danny get shot?' she whispered.

'Yes, I'm afraid he did.'

'He'll not be comin' after me no more?' Her tormented eyes searched his face for an answer.

Bradley shook his head. Suddenly a loud cry rose from deep inside her throat, and as if from a dream he heard it and knew it was the end of a terrible battle within her. Her eyelids were purple, her hair was streaked with silver and wet with tears. In one night, she seemed to have grown up and grown old.

'Kim?' he cried, staring at her in bewilderment. 'Are you hurt? Is your baby—'

'No, I think I'm OK,' she sniffed, and suddenly she hugged him tightly, her baby a bulky presence between them.

'But are you in pain then?'

She shook her head and shuddered. 'No, I'm fine.' And then she choked, and a sob broke from her throat, which was a nervous giggle of relief.

'You're lookin' a right mess, y'know, Brad!' she said, sniffing and wiping her nose on her sleeve.

'Come along, my dears,' Winnie called. 'Let's get you inside.' As they stepped through the door, the light and warmth from the house engulfed them.

The tiny person of Isobel Pentley sat on an upright chair in the lounge. She looked like a china doll dwarfed by two police officers, one on each side. Her thin wrists were hardly contained by the handcuffs that clinked together like cheap jewellery. Apparitions appeared to bewitch her, and occasionally she spoke, words tumbling from her mouth incoherently. The policemen eyed each other:

'Are you all right love?' one asked loudly, as though she was deaf. There was no response.

Oblivious of the policemen, her lips began moving animatedly as though she was in conversation with someone. Her eyes darted about and she wrung her hands, making the handcuffs chink constantly. Winnie went and spoke quietly to her, laying a comforting hand briefly on her shoulder. Then she came over to where Bradley and Kim sat huddled together on the sofa.

'Come along into the kitchen, dears, I've brewed some tea. We'll bring some in for Isobel when she's ready. We're just waiting for the doctor to come. Would you like some tea, officers?' she asked.

They both declined.

Sitting together beside the Aga in the kitchen, Bradley relaxed and let the warmth flood through his trembling limbs. Winnie poured them some hot sweet tea and Kim sat closely against him, her small hands covering his. Chattering away to him nervously, sometimes a sob would catch her voice but she pressed on urgently like an excited child:

'Remember, in the summer when we was kids, when we used to play at buildin' a tree house in the yard? Try an' picture it, Brad.' She nudged him to get his attention. 'We'd have some supper an' pretend we was by the sea, remember?' She gave a deep shuddering sigh and continued, 'You would catch a fish an' cook it, an' we had lovely chunks o' bread an' drippin'.' She watched his face, waiting for him to answer. She nudged him again. 'D'you remember?' she asked again, peering into his face like a demanding child at her father's knee.

Slowly, without saying a word, he shifted slightly and turned towards her. He put his strong arms around her and hugged her, feeling the firmness of her unborn child pressing against his side. She buried her head in his shoulder then, and began weeping softly.

'Shh, you'll be all right now,' he said, stroking her hair. Somehow he felt he was trying to comfort himself too, because despair was creeping up on him like a ghost. 'We'll both be all right now, sis,' he said.

Bradley lay awake, staring around the dark unfamiliar bedroom. It was a large room – the bed was bigger than he'd ever slept in before and the sheets were smooth and cool – but he couldn't sleep. So many times he would wake to see Danny towering over him. When he finally slept, it was daylight before he woke again with a start. Confused as to where he was, he looked at his watch. It was already after nine.

His room looked out onto the front drive. Below him the sight summed up the nightmare of the night before. A group of police officers stood talking, making notes and taking photographs of Tom's car. It looked as though it had been in a crash. The roof and bonnet were dented, and the windscreen was a white haze of splintered glass that spilled onto the gravel. Police incident tape fluttered all around the scene like bunting at a church fête.

Dressing hurriedly, he ran down the stairs and, as he came into the hall, saw Winnie replacing the receiver.

'Good morning, Bradley,' she said. 'That was the hospital. Kim's pains started during the night and the ambulance came about six – the baby's on its way.'

'Already?' A tight knot of dread started turning in his stomach. 'She'll be all right, won't she?'

'Oh, I'm sure she will. She's stronger than she looks, your sister. We'll phone again in an hour or so, shall we? A cup of coffee for us both, I think! We'll see if Lady Ashby wants one too.'

'But isn't it too soon?' he blurted out, fighting the urge to fling open the front door and go to her.

'Three weeks is a bit early,' Winnie replied. 'It was the shock probably. No need to worry – the baby was a good size. The little mite was ready to make an appearance, I'm sure.'

He stood in the hall for several minutes collecting his thoughts and then, responding to Winnie's call, entered the haven of her warm kitchen and sat down on the seat by the Aga where he and Kim had sat together the night before.

'There you are, dear,' said Winnie, handing him a steaming mug. 'Do you take sugar?' He nodded and she responded with a broad smile. 'I thought so. The hard-workers generally do.'

Chapter 18

As soon as Helen walked into the Welfare Hall she knew something had happened – it was so quiet. No Christmas music or cheerful banter, no cutlery rattling, no shouting, no laughing; the women were huddled together whispering.

'What's happened?' she asked.

'One of the scabs has been shot dead,' Jean said. Helen's stomach turned over. She looked at Jean as if she was about to faint.

'No, love, it's all right – it's not him.'

Helen put her face in her hands and sighed with relief. 'Who was it?' she asked, her heart lurching.

If something had happened to Bradley, how would she ever forgive herself? Lifting Sam out of his pushchair, she kissed him and put him down on a rug in the corner. All the while she was listening, waiting for her answer.

'Who was it, Jean?' she repeated.

'Y'know the lad, the one your Kim took up with?'

'Not Danny Stuart?'

'Yeah, it was him apparently,' Jean continued. 'He got into a fight down in Ebbingsfield an' got himself killed. Doesn't surprise me. He always seemed like a troublemaker to me.'

'Dead!' She couldn't believe it. 'Who did it?' she asked, looking from one to the other. 'Who shot him though?'

'Who knows?' another woman said. 'Bet he was asking for it, knowing him! He was a loser, that one. Bloody scab! Serves him bloody right!'

'You can't say that!' cried Helen, horrified.

'Oh, can't we!' they chorused, laughing at her. 'Whose side are you on anyway?' They were all giggling now. It was a great joke. 'We're not sending him any flowers, are we, girls!'

Their talk, gossip and speculation continued, but Helen's mind was racing. Asking them to watch Sam for her, she went home to fetch her pushbike. She just had to get down to Ebbingsfield quickly and discover what had happened.

Bradley was in the hospital waiting room, when he was surprised to find his son's little sock in his pocket. He'd quite forgotten about it! Since picking it up from the floor months ago, he hadn't stepped foot inside the house. What an honest, harmless little sock it was, the colour of a summer sky. He could envisage Sam's pink toes as though he had just kicked it off; the game they had often played came back to him with brutal clarity. 'You naughty boy!' he would chuckle, and slip the sock back onto his tiny foot and the baby would giggle, kicking his chubby legs until the sock was again on the carpet.

'Brad?'

He looked up, stunned to see Helen standing there. He stared at her as though she was an apparition.

'Bradley? You look awful!'

'Thanks. I'm just goin' to visit Tom,' he said. Realizing he still had the sock in his hand, he quickly slipped it out of sight.

'I heard what happened last night. I've just been in to see Kim. Did you know she's had her baby?'

'Had it – already?'

'Yes! A baby boy! And he's lovely!'

He was astonished. 'So quickly?' he said, half to himself.

'Brad? Does she know about Danny? I mean, that he's—'

He nodded and looked at her, his eyes full of pain.

'She knows. I was there with her when it—' He stood up to go. His head felt heavy and he couldn't think straight. 'I'm waitin' to see Tom; they told me to wait here. Tom was caught in the middle of it all.' He paused, facing her.

'You never told me she was expectin',' he said. 'Kim never told me

197

neither, not till a few weeks ago. I never knew she was havin' Danny's kid.'

'Brad! Such a lot's happened! I know I should've told you but look – we've got to talk.'

'I wish—' he said, stepping towards her. 'What I mean is, I wish we'd never split up. I wish none of it had 'appened'.

She ignored this, watching him curiously. 'What was that you had in your hand?' she asked. 'When I came in just now.'

He withdrew the sock from his pocket and held it out to her, expecting her to take it away from him; his last link with home. He cherished anything familiar, anything to rekindle in his mind the home he once knew and loved. It was his only lifeline. Would she destroy this too, like the newspaper cutting she had chucked on the fire? She took it from him casually.

'Oh, it's Sam's,' she said. Her pupils grew large and flooded with emotion. He wanted to say something, anything, to keep her there for a moment longer.

'Helen? You know, don't you, how sorry I am about all this?'

'No, I don't know, Brad, I wish I did,' she replied and pressed the sock back into the palm of his hand. 'You'd better look after this for him,' she said. 'He's always losing them, the silly bugger!' A giggle escaped through her tears. He looked her straight in the eye.

'OK, thanks.' Relief flooded through him. He put the sock back in his pocket and smiled, a sad, lonely smile. Suddenly she flung her arms round his neck and hugged him, and turning her face up towards his, she brushed his lips with a kiss.

'I've got to go, Brad,' she whispered. 'I miss you so much, you know that, don't you?' she whispered, and letting out a cry, she was gone.

Walking into the ward, he saw that a bandage partially obscured the old face he knew so well. Tom gave his crooked smile.

'My God, Bradley, that's a shiner you've got there!' he called.

'Not half as bad as yours, Tom! How are you then?'

'Heh! Never felt better!' he chuckled. 'They're doin' a grand job here looking after me so they are. Breakfast in bed! Nurses waitin' on me hand and foot! And yourself? Mighty whopper of a black eye!'

'So they tell me.' Bradley smiled. He was walking on air. Nothing could stop his heart racing after Helen's kiss.

'Heh, twas a rough night, so it was!' Tom sighed.

They talked about the hospital food, the nurses, and they laughed about the narrowness of the bed, everything except what mattered, what had really happened the night before. Gradually Bradley began to realize Tom had no idea Danny had been killed. How could he know? He was unconscious when the shot was fired and still out when he was rushed off in the ambulance. There was time, though, he considered, before he needed to break the bad news to him.

'Well, I've got some good news for you, Tom! I just met Helen outside – she told me Kim's had her baby this mornin'!'

'Her baby? Already? How long was I out cold, a couple of months?' he laughed. 'And what did she have?'

'A little boy.'

'Ah, tis grand when good things come out of bad, is it not?' exclaimed Tom, sighing with satisfaction. 'And yourself, Brad? You seem to be in good spirits considering the night you've had!'

'It's all the excitement, Tom.'

'And what about Danny then? It looks as if you came off the worst – he can certainly give a good punch when he wants to, can't he?' Smiling impishly, Tom was feeling the line of his swollen jaw.

Bradley's serious expression made him pause.

'What happened then, did he sober up? He'd had a few, hadn't he! And Kim, the poor girl, she was scared to death. Ah, tis shameful when drink gets to a man like that.'

Bradley took a deep breath. Whether it was right to give him the bad news yet he didn't know, but his face was already giving it away. 'Danny was shot last night, Tom.'

'Shot! Dear Father in heaven, who would have shot the man?'

'It was an accident, sort of. . . .' Bradley flexed his hands, studying every sinew of every finger.

'So how is he then? Was he badly hurt?'

'Danny didn't make it, Tom,' Bradley replied. 'He was shot in the head. He wouldn't have suffered.'

'Shot in the— No!' Tom's bruise grew even more ugly as the colour drained from his face. Below his eyes, the puffiness took on a yellow tinge. 'I can't believe it, Brad. Danny Stuart – dead? God rest his soul, the poor man.'

'Probably I shouldn't have told you, Tom, but it's true, yes. The nurses won't thank me for tellin' you, seein' the state you're in as well. I'm sorry.'

He looked at Bradley gravely. 'I'll be OK; I'll mend. An accident, you say? But I had no idea Danny had a gun out there, Brad! You could have been shot yourself!'

'Don't worry yourself, Tom, it's all over now.'

'Edith and Winnie, are they all right?'

'They're both fine – I saw Winnie this morning. Danny didn't bring the gun, Tom, it was one of the guests, Mrs Pentley – she kept an old rifle under the bed for emergencies or somethin'. I don't know any more at the moment but you rest now. We'll talk about it later.' Standing up, he added, 'I'll go back up to Chalkfield Hall today, make sure they're all right up there, see if there's anythin' I can do.'

'Thanks, you're a good man. Tell Kim she has my blessing. She'll have a lot on her hands now, but she'll be fine, I can feel it in my bones.' Tom gave a feeble wave of his hand before sinking back onto the pillows and closing his eyes.

A week later, Tom was still in hospital when a nurse came: 'Telephone message for you, Father! Your parents are on their way from Tipperary to see you.'

'But they shouldn't be coming, tell them! They needn't be troubling themselves to come all this way to see me!'

'Too late, they'll be on the plane by now!' She beamed, pumping up his pillows.

He wished he felt better. His recovery from the head injury had been slow, the doctors had told him it might be the weakness left after pneumonia. Past middle age and still can't look after myself, he thought. I'm not a strong man, hardly a tower of strength for the Church. Perhaps that's why my dear parents named me Thomas, doubting Thomas. Just as well they didn't call me Peter, the Rock of the Church – they'd have been bitterly disappointed, so they would.

Before his parents arrived, Tom made a special effort to look as fit as possible; he shaved, and one of the nurses gave him a haircut.

'My, you're lookin' a lot better today, Tom!' called Bradley, walking into the ward unexpectedly with Kim behind him. Tom was sitting in a chair.

'Ah, the new baby!' he called. They drew up chairs beside him.

'I can take him home today!' said Kim, cradling the baby in her arms.

'He's a grand little chap! Hey, little fella,' said Tom, taking hold of a tiny hand.

'I'm callin' him after you, Father: Daniel Thomas: Danny, after 'is dad like,' she added.

Tom looked pleased. 'I'm glad you feel you can call the boy after his father – it shows a charitable heart. I'm sure Danny wasn't all bad. Tis a sorry business things turned out the way they did.'

'Danny was askin' for it though, weren't he?' she replied. 'I ain't sorry he's gone. He'd never 'ave looked after us proper, would he, eh?' She nuzzled the baby's cheek affectionately. 'You're my new little Danny now, ain't yer! You're gonna be a good boy, not like your dad!'

Seeing his sister with her baby on her lap filled Bradley with hope for the future. One day he hoped he and Helen would get back together, leave history behind and start a new life, just as Kim had done.

'Brad?' Kim was staring at a man holding onto the door.

'Tis my father, Kim! Here, let me get up.'

'Dad?' The old man stared around the ward. His gaze fell on Tom and a glimmer of recognition lit up his eyes.

'Son?' said the man, clasping hold of Tom as though about to fall.

'Come and sit down. Where's Mother? Have you left her at home?'

'No, not at home. . . .' He trailed off, struggling to continue. 'Your mother took very bad on the plane.' Tom held his hunched shoulders, waiting on his every word. 'They couldn't do anything, son. The Lord's taken her. . . .'

'Tom, sit yourself down here,' said Bradley gently. Slowly, he managed to ease Tom into his own chair. Summoning a passing nurse

201

for help, he – and Kim with the baby – left the ward in silence. Glancing over his shoulder, he saw Tom and his old father crouched together in an isolated shadow of shock and grief.

Chapter 19

March 1985

Helen was clearing up after the meal at the Welfare Hall.

'I don't know what we're going do with all this stuff!' she complained, surveying the odd collection of boxes with dismay. 'We don't know what's in half of them.'

'Yes, remember when we ruined a meal frying sausages in engine oil by mistake,' replied Jean. 'They smelt revolting! We had to throw the whole lot out!'

Months ago they would have laughed themselves into stitches but now their reaction was one of frustration. Countless boxes of tinned food, lentils, bottles of chilli and sacks of haricot-type beans occupied a whole corner of the Welfare Hall.

'Hey, look at this!' called Helen, sniffing the top of a tin she had just opened out of curiosity. 'It smells fishy!' She held up a limp piece of white meat with yellow fringes on it.

'Ugh!' cried Jean. 'What on earth's that?'

'I don't know,' Helen sighed, 'but there's about sixty tins of it!'

'We won't need all this stuff, the way things are going – look at all that mashed potato we had left over today.'

'Not funny is it, when only a handful of people turn up.'

'It's bloody annoying actually,' Jean sighed.

They looked at each other, both knowing the fun had gone out of it. In sombre mood, they packed up and left, not knowing what the next day would bring. Helen went straight to her mother's to fetch Sam.

'You're quiet, my girl,' Beatrice said, sitting on the floor with her arms outstretched. 'Come on, Sam! Come to Nanny! That's my boy!' He tottered towards her and she swept him up in her arms. 'Who's a clever boy then?' she cooed. 'So come on, Helen, what's up? I can read you like a book.'

'I don't know, Mum, it's just—' Helen started to gather up a few toys. 'It's not the same now, with the strike, I mean. Loads of miners are going back in. There was so much food left today – they just aren't turning up for the meals. Seems pointless struggling to cook when half of them don't even bother. Once they've gone back, it's like they were never part of it at all.'

'Well, I always said they took you a bit for granted, my girl; you and your friends working away up there like skivvies, going out collecting money, working yourselves half to death to keep them all fed. Typical! Now the strike's breaking down, they all drift back to work as if nothin's happened and with not so much as a thank you!' Beatrice shot a glance at her daughter while she wiped Sam's nose with a tissue. 'You can't keep it going forever, love,' she continued. 'If the men have decided to go back in, well, that's it. You did them proud; if it wasn't for the likes of you they would have been starving no doubt! But they don't have the sense to realize that. I'm sorry, Helen love, but the truth is, at the end of the day they're only coal miners – they can only see as far as the end of their noses some of them.'

'Oh, that's not fair, Mum! They're decent hard-working men; they've been forced to end the strike because the union's losing ground. It's the government's fault. The miners have been forced into a corner. . . .'

'Well, they haven't made it any easier for themselves or the country, have they! Take your Bradley: a man like that with responsibilities should have known better than to go on strike.'

'Brad didn't stay out long though!' Helen retaliated.

'No dear, that's exactly my point. He showed a bit of common sense, thank goodness, more than can be said for some of them. Credit where credit's due. He didn't just follow the others like a sheep; he's showed me that he's a man of integrity.'

Helen stared at her mother incredulously. 'You never talked about him like that before! You always implied he was no good for me! Mum! How can you start talking like that about a man who turned his back on his mates and went back to work? You know he's dreaming about daft things now, don't you, like moving away and buying a farm or something?'

'Is that so daft, Helen?' Beatrice put the toddler down and turned to her daughter with burning eyes. 'He's fit and strong – seems to me it's quite the opposite. The colliery won't stay open forever, y'know. Once the government have their way – and they *will* have their way, believe me, dear – no government in its right mind would want to keep a pit open in the twentieth century when it's running at a loss. Silt Edge Colliery will close. Maggie Thatcher's right, you know, there are other jobs out there. At least Bradley's got the imagination to see that!' She finished crossly, angry for finding herself in the position of defending her son-in-law against her own daughter.

Helen fell quiet. Things were spiralling out of her control. From being at the helm of a new movement with strength and spirit, she was now beginning to flounder in a cross-current of different ideas and emotions. She must have some time to think.

'I'd better be getting back,' she said. Taking her bag, she began stuffing things into it impatiently, feeling tired and frustrated.

'Don't take it to heart, dear,' Beatrice said, giving her a quick hug. 'See you tomorrow, eh?' Helen nodded, and sweeping Sam up in her arms, she left. Beatrice stood on the step to wave, but Helen didn't glance back. Only Sam, looking over his mother's shoulder, grinned with a rosy-cheeked smile.

It was early morning. An overcast sky hurled a biting wind into every face turned towards the pit head. Everywhere in Silt Edge people lined the streets, hanging from open windows, standing at front gates, clapping their hands and waving flags. Helen watched the events unfold as she stood at her front gate holding Sam on her hip. She felt disorientated. For her, it wasn't a joyful occasion; she watched with mixed feelings of apprehension and loneliness. The strike was over. The miners were marching back to work.

Looking straight ahead at the pit gates, defiant but defeated, they walked with a resigned, funereal dignity. Four hundred or more in number, they formed a seemingly endless procession. Two words were hovering on their lips – *we failed* – but no one uttered them. As they passed by, a wave of applause followed them, rippling through the crowd. There was something about their skin and clothes, Helen noticed, which already seemed to have taken on the pallor of coal dust. Their eyes were dull, their fighting spirit was spent. The fire that fuelled the strike had been doused.

Bradley wouldn't be among them, she knew that. What kind of treatment he would receive when they all met face to face again down the pit she couldn't imagine. Seeing the leaders carrying 'back-to-work' banners, she encouraged Sam to wave his flag too, but she saw that some of the men were shedding tears, and they didn't even wipe them away.

The strike had been called off without the trumpet sound of victory. All their efforts, she felt, had come to nothing because no deal had been struck. So many had hoped the year-long wait would have produced results: assurances, job security, a mandate from the government. Instead, nothing had been achieved. She couldn't help feeling it had all been a waste of time.

As the march progressed through the streets, like a tragic game of sticky toffee, it picked up miners from almost every house, growing longer and longer and snaking into an army. More and more came, and the onlookers' applause escalated into a crescendo of encouragement. Helen noticed the police; they were relaxed now and off their guard, probably looking forward to climbing into their coaches and making for home for the final time. She saw all this and she knew – the show was over.

Once the march trailed off, she turned thankfully back indoors. Today she wouldn't be meeting the girls up at the Welfare Hall; they wouldn't be cooking, making lists or going out collecting. She thought she might make some cakes for their street party, celebrating the end of the strike. But after today, the days ahead stretched out before her like blank pages, frightening in their lack of content. What about tomorrow, and the next? She thought about her friends – how their focus had already shifted – already they were looking forward to when their men would get home. They would be planning their days around their husbands' shift patterns. But what about her?

Without Bradley, and without Jean and the others for support, her lifeline with the community was broken. How could she have allowed the strike to dominate her whole life? Now she was alone, with a child to support. Should she look for a job? Being so involved in the campaign had been like going to work – but without pay. Stupidly, she realized, it hadn't really occurred to her that her role as organizer would eventually disappear. Her purpose in life had been totally focused on the strike – and suddenly it had been swept like a rug from under her feet.

The street party everyone was talking about was going to start after the men finished their first day back. Oblivious of the cold March weather, tables, chairs and balloons began arriving outside. Unobserved from her window, she stood watching two women putting up bunting, giggling as they struggled with a stepladder, almost drunk with excitement. Dressing Sam up warmly, she put him in the pushchair and set off for the Welfare Hall. She hadn't gone far when she noticed a loud grating and grinding noise, echoing around the streets of the village like an invasion. It was the headgear up at the pit: it was turning again.

When Helen arrived at the Welfare Hall it was deserted; it looked smaller inside, shabby and neglected. If she put her brain to work, she decided, she might find something appetizing for the street party among the stocks of food they had left. But there were the same old jars: peanut butter, tinned beans and vegetables, luncheon meat and foreign food. It was hard to imagine it now, when the place had been buzzing with miners and their families heartily tucking into their hot dinner, and laughter echoing around the walls. She felt very tired, almost exhausted. In the quiet, surrounded by all the boxes, loneliness swept over her which hurt so much it made her head ache. Putting Sam on a blanket, she got out his toys and began to play with him –

but the first sobs broke from her throat like a fistful of marbles, like the heavy drops of rain preceding a thunderstorm. She peered around the hall trying to recapture some sense of reality, but her eyes fell on the noticeboard, with all its cards and messages from well-wishers, and the poignancy of it all ripped through her like a knife.

Early that same morning, as Bradley climbed into Mick's van ready for work, he was worried.

'Could be a bit o' trouble today, eh, Mick?' he said. 'Best keep our heads down.'

Mick shrugged. 'Up to them, isn't it?' He squinted as though the sun was in his eyes. With a deft flick of the wrist he started the ignition. They pulled out onto the road and he accelerated savagely. 'Just another workin' day to us, mate. We'll see what they're made of after sittin' on their backsides for twelve months, the lazy bastards!'

Bradley looked away without commenting. They had almost got used to the small-scale working pattern which they had adopted during the strike. The close band of men who had worked with them would be dispersed now because they had been shipped in from other pits. They might stay on to do a bit of maintenance work, make sure everything was safe, but then they would return to their own collieries up in the north or in Wales.

'We're gonna have to pull our weight, double shifts probably, that's what they'll be askin' for,' said Mick. 'As much overtime as we want. It'll be hard if we're gonna try an' make up our quota for the year. Stands to reason, don't it, so much ruddy time lost.'

Bradley reflected. Now the strike was over he knew, although he didn't voice it – but rather felt it with a quickening of his pulse – that the wheels for his application for voluntary redundancy would be set in motion. While these men were heading back to their future underground, his path of escape was in sight. He sighed, wondering about Helen and what she was doing that morning. He would hang on, work hard, save up for his smallholding, drive himself to the limit if he had to, anything to escape the pit for good; but how he wished Helen was behind him.

*

Tom was also at the crossroads in his life that morning. The last stragglers of the march were passing by his window; cars and delivery vans sped by portraying the fact that life was returning to normal. He put a new sheet of paper into his typewriter, shifted the carriage, typed his address and then paused, trying to think of what to say. The only sound in the house was the quiet whirring of the fridge and starlings squabbling outside on the telegraph wires. Occasionally, his father's dry cough came from the next room where he sat without an iota of meaning and purpose left for the final years of his life. To Tom's distress, since his mother's death his father just stared into space all day. Perhaps he looked at pictures within his mind, at home in Ireland with Nancy.

Her death had left more of a gaping hole in his own life than he had expected. After all, he had no other home to go to, nothing to look forward to other than the few weeks a year he spent with his parents. At home he had found rest, time slipped by as quietly as turning the pages of a book. It was where the eyes grew pleasantly heavy, and where his mother's wheezing was a comforting familiar sound – it was all he knew and loved. At heart, he had to admit, he was still a young boy. The celibate life hadn't armed him with the spiritual strength and detachment he needed to make a success of his ministry. Losing his mother had been a terrible shock; he had never experienced grief like this.

Finding his father still sitting in the same position as an hour before, he asked, 'Would you have a cuppa wi' me, Dad?' There was a long pause before the old man realized someone had spoken to him. He turned and looked at him vacantly. It was the closest thing to a reply Tom was likely to get.

He went through to the kitchen, filled the kettle and switched it on.

'*My Lord Bishop,*' he began in his head, as he took two mugs from the cabinet. '*It is a few weeks since I wrote to you last, and I have spent time and thought on the choices you so kindly laid before me.*' He put a spoonful of coffee into each mug as the kettle rose to the boil. '*However, I feel my work as parish priest, here in Silt Edge, is finished. The decision I have made answers the needs of my elderly father. Since the sudden loss of my dear mother after Christmas, his health is not good; he has taken her death badly. At present he is staying with me here, but my intention is to take him home to Ireland and care for him there, where he may recapture some of his old spirit. I regret to tell you that I therefore reluctantly submit to you my resignation. . . .'*

Pouring hot water, he watched the coffee froth and adding a drop of milk, reached for the whisky and sank a good draught into each mug. He put the coffee next to his father on the table and sat down opposite.

'I've got some news for you, Dad,' he said. We're going home. I'm taking you back to Tipperary, and I'll be stopping with you – my work here is done.' His father stared at him for several minutes and Tom wondered if he had understood. 'I'm coming to live with you,' he said. 'It's what Mother would have wanted.'

'Ah!' said his father, brightening. 'Your mother!'

Tom placed a hand on his shoulder briefly and, walking through to his study, typed the letter that had already formed itself in his head. When he had finished it, he sank his head in his hands and prayed. Time was moving on. With a satisfying sigh, he thanked God for the sense of utter completion he felt, picked up his pen and signed his name with a flourish.

Chapter 20

Bradley must have read the letter over five or six times. He looked away and saw the postman wheeling his bike back up Mick's path to the gate and along the lane. He tried to read but his eyes darted across the page dizzily. The 'Silt Edge Colliery' letter heading looked so grand.

'*Dear Mr Shepstone,*' he read and then the words '*redundancy confirmed*' leapt out from the page almost knocking him over. The amount, '*£18,742.20p*' was exact, down to the last penny. The cheque itself was folded into the letter loosely like nothing more than a coupon.

He didn't dare believe it and read it over again and again, exhilaration rushing through his bloodstream. He felt hot and unsteady and sat down on the logs in a daze. Chaffinches chattered in the hedge and the distant boom from a cross-channel ferry sounded in the distance. It must be like winning the pools, he told himself, and he tried to smile – but the smile wouldn't come. He tried to feel joy, excitement, relief even, but to his horror the only emotion that he became aware of was fear. You can sit and dream away your whole life, he thought, but when your dream actually comes true. . . .

'Oh my God, it's happened,' he said out loud, sinking his head into his hands and feeling his fingernails dig into his scalp.

His mind went straight to Helen. How could he tell her? He felt vulnerable, as though he was looking down over a precipice. Holding that piece of paper, momentarily, he felt so uncertain he thought he could almost fold the cheque into a paper aeroplane and hurl it into the wind. Should he tear it up and pretend the day was still the same as it had been minutes before? The saw still lay innocently where he had rested it against the shed as the postman came up the path. He looked around him – buds were bursting on the trees with pink and lime green leaves and all looked as peaceful as before. But in those few minutes, his life had changed forever.

Carefully he put the letter and cheque back into the envelope and slipped it safely into his jacket pocket. The action took him back to the advertisement he had kept there for weeks until the night Helen had cast it into the fire. Now the envelope rested alongside Sam's little blue sock, a humble but treasured possession. He let his eyes soak up the green hedgerows, the trees, the great space of landscape beyond. 'At last,' he sighed. 'At last I'm free!' With a racing heart he stacked the logs; the task gave him time to digest the news, time to quell the inner turmoil fizzing from the pit of his stomach. Just as he was finishing, a familiar figure came into view, striding along the lane with the dog at heel. Since Bradley had broken the strike, all his so-called *friends* had passed him by without saying a word. Somehow he had hoped Gavin, who was always a loner, would behave differently. Bradley raised a hand in greeting, hoping he would stop and speak.

'You all right there, Gavin?' he shouted with a newfound confidence.

The lone figure moved on, unflinching. His collie gave one glance in his direction but it cowered to one side as a hand struck its ear. Bradley heard the low voices of ghosts echo in his ears: '*Scabs. They're all dead men.*' The man and his dog were soon in the distance, leaving him alone again with his joyful yet unbearable burden of good news. There was no one to share it.

However hard he tried to regain his enthusiasm, the freedom opening up before him began to look as frightening and dark as the underground tunnels themselves. Having to make a decision about what to do with the money filled him with anguish. To leave Silt Edge Colliery was one thing, but to put real distance between himself and Helen and little Sam, and sever the connection with all his friends, however unforgiving they were, seemed so final. To leave it all, to start his life over again in a new place – it seemed impossible. Where would he go? He pictured the advertisement he had cherished for so long: the small tumbledown cottage by the sea with outbuildings and land in Wales. It was easy to imagine making a new start before; now, without Helen and Sam, the responsibility for the decision rested solely on his shoulders. But his dream had to become a reality or he was a lost man. He might as well go and throw himself down the pit shaft there and then.

Looking at his watch, he decided it was time to put the tools away and get changed. Having accepted an invitation from Lady Ashby to a celebration for the opening of the new apartment block, it meant that he was expected that very evening. Glad of the distraction, he turned towards the house. At least, he told himself, when he got to Chalkfield Hall he would be able to share his news with Kim.

'It's you!' said Bradley, opening the front door, dripping wet from the bath and a towel slung round his waist. 'Come on in. I was just gettin' ready to go out.'

'Would it be Chalkfield Hall you're off to?' Tom asked. 'I'm about to head for there myself!'

Having accepted his offer of a lift, Bradley reappeared minutes later smartly dressed in a dark suit, white shirt and tie. He was ready to burst with his good news but found Tom off-guard, sitting on the sofa with his head in his hands.

'Hey, are you all right, mate?' he asked. 'It's a while since I've seen you. Is everything OK?'

'Yes, yes,' Tom replied, recovering himself and giving a dismissive chuckle. 'Just look at the state of me,' he said, brushing a few imaginary crumbs from the front of his emerald green waistcoat. 'D'you think Edith will allow me in, eh, looking like this?'

'You're lookin' fine, Tom, just fine.'

'Y'know I'm leaving this parish in the same state I arrived in all those years ago – as scruffy as a dog's dinner!'

'Leaving?' protested Bradley 'You're not leavin' us, are you, Tom?'

'I'm sorry to say I am. Things being the way they are – my father needs taking care of, now Mother's gone, God rest her soul. He needs to be back home in Ireland, y'know, to get his bearings. He doesn't know where he is at the moment, poor chap. To be honest with you, Brad,' he added, looking him in the eye, 'I'm not up to much myself these days.' Taking a deep breath and inflating his cheeks for a moment, he contemplated his fate. 'Heh, I've submitted my resignation to the bishop and it's been accepted, as he put it, "*on compassionate grounds*".'

Bradley was shocked. 'I'm sorry, Tom, I'd no idea you were. . . .'

'You've had your own troubles to sort out, so you have. I've done my best here in Silt Edge. Gave it my best shot, eh?'

'Life's changin' for me too, Tom, as a matter of fact. I got the letter today – my redundancy's come through.'

'Well I'll be! Congratulations, my man!' The priest thumped him on the back. 'You know, Brad, your father would be very proud. It was his dying wish you got yourself out of that pit. It's not been easy for you, I know that.'

'At least I've got a choice now, Tom. Can't say I'm a happy man though, the way things are between me an' Helen. Little Sam's walkin' now, I hear, but I'm a stranger to 'im.' He shook his head miserably and the tie he had so carefully knotted he pulled apart again savagely, struggling to remain calm.

'She'll come round, Brad,' he said, resting a hand on his shoulder. 'Give it time.'

'I want her back so badly, Tom – but not the way it was. I can't ever go back to live in Silt Edge. You understand that, don't you?'

'I do. Helen's not happy there either though, I understand – not now. The other women, well, they've all moved on. She's not really a part of it, if you see what I mean. They've got their men back at work, money in their pockets and they're having a whale of a time going out spending it. All that campaigning and fund-raising Helen and the others did – well, it's virtually forgotten, almost like it never happened at all, heh! I think they deserve a medal myself those women – but that's the thanks you get!' Tom sat down heavily again as though his thoughts were making him feel dizzy.

'But the pit?' Bradley said. 'Does it have a secure future after all? Can they be so sure they won't shut it down anyway, come a year or two?'

'Who knows!' Tom slapped his thigh. 'You've no need to worry yourself about that now, have you! It's torn the village apart, that strike, that's the truth of it. Don't think it will ever be quite the same again. There's those even now who still want to stop out, even now the strike's over and done. Given half the chance they would too, believe it or not. Rather starve they would, I think, than let the government win. They're stubborn men – strong and faithful, but stubborn, not open to compromise. I would've taken my hat off to them once; it takes courage, Brad, stamina, and self-control to keep a strike going. They were prepared to do without luxuries, necessities even, but they're bitter now and it won't be easy in the days and weeks to come.' He shook his head glumly. 'Once a scab, always a scab. Y'know, if a scab dropped down dead in front of them, I'll bet you they wouldn't even dig a decent grave and bury him.'

Bradley had never seen the priest so depressed. 'Forgivin's not easy, Tom,' he said quietly, 'when there's so much at stake. I know the miners won't accept me back but I've got used to the idea now. What about Helen though?'

'She's a bit left out, to tell you the truth,' Tom replied. 'She won't admit it, not to me anyway. If you ask me I think she's a bit down in the dumps.' He pursed his lips. 'Her friends are all too busy enjoying life again.' He drew a breath and seemed to decide he might as well finish off what he was saying: 'The truth is they don't need your Helen any more. It was fine while they were all busy campaigning, but. . . .' He seemed at a loss what else to say.

Hearing this, Bradley put his hands in his trouser pockets thoughtfully and went to stare out of the window. 'Thank you for comin' and tellin' me this, Tom. It's good of you – I appreciate it.' While he stood with his back to Tom, he struggled to come to terms with his change in circumstances. Helen's position was difficult, unusual, he could see that. But he had never intended to abandon her, surely she knew that. He must see her, talk to her. Straightening his tie in the mirror, they prepared to set off.

As they stepped outside, a silence hung between them as both men contemplated their own futures.

'I'm sorry you're leavin' us, Tom. I'm sorry about all that's happened, you losin' your mother an' all.'

'Ah, tis the Lord's will, Bradley lad. Who are we to ask the reason why? My poor mother, God rest her soul, she'd want me to take care of Dad, so she would. I told your Kim only the other day, it sometimes happens that good things come out of bad. It's about time I went home – the way things are. Now let's get to Chalkfield Hall and cheer ourselves up, eh?'

Shortly after Christmas, Edith was called away '*on business*' as she put it, leaving Winnie and Kim to plan the preparations for the opening of the new apartments alone. Shortly after her return in March, however, Kim was unexpectedly summoned to Edith's room, only an hour or so before the guests were due to arrive.

Kim climbed the stairs with trepidation. After tapping on the door, she entered the dimly lit room when she heard Edith's voice.

'Come in, my dear, and close the door behind you, there's a good girl. I do suffer with the draughts so!' Edith was sitting at her dressing table doing her hair. 'Come, child, sit here beside me, there! I'm pleased you've come to see me. We need to have a little talk. What with all the goings-on, I've hardly had time to set eyes on you since I've been back. Oh, I do find London so tiring dear! Lawyers! They're enough to drive one up the wall.'

'I wanted to say sorry, like,' said Kim, 'about when Danny come at Christmas, y'know, all drunk an' upset everything.'

Edith inclined her head to show she was listening, but still looked at herself in the mirror. She turned a kiss-curl expertly, pinning it in place above her ear and puckering her lips at her own reflection in approval.

Kim continued, 'He shouldn't 'ave come after me, ma'am, shoutin' out like that an' smashin' up cars, it weren't right.'

Edith raised her pencilled eyebrows and her marble eyes shot a sideways glance. 'You've no need to apologize, my dear, it was none of your doing. An unfortunate incident happened, yes, with the tragic loss of a young life, and not one I would wish to go through again, but still.'

Edith turned away from her mirror and gave Kim her full

attention. 'I was very impressed by the way your brother, Bradley, intervened on that unfortunate night. In my view he showed himself to be a gentleman of strong character, courageous in fact! He seems to me to be the kind of man who can be trusted.'

Kim was awestruck. 'He was always stickin' up for me when I was little an' that, ma'am. I wish he weren't goin' away. I don't know why he can't have his farm round here, so's I can still go an' see 'im like, with little Danny when he's growin' up. He would've loved it, playin' with all the animals. I won't never see him again if he goes away.'

'He's moving away? To a farm?' asked Edith. 'But I thought your brother was a coal miner, dear?'

'He is! But as soon as he gets his redundancy come through, he told me he's gonna buy a farm or summat. It's what he wants cos he hates workin' down the pit. Our dad hated it an' it killed him in the end. Brad says he ain't gonna hang around for it to choke him to death too. That's why he wants to have a farm an' have chickens an' that. . . .' She paused uncertainly, seeing Edith's face melting into a smile.

'He's always been good at gardenin',' she continued, 'an' we used to dream when we was kids that we would live in a tree-house by the sea one day an' catch fish an' that. . . .' She trailed off. The childhood image faded rapidly as the reality of Edith's shrouded room and the memory of that tragic night rushed back to her.

Putting some rouge on her cheeks, Edith picked up her pearls and held out the two ends. 'Would you mind, dear?'

Kim stood up and fastened the necklace at the nape of Edith's neck. 'Ma'am? You know that old lady? She didn't mean to shoot no one, I know she didn't. She was always seein' things an' that – she must've got mixed up, that's all. I don't want her gettin' locked up in prison when she's so old, it ain't fair!'

'Kim, if you mean Mrs Pentley, the charges against Isobel have been dropped. You are quite right, she was, shall we say, *misguided*. The whole episode was very unfortunate, and thank you for your apology, but it really isn't necessary. The matter is closed, dear. She will be coming to live here with us, where we can keep an eye on her. Now! You must put all that out of your mind, and stop worrying. After all, we have your future to think of!' She patted the seat beside her. 'Now

217

sit down again, I have something important to tell you: I've chosen which of the new apartments you shall live in. That room you've got at the top of the house is far too small for a growing baby. But if you accept, it means you will continue to work here permanently – what do you say to that? It would mean helping Winnie as best you can; she isn't in the best of health, poor dear. Arrangements will have to be made around the baby, of course, but I'm sure we'll manage.'

'You mean I can stay 'ere, ma'am?'

'That's right, Kim; rent for the apartment will be taken out of your wages, just as your board and lodging is at the moment. Now, what do you say? Do you want time to think about it?'

Kim was wide-eyed. 'Me an' little Danny? Our own place?' She could hardly believe it. 'Oh, ma'am!' Her face was luminous with joy. 'Thank you,' she whispered. 'I don't need no time to think. I love it 'ere, ma'am, an' I got nowhere else to go.'

'That's settled then, dear,' replied Edith. 'Tomorrow afternoon we shall go across together and take a look, and then if you like it you may have the keys.'

While Winnie continued to set the table, taking crystal decanters and wine glasses from the glass cabinet, Kim walked to and fro from the kitchen carrying plates of sandwiches, dishes of gherkins, nuts and delicacies. An appetizing aroma began to permeate the house.

'Now, all we need is to fetch up some bottles of wine and sherry from the cellar, dear,' said Winnie.

'I'll go an' check the oven first, shall I?' Kim suggested. 'Them sausage rolls smell good an' ready!'

As she entered the kitchen, she paused beside the carrycot where her baby was sleeping soundly; she adjusted his blanket and kissed his damp head tenderly.

The drawing-room was furnished with Edith's finest furniture, which had been burnished with beeswax for years, having been in her family for generations. A thick gold carpet ran the length of the room and on each side of the inglenook fireplace, two leather sofas were placed opposite each other. They had ornamental gold-lacquered scrolls across the top. In front of the fire was a sculptured Chinese rug

218

in wedgwood blue. Sitting on an armchair with her legs elegantly crossed sat Edith, relaxing with a glass of dry sherry.

'Ah! Winnie,' Edith began, 'we ought to start thinking about planning the garden again, dear. We need to smarten it up, plant some new shrubs and get some seedlings in.'

Winnie steadied herself, holding the back of the sofa and breathing heavily. 'The builders have made rather a mess but the gardener will soon get on top of it again, I'm sure. No need to worry ourselves!' She returned to the kitchen, leaving Edith to enjoy her aperitif.

Resting her eyes on the soft furnishings, time and history seemed to stretch out before Edith like an open landscape. In her mind's eye a pattern was taking shape, as though fate had taken a hand in determining her future. She felt more relaxed and unhurried than she had for years. The grandfather clock against the far wall began to chime the hour of seven.

Some starlings started squabbling over a few crusts of bread on the patio. Immediately, Edith's memory jumped back years to that raw wound. Over the mantelpiece hung the large mirror which echoed the reflection of the garden. It was here that her father had towered over her almost seventy years ago, in solemn condemnation of her condition. His face and neck were flushed livid red while her mother, unable to cope, had rushed from the room, weeping hysterically. The same blue and white jardinières still stood each side of the french doors through which she could see the new apartment block and the pink-paved area surrounding it.

It was a fancy of hers to imagine her sweetheart as he might be now, sitting quietly in the captain's chair near her, wearing his naval uniform and puffing on his pipe. He would be reflecting on the war, and how his men had lost their lives beneath the waves.

'George, dear,' she whispered, 'if you had lived, our daughter's heritage would have been secure. Sadly, I don't know what became of her. As it is, all I can do is honour her memory by offering a helping hand to another poor girl in distress. I know you would have done the same.' A great sense of providence swept over her. The years seemed to fly before her, to a time when she would no longer be there to oversee the running of Chalkfield Hall. Time, she knew, was slipping fast through her fingers. 'The house will be in safe hands now, George,' she sighed. 'I can feel it in my bones.' With a sense of peace, she sank into a nearby chair and closed her heavy eyes.

The doorbell sounded, and the house sprang to life. Ben began barking excitedly as Winnie went to open the door. Edith, roused from her reverie, rose from her seat with graceful serenity, gave a cursory glance across the table laden with food and wine and, as all appeared in order, straightened her shoulders and stepped forward keenly. The first guests to arrive were Tom and Bradley.

As Winnie took their coats and chatted, Edith became agitated. 'Would you mind going through to the drawing room, Tom? Winnie will pour you a drink, won't you, dear? Bradley, I'd rather like to have a quiet word with you in private. Would you mind stepping this way?' She accompanied this request with an intense sparkle and such girlish excitement in her eyes it made Bradley hesitate momentarily.

Some time later Bradley returned to the now-crowded drawing room to find Tom reminiscing about the years he had spent in the parish, surrounded by a group of enthusiastic guests. He longed to be able to get him on his own, to be able to tell him his latest news; the offer he had just received was so amazing he needed to tell someone. He thought about going to seek out Kim from the kitchen, but she was still busy helping Winnie prepare the food. Still holding the unfamiliar crystal glass of sherry that Edith had handed him, he appeared to be listening to the conversation, smiling and nodding appropriately, but his thoughts were flying away from him, back to the fields, to the allotment where he used to find refuge at times of crisis. He felt as though his chest was going to burst if he couldn't talk to someone soon. The doorbell went again and there was another flurry of activity in the hall. Tom, recounting one of his stories, paused mid-sentence: 'And there was this huge crucifix slap bang right across my front door, so I thought the best thing to do. . . .' Glancing towards the door, he turned and winked at Bradley. Helen was being shown into the room.

Winnie led her over to the table and poured her a drink.

'Helen?' said Bradley, walking towards her.

She smiled. 'Kim was asked to invite someone,' she began, as though answering a question. 'Where is she, by the way?'

'Still busy in the kitchen, I think,' he said. 'Shall we sit over there?' He gestured towards a quiet corner and she walked ahead of him to take a seat, holding her glass of red wine. He noticed her rose chiffon dress hanging from her hips like wilted petals; she was thinner, he thought, and more delicate than he remembered.

'Are you OK?' he asked, when they were both seated.

'I'm fine. I've left Sam with Mum tonight. He loves staying with her, the little monkey.'

'Tom's got plenty of stories to tell!' he said, tossing his head to where the priest had attracted an audience. 'It's his last night tonight. He's off to Ireland tomorrow, for good.'

'He's leaving us? Oh, it's all change now!' she sighed.

'And for me too.'

Helen looked at him. 'So you've found the farm you were looking for?'

He nodded. 'My money's through; it's all sorted.' He heard her take a sharp intake of breath.

'You've got it? The redundancy?'

'Yes, this afternoon.'

'So you're going away?' He noticed her bite her lip.

'You know, I always thought you an' Sam would come with me,' he added quietly. 'I only did it for us, an' how I promised my dad. I wanted all of us to 'ave a better life – you do know that, don't you?'

Ignoring this, she asked: 'Is it far away, your new place?'

He shook his head.

'Another picture to show me, Brad?' she said, looking at him quizzically. 'Another advert? Some old tumbledown place in the middle of nowhere? I can't come with you, you know I can't. I'm sorry. It's not my sort of thing, knee-deep in mud and getting up at dawn to milk cows!' She was smiling now, to his surprise. 'Brad, I've been thinking. I'm going to teacher-training college. Mum says she'll support me and have Sam for me during the day. I'm going to be a primary school teacher! I know I'm a bit late starting but – I didn't know what I wanted to do when I left school.'

'And now you do?' asked Bradley, trying to keep his voice level. He was watching her slender fingers clasped around the fragile stem of the glass and he felt as though she had his life in her hands. His heart pounded and his throat became parched.

'You said once,' Helen continued, 'there's always a choice, an alternative. I argued with you at the time but I was wrong, I admit it. When the strike finished I didn't know what to do with myself; I felt I'd still got so much more to give!' Her voice broke, 'If I can't make a success of this then—' Putting the glass down clumsily, her face disappeared into her hands and he watched her shoulders shudder as she struggled to control her tears.

'You'll make a good teacher,' he said gently, resting his hand on hers. Letting her have a few moments to recover herself, he cherished being close to her and longed for the moment never to end.

'Will you at least come to visit me, bring Sam to see me?' he asked finally.

She retrieved her hand. 'Sometimes perhaps, but when I'm studying it won't be easy. Wales or wherever you're going – it'll be such a long way to go,' she replied, regaining her composure and taking a tissue from her bag.

'Oh, I wouldn't say it's that far,' he said.

She gave a little amused frown. 'No? Where is it then? Scotland? Cornwall?' She sniffed, resisting a smile. 'Honestly, Brad, what godforsaken place have you found this time?'

'Lady Ashby's offered me a job here,' he said, 'as groundsman to the Chalkfield Hall estate.'

She looked up in amazement.

'Yeah, I'm free of the pit at last, Helen, just like I promised Dad. All I ever wanted was somewhere to work where I can breathe fresh air and feel the wind on my face.'

'But where will you live though?'

'Wait here just a second, Helen, please.'

Minutes later, Edith came, unlocked and threw open the french doors. 'It's all yours – enjoy your walk,' she said. 'Take your time, dears, we won't eat for half an hour or so. The garden has been here for over two hundred years; one can't hurry the gift of nature, only hinder her at times, I fear.'

Helen caught her eye. Edith's expression surprised her, because her eyes were brimming with tears.

'Thank you, ma'am,' replied Bradley, as they passed through into the lush evening air.

He felt as though he was stepping under some kind of spell as he walked outside with Helen, across the moss-covered patio and down into the well of shrubs and tangled honeysuckle. The evening air was beginning to chill; birdsong rang in the overhead branches and mosquitoes clustered in clouds above their heads. Presently they came to a clearing where the roof and crumbling chimney of a house rose above the trees, the tiles rusty red and covered with ivy and lichen.

'Oh, look at that cottage, Brad!' cried Helen.

'It's the old gamekeeper's cottage. He died years ago; it needs a bit o' work, I know, but after a few repairs it'll do us all right.'

Helen looked at him steadily. 'You're intending to live there?'

Bradley swallowed. 'It'll be OK. There's ten acres or so of land to look after here – should keep me busy for a while.' He turned to face her. 'Will you . . . will you come and see me, an' bring Sam?'

'What about your dream though, Brad – your smallholding by the sea?'

Her face was as pale as the moon now, in the fading light.

'The sea's in here' – he tapped his temple – 'an' it was all along I suppose. I don't need it out there, Helen, not like I need you an' Sam. All I really want is right here – you an' this garden, an' bein' able to hear the wind in the trees.' He reached out and gently moved a strand of hair from her cheek. 'Wouldn't you like that too?'

'We'd best get back to the house,' she whispered, without answering his question. But as they turned back up the path, he felt her warm hand slip into his so naturally that when he glanced at her, he knew he had his answer.

The boom of the cross-channel ferries sounded distantly from off the coast; a fog seemed to be coming down. Somewhere, not far away, a young boy out sea fishing with his father was just setting off from the harbour, his life stretching out before him, as dark and mysterious as the ocean.

All those years ago, Bradley thought, he too had cast his fishing line into the darkness and dreamt of what he might become. But it was only now he knew for certain what the future might hold.